A MATCHMAKER for a MARQUESS
Heart of a Scandal Series

For more information about the author:
www.christicaldwellauthor.com
christicaldwellauthor@gmail.com
Twitter: @ChristiCaldwell
Or on Facebook at: Christi Caldwell Author

For first glimpse at covers, excerpts, and free bonus material, be sure to sign up for my monthly newsletter!

Printed in the USA.

Cover Design and Interior Forma

© THE KILLION GROUP INC.
t

A Matchmaker For A Marquess

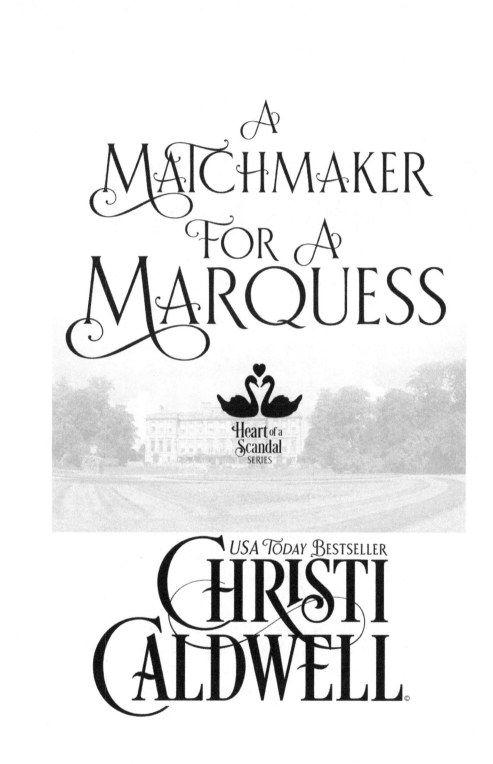

Heart of a **Scandal** SERIES

USA Today Bestseller

Christi Caldwell

Captivated by a Lady's Charm
Rescued by a Lady's Love
Tempted by a Lady's Smile
Courting Poppy Tidemore

SCANDALOUS SEASONS
Forever Betrothed, Never the Bride
Never Courted, Suddenly Wed
Always Proper, Suddenly Scandalous
Always a Rogue, Forever Her Love
A Marquess for Christmas
Once a Wallflower, at Last His Love

SINFUL BRIDES
The Rogue's Wager
The Scoundrel's Honor
The Lady's Guard
The Heiress's Deception

THE WICKED WALLFLOWERS
The Hellion
The Vixen
The Governess
The Bluestocking

THE THEODOSIA SWORD
Only For His Lady
Only For Her Honor
Only For Their Love

DANBY
A Season of Hope
Winning a Lady's Heart

THE BRETHREN
The Spy Who Seduced Her
The Lady Who Loved Him
The Rogue Who Rescued Her

BRETHREN OF THE LORDS
My Lady of Deception
Her Duke of Secrets

A REGENCY DUET
Rogues Rush In

MEMOIR: NON-FICTION
Uninterrupted Joy

DEDICATION

To Riley

I'll never forget the first time you played soccer. You were not so very excited about the game of soccer itself. During practice, in the middle of the field, you dropped to all fours and opted to play your own game instead— that of horsey for a little friend.

I laughed from the sidelines as children kicking soccer balls navigated around you, as you 'galloped' about.

On that sunny, happy day, Meredith and Barry's story was born.

Thank you for the memory. And thank you for being such a special, clever, nurturing, loving, spirited girl.

I love you.

PROLOGUE

Berkshire, England
1811

FOUR HAD ALWAYS BEEN MEREDITH Durant's special number.

She'd entered the world in the early morn hour of four o'clock on the fourth day of the fourth month.

She'd had four best friends in the world when a girl was fortunate if she had but one person in whom she could confide.

And it had taken just four days for Meredith's life to fall apart.

She stared blankly at the collection of valises packed and positioned neatly alongside the door, ready to be carted off tomorrow morn. And four valises were all it had taken to stuff all the things she'd accumulated in her nearly twenty-year existence.

Her lips twisted up in a painful smile at the recurrence of that damned number.

Perhaps it was the shock of being turned out after she'd spent her entire life at Berkshire Estates. Or perhaps it was the abrupt and unexpected sacking of her father, the Duke of Gayle's loyal man-of-affairs. But there was nothing more than an absolute numbness to her and Papa's impending departure.

Though, in fairness, the numbed state had begun four days ago with the arrival of the letter that had broken her heart and made a mockery of the time she'd spent loving and mooning over a worthless cad who'd never truly had honorable intentions where she was concerned.

"Where did I put it? Where did I put it?" Her father's mutterings as he flew between the small rooms of their cottage—nay, the Duke of Gayle's cottage—managed to penetrate Meredith's misery and proved a welcome distraction.

Dusting at her cheeks, she quit her place at the window and joined her father. "What are you looking for, Papa?" she asked in the same gentling tones the head stable master and her former sweetheart had used when talking to the most fractious mares.

Alas, her father continued to mumble to himself, a man in a trance.

"I've left them somewhere. My letters. The letters. Where did I put them?"

The letters. As in the Duke of Gayle's letters of reference.

A healthy fury pumped through her chest at the thought of the duke. A man who'd been like a second father to her and who'd so easily replaced his friend with a younger man-of-affairs. "Have you checked...?" Her voice faded off as she pulled open the center drawer of his desk.

Meredith collapsed into the empty chair. Balled pages stained with ink filled the narrow space. "Papa," she chided gently. He'd forever been meticulous with his work. He'd instilled in Meredith the essentiality of proper organization and keeping one's papers tidy.

Her father, however, gave no indication he'd heard her. Instead, he continued his frenetic movements, darting around the cottage and talking to himself. In short, the greying, stoop-shouldered figure was a shadow of his former self.

Her mouth tightened. But then, that was the effect of this place on a person.

Berkshire, this country estate that had once been a place of joy, had changed. It had been altered by the people who dwelled here, their unkindness replacing the warmth and love and sense of family...

Her lips twisted again, and she caught the grimace reflected in her father's silver inkpot.

"Unkindness," she muttered to herself.

Is that what you call removing a trusted friend and man-of-affairs from a post he's held for more than two decades?

Is that what you call the stable hand professing his love, vowing to marry you upon his return from fighting Boney's forces and then instead penning you a note to share that he's had a change of heart? That his heart, in fact, belongs to another young woman he's met in his time away?

Her lower lip quivered, and tears filled her eyes, blurring her father's sloppy work space. She yanked out drawer after drawer, sifting through piles of stained and wrinkled pages.

There was something safer in focusing on the sorry state of her father's belongings than the splintering of her heart. "How could you have so horribly neglected your work?" she asked sharply as her father stopped at her shoulder.

Papa frantically wrung his hands. "Afraid I've been more distracted than usual."

"Distracted?" Her voice crept up in pitch. "Distracted?" And then all the resentment, fear, and pain of these past four days boiled over. Meredith grabbed fistfuls of the balled paper and tossed them onto the floor at his feet. "This isn't 'distracted.' This is a blasted disaster, Papa."

He rubbed at his temples. "I know, I know, poppet."

"You know?" Meredith jumped up. "If you knew, then you'd have taken care before it came to this."

"I'm afraid my mind's been elsewhere," her father whispered, claiming the chair she'd given up.

"And mayhap if it hadn't been, you'd still hold your post, and we'd still have a home here, and—" Her words cut out at her father's stricken expression. "Papa," she whispered. "I'm so—"

He waved off her apology. Removing his glasses, he cleaned the smudged lenses. "I deserve that," he said, his voice cracking.

"You don't." She perched herself on the arm of the chair. "But you should have asked me for help."

"I didn't want to ruin your happiness with work that isn't yours to see to."

Ruin her happiness…? How…?

A sad smile was on his lips. "I'm your father. *Of course* I noted you and the boy."

The boy.

Only, Patrin hadn't been a boy. He'd been two years older than she—a man and now a soldier. A lone tear trickled down her cheek, and she angrily swatted at it.

"He wasn't more important than this." It had taken a betrayal for her to realize as much, and now it was too late. Too late to protect her heart from hurt. Too late for her father to receive the help he'd required. And because of it, they'd lost their home.

"He's seen us taken care of. We'll be fine, Camila."

The mother she'd never known, who'd died birthing her. "Meredith," she gently corrected.

Her father scratched at his heavily furrowed brow. "I know. I know. It's just every day you remind me more and more of your mother." Her father patted her hand. "Run along. I've work to see to for the duke."

Work to see to? They were set to leave. What manner of work would the duke require her father to see to?

But then, what else could she expect of an all-powerful ducal family who thought nothing of replacing their loyal man-of-affairs? Oh, how she missed Emilia.

Except the ducal daughter had been a best friend to Meredith and then had completely forgotten her when she'd gone off to London and fallen in love.

Yes, they were better off with this place behind them. And yet, she couldn't quite make herself believe that.

"Where is it?" His gaze slightly unfocused, her father glanced about. "Where is it?"

"Papa?"

He was already off, pacing the rooms again and resuming his ramblings.

Meredith's eyes slid closed. She didn't want to be the parent in this situation. She wanted to be the young woman entitled to nurturing her broken heart while at the same time railing at the unfairness with which she and Papa had been treated by the Duke and Duchess of Gayle. Meredith wanted to be able to give in to the tears at having to leave the only home she'd ever known and facing the search for a new one in London.

"Camila," her father called from his bedroom. "Do you recall what I was looking for a moment ago?"

It was too much. Her pulse pounding in her ears, Meredith bolted to the door of their modest cottage. She caught herself on the handle. Struggling with it for a moment, she managed to wrench the panel open. She slammed it hard behind her and took off. She continued running, stretching her legs as far and as fast as they would carry her.

She ran until perspiration beaded her brow and slid down her cheeks. Raced on until her lungs felt close to exploding.

Panting, she staggered to a stop—at the stables. The place she'd come whenever she'd needed to smile or laugh. Or simply talk.

Meredith hugged her arms tight around her middle and struggled for a proper breath.

Damn you, Patrin, for breaking my heart. Damn you, Emilia, for breaking it, too, when you forgot me. Damn you, Duke and Duchess, for caring more about your titles than the people who've been like family to you.

But then, that was the truth, wasn't it? *Like family* was not the same as *family*.

With a shuddery sob, she burst into the stables.

This time when the tears fell, Meredith let them cascade unchecked down her cheeks. The familiar scent of horses and hay proved calming, an odd pastoral balm. As she closed the door behind her, the duke's mounts whinnied and stomped the ground. Others danced restlessly about their stalls.

Meredith moved deeper and deeper through the empty stables and stopped beside a familiar stall. "Hullo, Gabby," she greeted. Stretching her fingers out, she scratched the mare in that spot between her eyes that she so loved to have rubbed. "I trust you're disappointed in me for not coming sooner."

The chestnut mare gave a toss of her head.

"And with good reason," Meredith allowed, favoring her with another stroke, while with her other hand, she dusted away the remnants of her tears. "I should have come sooner to say goodbye. You deserved far more than a visit on the eve of my departure."

As if she understood and shared in that misery, Gabby rested her chin atop Meredith's shoulder. Angling her head, she snuggled the mount. "I'm going to miss you most of all, you know."

A faint creak was followed by a splash of light. Meredith went motionless. Even this was to be taken from her. When the stable door was shut once more, she glanced over her shoulder and squinted, searching for the identity of the thief.

His hands clasped behind him, Barry Aberdeen, the Marquess of Tenwhestle, made his way slowly through the stables. "Hullo," he called out hesitantly.

"Hello, Barry."

Four years younger than she, he'd been the bane of her girlhood existence, delighting in tormenting her and teasing her with a ferocity second only to that which she'd teased and tormented him.

How long ago all that seemed. How much time had passed. Had she ever been a child so carefree? Dropping her chin on the stable door, Meredith returned her attention to Gabby.

Barry took up a place next to her. He was at least four inches shorter than she was, but at some point since he'd been gone, he'd put some muscle on his scrawny frame.

She looked at the two roses in his hand, one red and one yellow. "Barry, did you bring me flowers?"

He stared at the small bouquet and blushed. "I... uh..." As if he were being asked to relinquish the Aberdeen heirlooms, he reluctantly held them out.

"I was only teasing," she assured. "I'm sure they're intended for some very fortunate young lady."

"They're not," he blurted. "You take them."

She hesitated.

"Here," he insisted, and this time, he pressed them into her palm.

Meredith accepted the collection of brightly colored flowers, raised them close to her nose, and inhaled deeply. "You don't have to give me your flowers, Barry."

No one had ever given her flowers. Not even Patrin.

The damned tears started again, and she blinked them back.

"Don't cry," he said frantically, with a seriousness she'd never heard from him. With a seriousness she'd never believed him capable of.

She sniffled, and then a kerchief was dangling before her blurry vision.

"I *want* you to have them, Mare."

No, he didn't. She'd seen the longing in his gaze to keep those flowers, but he'd relinquished them anyway. That unexpected tenderness sent a welcome warmth to her chest.

"I w-wasn't crying about the fl-flowers," she assured him.

"Here," he murmured, reaching up to wipe the tears from her cheeks, and somehow this grown-up side of little Barry made her cry all the harder.

"Please don't cry," he implored, searching about. Mayhap for escape? Which was a sentiment she'd become all too familiar with these past four days.

Meredith wept all the more. Big, noisy, ugly tears.

Barry awkwardly pulled her into his arms, and then oddly, there was the greatest of role reversals as the boy who'd always been like a bothersome younger brother to her became a protector. Barry was growing up, and a pang of sadness struck in her chest. It was just another change.

He continued holding her until her tears abated, and still for some reason she could not make herself step out of his embrace. Because with that move would come a finality to her time and place here.

In the end, Barry was the one who broke the embrace, jumping back with the awkward relief that only a fifteen—almost sixteen—year old boy could muster. He jammed his hands into his pockets. "You're leaving."

I'm being forced out. "Yes."

"I'm sorry."

He spoke in a solemn tone, sadness spilling from his gaze, and she believed him. Only, it was far easier to believe he'd be as indifferent as the rest of the Aberdeens. "And here I thought you'd be happy to see me go," she said in an attempt at levity.

By the frown on his lips, she'd failed. "I'm not heartless, you know."

She sighed. "I... know." Only, she hadn't known. Barry was, simply put, the unlikeliest of the Aberdeens to be offering comfort to her. How funny to learn that it was his parents who were, in fact, heartless. Even his sister, who'd barely spared her a note in their time apart, was without that organ.

Barry stroked Gabby in that place between the horse's eyes, and Meredith started. "How do you know about Gabby's favorite spot?"

He briefly paused in that stroking. "I'm aware of far more than you give me credit for, Mare," he said quietly. "I could always marry you, and then you could stay."

She managed her first smile, this one watery and slow. Knocking her shoulder into Barry's, Meredith tousled his already messy golden curls. "That's a very generous offer I'd almost take you up on if you were three years older."

She lied.

She wanted no part of this place or this family.

They settled into a comfortable silence, one occasionally broken by the whinnies of horses. And she recalled Patrin and his betrayal. With that unwelcome reminder, reality was revisited upon her. Meredith gave Gabby one final stroke. "Goodbye, girl," she whispered and stepped away from the stall.

Barry hurried to place himself between Meredith and the path to the exit. The large Adam's apple in his throat wobbled. "Will I ever see you again, Meredith?"

No. That was the most obvious, truest, and honest answer to his question. "Perhaps," she said with a forced smile, because ultimately, the stridency in Barry's voice said her answer mattered and reminded her that, for all the ways in which he'd grown and the maturity he'd shown while she cried, he was still a boy. Meredith drew the pair of roses he'd given her close and plucked forth the yellow bloom. "Here," she said, handing it over. "We'll each keep one as a way to remember one another."

He hesitated a moment before accepting it. "Do you know they say yellow roses signify friendship shared?"

"I didn't know that."

His blush matched the shade of the rose she still held. "Or I may have heard something like that in one of my classes at Eton. I can't really recall." Directing his boyish gaze to the ground, he scuffed the tip of his boot in the dirt.

"Then I'd say that is a perfect flower for you to hold on to and remember me."

Again, his throat moved spasmodically.

She cleared her throat. "I should go. There's much to see to before…" *I leave.*

Barry stayed her with a hand on her shoulder. His gaze moved over her face. "You'll return to visit?"

Never. "When life permits," she settled for.

Some of the tension left his narrow shoulders. "Goodbye, Mare."

"Goodbye, Barry."

As she dashed off, making for the cottage where she'd spend one more night, she was besieged by a new sentiment—guilt. For despite the kindness Barry had shown her this night, for the friendship he'd provided, she'd met that kindness with a lie.

The moment she left Berkshire, Meredith would never return. *Ever.*

CHAPTER 1

London, England
Spring, 1822

THERE WAS NOTHING MORE ALLURING than a man with a book.

That allure, of course, was even greater when a tall, broadly powerful gentleman held a book of poems by Byron in the middle of a botanical garden.

No woman could resist this.

It would appear that universal truth held true even for matchmaker Miss Meredith Durant. Notoriously straitlaced, strict, and generally unaffected, she found herself hard-pressed not to peek at the stranger with tousled golden curls.

Though, to be accurate, she wasn't *really* peeking.

She was blatantly staring. One of those bold looks that would cost her the hard-earned reputation she'd secured for herself and, along with it, any future work and security.

If the gardens were busy.

If there were passersby in the same area as she and the specimen before her.

If he weren't engrossed in his book.

But he was engrossed, and his back was to her, and it was because of his fixation on Byron's sonnets that Meredith was able to stare unabashedly.

Which was preposterous.

She, at nearly thirty-one years of age, didn't stare—at anyone. Most certainly not a gentleman in tight-fitting black trousers and a tailcoat that, in just a shade deeper than red, gave an illusion of sin.

And yet, nothing about the stranger being here made sense. Sin didn't belong at a horticultural society. It was also a universally known truth that places of science and study were entirely safe from scoundrels and scamps and rogues. Therefore, they were the only safe places to escort one's charges, such as ladies who were still innocent, having hope in their hearts and entirely too impressionable minds.

The gentleman licked the tip of his finger and turned the page. And then he began to read aloud.

"But mighty Nature bounds as from her birth;
The sun is in the heavens, and life on earth…"

Meredith's eyes slid closed. *My goodness.* Her fingers reflexively went to the necklace she always wore at her throat, and she gripped it tight. The stranger's voice was a deep, melodic baritone with the quality of warmed satin on a summer's day. It brushed over her skin as real as a touch.

It was a heady moment when she'd believed herself long past heady moments.

Of course, that had been before him… Lord Captivating. Because there could be no other name for one such as him, a gentleman reading poetry at the Royal Horticultural Society. He proved that age-old warning she provided to each of her charges and their mothers at first meeting: A charming gentleman was a dangerous thing, and all women—all of them—could fall prey to one.

She, even with a heart long ago broken and then healed by a good hardening, proved no exception to those rules of weakness.

That reminder brought her eyes flying open.

Logic, which she'd always had in spades, urged her to flee.

"Flowers in the valley, splendor in the beam,
Health on the gale, and freshness in the stream."

Alas, if the spell had been shattered and reality had intruded, why did her serviceable boots remain rooted to the ground? Why couldn't she rush off in search of her charge, loose somewhere in the gardens?

His quiet reading stopped, and all that was left was the hum of his hushed words. Words that had, in the moment, felt as if he'd intended them for her. Which was further foolishness. Men, as a rule, didn't intend any of those seductive words for her, the pinch-mouthed Lady Matchmaker, as she'd come to be known. The only one who had proven false, and that had been before she'd refashioned herself in life.

Read another...

"Shall I read another?"

So quiet were those words spoken, she might have imagined them, a gust of the soft early summer wind, a compellation born of her own secret yearnings. His husky invitation tempted her with the promise of more Byron falling from his lips.

"If I do, love, will you remain standing there, staring?"

The truth slammed into her. He knew she was there. That was why he'd read those words. And selected that book.

Rogues. Rakes. Scoundrels. She knew all the tricks they employed to seduce, and yet, had allowed herself to be entranced.

"No need to be shy."

Bringing her shoulders back, Meredith opened her mouth to deliver a stern dressing-down to the conceited bounder... when he turned to face her.

Shock and horror filled her, those keen sentiments battling for supremacy.

In the end, humiliation won out. A rush of heat painted her from the tips of her toes to the roots of her hair.

The gentleman widened his eyes. "Well, now I see why you are staring! Meredith Durant, as I live."

Oh, saints be preserved on Saturday.

"*Barrrry?*" she said dumbly.

As in little Barry Aberdeen, with his voice prone to breaking, four inches shorter than she. Only... this man was a taller, wider, more masculine, more enticing, more... *everything* version of his younger self.

Her former best friend's younger brother bore no hint of the bothersome sibling who'd long been underfoot.

With a fluid gesture, he whipped off his hat by its brim and sketched a bow over it. "A pleasure as always," he said, flashing a flawless, gleaming, white smile. "And an unexpected one at that."

Barry flipped his Oxonian with a flourish that would have impressed the jugglers at his family's summer picnics and set the article atop his luxuriant strands. Luxuriant? Egad, this was Barry?

"Goodness, it's been ages, Mare."

Oh, God... that child's moniker he'd had for her as a boy of three insisting she, a girl of seven, ride him atop her back 'round the nursery. Or the grounds. Or the parlor. Or the halls. In short, wherever he'd felt like, because even as a babe, he'd had an inherent sense that all wishes would be granted him as a future duke.

Alas, garrulous as he'd always been, he had no problem carrying on a conversation. "Missing all these years, and you're here, right under my nose. How long has it been now?" he asked, so conversationally that she could almost believe they were the young pair bickering across the dessert table over the last cherry tart.

"Ten years," she said softly. And much had come to pass since she'd been a young woman in the Duke of Gayle's stables, crying in Barry's arms. Her heart had been broken not by just one man, the man who'd proven faithless, but by two, the second being the father who'd died, leaving Meredith on her own and needing to begin again.

"Ten years," he murmured almost wistfully. Then he looked at her as if seeing her for the first time in this garden. He lingered his gaze on her chignon. Her wire-rimmed spectacles. And then, ultimately, her puce dress. He grimaced. "You've... *changed.*"

She narrowed her eyes on him. Grimaced? He'd *grimaced.* Furthermore, she'd have to be deafer than Old Lucy, the mount who'd lived to near fifty in his family's stables, to fail to hear the cringe-worthy edge to his judgment.

"Yes, well... time does that," she said with all the aplomb one could muster when presented with one's childhood nemesis all grown up and a splendid specimen of a man, while one found oneself... not at all splendid. Whatever she'd become was the product of what his family hadn't done or been for her and her father.

"Would it be impolite, love, to ask how long you intended to stare without saying anything? Or..." He drifted closer, snapping his book closed as he walked. "Were you waiting for me to finally notice you?"

She choked. Good God, did she imagine the double-meaning there? Because she'd not—then or now—ever wanted Barry's notice. "What are you doing here?"

He pressed a hand to his chest in mock affront. "Am I prohibited from visiting public gardens? Is there a scandal in it?"

"Of course not," she said quickly. It was just that gentlemen didn't normally visit botanical societies. That was one of the reasons she'd begun taking her charges to them.

"There you are!"

She froze as her charge came sprinting down the graveled path, her loose curls bouncing about her shoulders, her cheeks flushed, her eyes bright. In short, all the things that Meredith hadn't been in ages and would never be again.

Also, in short, now the object of Barry's keen notice.

Frowning, Meredith slid herself between them.

"Well, hullo," Barry greeted with a rogue's smile.

Her frown deepened. Over the years, Meredith hadn't given much thought to Barry Aberdeen, the Marquess of Tenwhestle because, well… he'd simply always been *Barry*. Her former best friend's little brother. A man who belonged to the family who'd turned out her father and seen them on their way. Nor did they move in the same social circles.

And now she knew why. Her charges did not company with a rogue keep.

Miss Saltonstall dipped her gaze and giggled. "I'm sorry. I was looking for my companion."

Companion was the word used by Meredith's employers so as to spare them the ignominy of hiring a matchmaker.

"Your… companion, did you say?" Barry slid his gaze back toward Meredith, so much interest and humor there that she gritted her teeth and nearly forgot every lesson on propriety and politeness she'd beaten into her brain.

"Oh, yes," Miss Saltonstall whispered. "She is one of the best and most in demand."

Just like that, her charge reduced Meredith to the status of object, which was no surprise. That was how those in Polite Society who wished to hire her services saw and treated her. It was, however, an altogether different matter for Barry to bear witness to her status. *It was always your status. Even when you lived alongside him at the Duke of Gayle's country seat.*

"We should be going, Miss Saltonstall," she said, her voice sharper than she'd intended, earning a sad little frown from her charge.

Barry, however, dropped an elbow on the side of the urn of roses, blocking the path forward so Meredith would be forced to turn her charge entirely around and march them off. "Far be it from me to tell you how to do your job, Miss Durant."

"Good, then do not," she gritted out.

"But this is where introductions are generally forthcoming," he said in an overly loud, teasing whisper.

It was on the tip of her tongue to point out that she saved such introductions for respectable gentlemen in the market for a wife. And there could be no doubting, with his cocksure half grin and twinkling eyes, Barry was in the market for only one manner of woman. And it was decidedly not a debutante new to the market. Nonetheless, he was a marquess and a familial *friend*. Or he had been before his family had cut her family loose.

In the end, the bright-eyed debutante broke the tense impasse. "Miss Duranseau."

They both stared at the girl.

"It is just that you called her Miss Durant," the girl said, "and her name is, in fact, *Duranseau*."

"You're married?" Barry blurted.

Would this exchange never end?

"Miss. It is *Miss* Duranseau."—Just as it had been since Meredith had begun a new life for herself and sought to sever all connections to the girl she'd been.—"Not Mrs.," Miss Saltonstall whispered loudly, as if there could be no greater crime committed than a young woman being unwed. But then, that was generally Society's opinion. It was also the reason Meredith, the most successful matchmaker, had been able to survive since her father's passing.

"Fascinating," Barry murmured, and in the gaze he turned once more on Meredith, there could be no doubting the veracity of that statement. He opened his mouth to speak, and before he said anything further that might raise questions about Meredith, she hurried to introduce him to Miss Saltonstall.

"Miss Saltonstall, may I present the Marquess of Tenwhestle. Lord Tenwhestle, my charge, Miss Saltonstall. Now, if I may—?"

Barry dropped another practiced bow, and despite the properness she'd drilled into herself, she couldn't stop herself from rolling her eyes.

Not that he or Miss Saltonstall noticed. Both were entirely

focused on each other.

"Is Miss *Duranseau* always this dour?"

"Oh, not at all," the younger woman returned in a like whisper and without inflection, simply stating a fact. "She's usually less dour than this."

Barry laughed, and Miss Saltonstall joined in with her atrociously high-pitched giggle.

Meredith gritted her teeth. What did it matter if her charge was correct? Having cared for her sick father until he'd died and then having devoted every moment since to amassing funds with which to survive, she'd long ago accepted that those experiences had changed her. And yet, neither did she take to being teased by Barry in the middle of a public garden.

He looked in her direction and winked.

Barry, who for all the ways in which he had changed, proved remarkably the same—he knew just how to needle her.

"But she is quite good at her job," her garrulous and painfully innocent charge confided.

That brought one of Barry's golden brows winging up. "Indeed?"

Meredith cursed her pale cheeks and the telltale blush burning them up even now.

"This is where you've been?" he asked. "In London?" For the first time since they'd collided at the Royal Horticultural Society, he displayed real curiosity and not the practiced teasing he'd perfected in their time apart.

A memory traipsed in of Barry her last night in Berkshire.

Will I ever see you again?

Given her work, she'd expected their paths would one day cross. Just... not in this way.

Miss Saltonstall glanced between them. "You... know one another, then?"

"No."

"Yes." Barry spoke over Meredith's denial.

At the conflicting responses, the girl's furrowed brow creased all the more. "I... see?" Her tone indicated anything but.

"We rode together as children," he said smoothly, and as Miss Saltonstall looked to Meredith, Barry winked.

Oh, the bounder. Rode together, indeed. If her cheeks grew any hotter, she was going to catch fire.

"Isn't that right, Ma—" Meredith leveled him with a look, and he wisely supplanted the familiar moniker with, "*Miss Duranseau?*"

"Quite, my lord." It was curiously the first time she'd ever referred to Barry in that formal way. He'd simply always been... Barry. Emilia's younger, underfoot brother. Life invariably changed everyone and everything, though.

Silence fell, and Meredith took that as the cue to end her—their—meeting with the young marquess. She sank into a curtsy. "It was so very good meeting you again, my lord," she murmured, and her charge dropped a flawless curtsy to match.

Berry jammed his hat atop his head. "The same, Miss *Duranseau,*" he murmured in the silken tones he'd adopted moments ago while reading Byron, when he hadn't known who she was. Only now he knew...

He winked again, and tamping down a groan of disgust with herself, she turned on her heel, took Miss Saltonstall by the hand, and marched off.

As Meredith and her charge took their leave of the garden, Meredith felt one certainty: No good could come from being around the grown-up version of Barry Aberdeen, the Marquess of Tenwhestle's once-troublesome self. None at all.

And given the gentleman's roguish existence, there was little likelihood she'd have to worry about seeing him again.

CHAPTER 2

THE DUCHESS OF GAYLE WAS a woman to be avoided at all costs.

Especially if that woman was one's mother. As such, Barry had made it a life goal to steer clear of her.

This moment would mark the one exception in all of Barry's twenty-six-year existence and also the reason he'd quit the Royal Horticultural Society and made a frantic ride through London.

After all, it was not every day a gentleman came across a ghost.

In this case, a living, breathing, dour ghost who went by an altogether different name than she once had.

Jumping down from his mount, he handed the reins off to one of the liveried servants who always stood at the ready outside his parents' Mayfair townhouse. Offering a hasty word of thanks, he bounded up the steps.

The dutiful butler was already drawing the door open and admitting Barry before he'd even a chance to knock.

"Hamilton," he greeted as the door was shut behind him. Removing his top hat, he tossed the article to the greying servant.

Catching the hat and passing it off to a footman hovering in the wings, Hamilton bowed. "My lord."

"My mother…?" he asked, glancing about.

"Is occupied."

Which was polite butler-speak for *She's not accepting visitors, even from her son.*

Alas, if he'd made an exception on this damned day, the Duchess of Gayle would, too. Meredith Durant was employed as a companion. Not that there was anything wrong with a woman being employed, but this was Meredith, and there'd been nothing at all happy today about the girl from his past. And what was more, she went by a different name and had been cloaked in secrets. He steeled his jaw. All of which required immediate research and answers.

"She is in her office, then. I'll show myself there." Barry started down the hall. "And see that my father is summoned immediately and be clear that I've requested his presence." Both of his parents needed to be made aware of his discovery today.

"But…" Ignoring Hamilton's futile protestations, Barry increased his strides, not pausing until he'd reached the duchess's Pink Parlor. He tossed the door open. "I've stumbled upon some disconcerting information ab—oh, *bloody hell.*"

He silently cursed Hamilton. The damned butler hadn't mentioned the duchess was in the middle of one of her blasted Meeting of the Duchesses, as they'd come to be called by Polite Society.

The two duchesses exchanged a look.

"Allow me to give you a hint, son," his mother said crisply. "*This* is the moment where you dip bows to the ladies present and make your apologies for an abrupt interruption. And then only after you've made proper apologies for cursing in front of ladies."

The Duchess of Sutton made a poor attempt at hiding a smile behind her teacup.

"My apologies, Your Graces," he returned, waffling between the requisite greetings and the need to exit.

In the end, the decision was made for him.

"Come, come. I trust by not only your… unexpected visit and the rapidity of your entrance that yours is a matter of… some importance."

At one point in his life, he'd have failed to hear the snark and sarcasm from his mother. No longer.

Barry cleared his throat. "I can return after your company is gone."

"Not at all," the Duchess of Sutton protested and remained firmly seated, showing no indication she'd be leaving.

"And I'd point out that Lady Sutton is not just any company."

Nay, the duchesses were as close as sisters. Plotting, gossiping, terror-inducing sisters who handled the strings of Polite Society like two master marionettes. That did not, however, mean Barry intended to divulge before the other woman the discovery he'd made a short while ago.

His mother sipped from her teacup. All the while studying him over the brim.

The door exploded open, and his father staggered into the room. "What is the crisis?" he panted, out of breath.

Barry wiped a hand over his eyes. "There is no crisis." Not in the traditional sense, per se.

Resting his palms on his knees, the duke sucked in great, noisy, heaving gasps of air.

"Perhaps I should return later." The Duchess of Sutton set her porcelain cup down and came to her feet.

The duke wiped at the sweat at his brow. "Sutton," he gasped out a greeting.

"A pleasure as always, Gayle," she returned and, with a smile, took her leave.

His mother pursed her lips. "I swear, Barry Aberdeen, you leave me wondering every day at the tutors who instructed you. Driving off a duchess?"

This wasn't the time for lectures on propriety. No time, in fact, was. But certainly not this one. "I'd ask that you both sit." Barry took up a place in the middle of the Aubusson carpet.

"He's going to make an outlandish request," the duke grumbled to his wife… as if Barry, the very son they spoke of, was not, in fact, present. "Funds for flowers."

That briefly distracted him. "They aren't funds for flowers. It's a—"

The duchess gasped. "Surely you aren't blaming *me*?"

"This is about your *flower* garden. Isn't it, Barry?" his father demanded.

Bloody hell. Barry swiped a hand over his face. "It isn't a 'flower garden,' Father." His neck heated as he faced the same disdain and lack of understanding he'd always faced. "It's an experimental garden proposed by the Royal Horticultural Society of London."

"I *told* you that's what this was about," his father groused. "This is why you'd summon me from important matters?"

"You were sleeping," Barry pointed out.

"You want me to lease out my—"

"Our," Barry and the duchess said as one.

"—properties for these meetings. I don't see the Duke of Devonshire offering his for your experiments."

"They aren't my experiments. They are the society's, and either way this is not the reason for my visit." He'd given up on petitioning his parents for the acreage desired by the Royal Horticultural Society some two months ago.

The duke pointed at his wife. "You've encouraged this."

Neither of them had encouraged Barry's appreciation of botany. They'd done quite the opposite, by dismissing the tutors who had promoted his fascination with that very particular science. Either way, he'd long ago accepted there'd be no support for his endeavors from the regal pair standing before him.

"Will you both please *sit?*"

They must have heard something in his voice, for this time he effectively silenced the pair, who sank into the nauseatingly pink sofa.

Barry took a deep breath. "I've discovered something quite alarming today." The memory of Meredith Durant from a short while ago… pinch-faced, world-weary. And not at all the Meredith of his remembrance. His lips tensed. "Something… horrifying," he added to properly prepare them.

His mother slapped a palm over her mouth. "You have an illegitimate child."

"What?" He furrowed his brow. What in hell…? Barry shot a frantic look at the door. "Good God, have a care lest a servant hears you."

"I knew it," the duchess cried out. She glared at her husband. "I told you with his reputation he was going to be careless."

His reputation? Barry attempted unsuccessfully to get a word in.

"Surely you aren't blaming *me* for him getting a babe on some woman." His father flared his nostrils.

Good God this was really quite enough. "Would you both stop?" Mindful of the possibility of passing servants, even if his parents weren't concerned, he dropped his voice to a hushed whisper. "There is no babe. I do not have a child. I don't intend to have a child. There's absolutely no babe. None."

That silenced his parents.

Briefly.

His mother twisted her hands together. "Are you certain you're not now saying this because of our reaction—"

"I assure you," he said swiftly. "I'm very certain."

"Because if you do," his mother continued over him, "I'd have you be sure you're caring for the child properly. Isn't that true, Geoffrey?"

"Absolutely." The duke stole a longing look at the doorway, and Barry commiserated with his father in that instant. He himself was nearly regretting this impromptu visit.

"You've no worries about an illegitimate child. I've taken care..." he said before thinking and then promptly wished he could call the words back.

Both his parents inched closer to the edge of their seats, eyeing him carefully. "Oh?" his mother pressed.

Barry yanked at his suddenly too-tight cravat. This was all really enough. "There is no babe," he repeated with greater insistence.

Even with that, however, his mother caught her chin between her thumb and forefinger and angled her head to study him. "Hmm," she finally said, noncommittal.

He didn't know which to be most horrified by: having to explain the measures he'd taken to avoid the possibility of having an illegitimate issue, or his parents' absolute lack of faith in him and his trustworthiness. "I came upon Meredith."

That pronouncement managed to usher in another blanket of silence, this one heavier. He frowned. Surely they'd say... something. "Meredith Durant," he said, as if he needed to clarify. As if there were another woman who'd been so very important to their family who bore that name.

"I... see," his mother said slowly, revealing nothing. Though the duchess was a master of emotion, a woman rumored to have not cracked so much as a smile or sigh at the birth of either of her children. What had made him believe this moment should prove any exception?

A bleating snore split the quiet.

"Do wake up, dear," his mother chided, lightly tapping her husband.

The duke jerked awake. "What... where?"

Oh, this was really quite enough.

Barry didn't give a jot either way about his parents' indifference toward him. This showing toward *Meredith*, however, was altogether different. "Can we please return to the matter at hand?"

"Meredith?"

Barry tossed his arms up. "Of course, Meredith," he cried out. How singularly focused they were. Concerned solely about the Aberdeen family and the Gayle title. All the while missing the entire point of Barry's visit, the one true person they required answers about.

In the end, it was the duke who responded. "I've... wondered where she'd gone on to."

Barry waited.

And waited. Expecting... something more from either of his parents. Nay, not necessarily his father. The duke was quite content to cede any and every discussion—important and not—to his wife. This instance proved no different.

"Hmph. And to think, all this time, she's been living under our very noses," the duchess said, at last finding her voice.

As much as he loathed admitting it, even to himself, he'd had the same thought upon catching sight of Meredith at the horticultural society, a woman he'd been raised alongside, as almost a sister. How had he failed to come across her—ever—in London?

"Mayhap she is new to London?"

Only, there hadn't been anything fraternal in the peculiar desire to tug free the pins from her severe hairstyle and let those curls tumble free, as they had when she'd been a girl. He gave his head a clearing shake and held up a palm. "There is more."

His parents stilled on the sofa.

"She goes by the name of Duranseau."

The duke's brows dipped. "Has she gone and married a *Frenchman*?"

"No. As I was able to gather, she's still unwed and using an alternative name..." For maximum effect, he held his parents' gazes separately. "And she's a... companion."

His mother gasped. "For who? Surely not... *yours*?"

His companion? Bloody hell, had his parents always been this obtuse? "A *companion* companion. Not... anything that's inappropriate."

"Oh."

That was all? They were generally fixed on their place in Society, and he'd expected they'd not be as horrified as Barry had been with his discovery, but he'd certainly expected more than this.

His father made a throat-clearing sound. "This is all very... shocking, to say the least. And all really confounding."

At last, he'd penetrated the wall of apathy his parents showed... well, to everything, really.

"Well?" Barry asked impatiently when no further words were forthcoming.

His mother sailed to her feet. "I'm not really certain what you expect, Barry. It's been some time since we've seen Miss Durant. I can hardly give answers as to what she has been up to."

A muscle pulsed at the corner of his eye. Was that why they believed he'd come? In search of answers? Except... hadn't he? And the better question was: Shouldn't he have?

Because he'd not seen Meredith since he'd been a boy of almost sixteen and she'd been crying in the stables, and but for fleeting memories of her that would occasionally intrude, he'd not thought of her. And in that, he was as guilty as his family.

"Neither of you have given thought to—"

A snore cut into Barry's question.

"You are sleeping?" Barry asked incredulously, and his father startled awake with a bleating snore.

"Who? What...?"

The duchess lightly nudged her husband. "Barry seems to be of the opinion that we should... do something where Miss Durant is concerned."

"And what would he have us do?" His father put that question to his wife.

Both of Barry's parents looked expectantly at him.

Surely... "You are asking *me*?" Mad. They'd gone utterly mad. Alas, by their expressions, they were of a like opinion where Barry's sanity was concerned.

"You are the one who has come to us, Barry," his mother said impatiently. "What would you have us do?"

Fury licked at the edge of his temper, and it was all he could do to retain control of it. "You have an obligation to her father's memory to… to… see that she is well."

"And can't you do that?"

He balked. "Me?" he sputtered. "Of course not. You are Society's leading matron. And you are her godparents," he snapped.

That seemed to reach the couple.

They shared a look.

The duke shook his head slightly and then pointed to his wife.

The duchess released a beleaguered sigh. "Oh, very well. I'll discreetly inquire after the young woman and ensure she is well. Will that suffice?"

Actually, it would. And as he gratefully took his leave of his parents, the worry that had dogged him since he'd come upon Meredith eased.

His mother would see the young woman was settled. There was nothing to worry about.

Except generally for the person whom the duchess was meddling with.

Mayhap he'd not done Meredith Durant any favors, after all.

CHAPTER 3

Two months later
Berkshire, England

THE LONDON SEASON HAD AT last come to an end.

And in his relish of that very time of year, one might say Barry Aberdeen was not Society's typical rogue.

Of course, there were many ways in which he was different from most other gentlemen: Barry didn't despise his family. On the contrary, he quite liked them and their company. Most of the time, that was.

He preferred fishing to wagering. Though not a soul in Polite Society knew as much.

And he enjoyed his mother and father's annual summer party. In fairness, it was less the party and more the place where those festivities were hosted. With its endless rolling green hills and crystalline waters and falls, it had been, plainly put, the only place he'd truly enjoyed being since he'd been a boy. As such, even he, admitted scamp, rogue, and scoundrel, could endure a fourteen-day house party hosted by his mother, the Duchess of Gayle.

This moment proved no exception.

Well, this moment *had* proven no exception.

"You do know how desperately I love you?" The husky endearment reached him first. The crunch of dried leaves and squelch of moist earth marked a pair of matching footsteps moving alongside the riverbank.

Barry froze in midcast of his fishing line. The gentleman's voice came faint and horrifically familiar…

"Do you? I do believe you've not told me how much… today." And those soft, definitely familiar female tones belonged to—

Egad. His damned *sister*. Barry cringed, and he resisted the urge to clamp his hands over his ears. Had he truly thought he loved this place? There could be no doubting this place was ruined to him forevermore.

"Ah, yes, love," his brother-in-law, the less-staid-than-Barry-had-credited whispered. "But have I shown you?"

His sister giggled and then sighed, and then it was really quite enough.

"You are not alone," he said quickly. He tossed his line out. The lead landed with a plunk. Otherwise, only silence met his announcement.

"Barry?"

"The same," he drawled.

Another giggle was followed by a sigh.

Oh, good God. He was really quite happy that his sister had gone and fallen in love, but this was simply too much to expect a brother to suffer through.

"Did you hear me?" he frantically called to the pair. "Because if you did, you would certainly cease all *activity* around me. It is I. Your brother. I said I am h—"

"You were heard," his sister assured, parting the brush… and then righting her gown with one hand, her other palm firmly tucked into his brother-in-law's hand.

He blanched. Egad, that was the manner of stuff to ruin one's day, indeed. The manner of sight that couldn't be unseen. "If that were the case, then I'd expect you and your husband would continue on your way." Barry directed that out to the light tug at the end of his line.

"We are here on a matter of business," she informed.

"Indeed?" His neck grew hot.

"With you," his sister said impatiently. "I'll have you know we were, in fact, seeking *you* out."

Given the amount of sighs, whispered endearments, and wrinkled garments, he believed his sister about as much as he believed Lady Jersey didn't give a jot about gossip. "Consider me found," he said dryly.

Emilia frowned and moved into position beside him. "We were," she insisted. "Isn't that right, Heath?"

His brother-in-law dropped a shoulder against a nearby oak tree. "Your sister is endlessly loyal to you."

"Oh?" Given the fact that not even six months earlier she'd sacrificed Barry, forcing him to sing Christmastide carols before all at the Duchess of Sutton's winter party, that sisterly loyalty was certainly up for debate.

Emilia released a long sigh. "I really should just leave. You're an unappreciative blighter."

"He doesn't know," Heath said for his wife's benefit.

Emilia glanced from Barry to her husband. "No. No, he doesn't."

Barry knew precisely what their speaking over him was all about: They were toying with him. Aside from clandestine escapades, he was equally familiar with how to bait a person. Which was why he knew precisely what his sister and her husband were up to.

Drawing his line back in, Barry assessed the nibbled end of the bait at the end of his hook and then recast it.

"Don't you have a question for me?" his sister asked.

"I'm hardly going to seek any information that might or might not pertain to me from someone who can't determine whether I have a question for her."

"It would serve you right if I allowed you to return to Berkshire and find out all on your own what you're up against."

He stilled.

"I see I have your attention now." Emilia smirked. "The paper, please, Heath." She lifted a palm up.

Her dutiful husband immediately abandoned his repose and came forward. Fishing a sheet from his pocket, he handed it over.

This time, despite his determination to not give in to their needling, he glanced over. The faintest warning bells went off. Distant and faint. Something was afoot. Something his sister was enjoying entirely too much. "What is that?"

His sister gave the official-looking page a little wave. "It is Mother's guest list."

He snorted. "And you expect I should be bothered either way about who is coming to stay?" Given he intended to spend his days largely outside amongst nature, he hardly cared what pinch-mouthed matrons she'd brought together for the fortnight.

"I'll have you know, Barry"—his sister took a step closer, and that page clutched in her fingers danced on a light summer's breeze—"it is not a guest list like last year's, or even the year before."

"Why *should* it be? The entire purpose was to see you wed, and now that you have?" He pointed at his silent brother-in-law, who wore the ghost of a smile. "There's hardly a reason to fill our household with potential..." Barry's words trailed off as he went absolutely motionless as a horrifying possibility crept in. "Surely you're not *suggesting*..."

"That is precisely what I'm suggesting."

After Emilia had been jilted during her first London Season, their mother had made it her life mission to see her wed. Every engagement, every soiree, every house party in summer and winter had been dedicated to the intention of making a match. Now, there was no daughter to worry about wedding. He laughed. "Impossible."

"You're nearly twenty-seven, Barry."

"Positively ancient. In my dotage, I am," he drawled.

Merriment danced in his sister's eyes. "Ah, try telling that to your mother."

His mother? "I'll remind you, she's your mother, too."

"Yes, but when she's being vexing, she's entirely yours."

"Vexing? If your concerns are, in fact, real—"

"They are."

"Then I'd categorize them as a good deal more than vexing." Terror-inducing. Infuriating. Stomach-churning.

His sister let out a patronizing sigh that only an elder sister could manage. "Surely you didn't think you'd escape her matrimonial maneuverings?"

"Of course not. By my calculations, I've at least another two years before it is expected I fulfill my ducal heir responsibilities."

She stared at him incredulously. "And what have you based that on?"

"You were twenty-eight when you wed. I thank you for your warning," he said and retrained all his energies on fishing. He'd fallen for his elder sister's baiting enough times through the years. He had no intention of doing so now. "If I may resume my—"

Emilia wagged the page at him. Daring him. "As I have your

attention—"

"I should point out," her husband interjected, "that he's in no way attending you. He seems content to return to fishing."

Barry inclined his head, but otherwise didn't look out from the pond. "Well-noted, Mulgrave."

"Thank you," his brother-in-law put in.

"Hush, the both of you. You men are insufferable." Emilia stomped over, joining Barry at the shore. "I *should* take myself off. Leave you to your own devices. I was wrong to assume that you would care that the guest list is comprised not of her usual guests but entirely of unwed ladies and their families—"

He spun so quick on the shore, his boot caught the slick earth, and he came toppling down, landing with a hard thump in the water. "What is that?" he called after her and Lord Heath's retreating frames. Scrambling to his feet, sloshing water as he went, he rushed after the pair.

Stumbling over a tree root, Barry righted himself. As soon as he reached his sister and brother-in-law, he made a grab for the sheet in their possession.

"Uh-uh," his sister admonished, holding the page beyond his reach.

He glared at her. "Emilia," he warned, making another attempt.

She kept a tenacious hold on it. "What did you think this house party was, Barry?"

He dragged a hand through his hair. "I thought it was every other annual summer event. Same fare. Same festivities. Same guests." *Same* was the way of Polite Society. Everyone was expected to be the same, as were the activities they were expected to conduct.

Emilia's smile widened as she made a show of studying the paper in her hands. "As I was trying to tell you earlier, the guests are not at all Mother's usual guests…"

This time, Barry did spare her a glance.

And shivered.

There was a ruthless glitter in his sister's eyes. The same sparkle she'd had when she and her friend Meredith Durant had emptied his fishing bait in his picnic basket, thoroughly spoiling his lunch.

"You're enjoying this," he mumbled.

Her grin widened. "Immensely."

She taunted him. In fairness, given his blasé attitude of before, he was certainly deserving of it. But that was neither here nor there. "Emilia," he said once more.

Heath took mercy and plucked the page from his wife's fingers, handing it over to Barry.

"Traitor," Emilia muttered, sticking her tongue out at her husband, who reached for her hand to soften the blow.

Ignoring the nauseatingly handsy pair, Barry worked his gaze swiftly over the page, and with each name that he read, his horror crept up.

There were six families who would be in attendance. As his sister had pointed out, entirely different guests than those who attended the duke and duchess's usual annual summer house parties. Twelve unmarried ladies. Only two unattached bachelors—himself included in that small number. And two more brothers to the unwed ladies.

There could be no doubting the purpose of his mother and father's summer house party at Berkshire Manor: changing his marital state. Or as he preferred to think of it—and keep it—his bachelor state.

With a curse, Barry let his arm fall to his side.

He'd simply deluded himself into believing there was more time. With Emilia happily married, the duchess would—and had, by his sister's visit and warning here—turn her matchmaking sights on him. Such was the way for a future duke and peer of the realm. Ultimately, all the world, his mother leading the charge, expected those young lords to make a match.

Expectations.

That was what it always came down to. What a gentleman should study… or not study. What pursuits a gentleman should take on. Whom he was expected to marry—and when.

"Bloody, bloody hell."

"It might not be all bad." All earlier levity had gone, replaced with a terrifying somberness from his sister. And something more… a sad, commiserative glimmer in her eyes.

Barry whipped his gaze over the sheet once more and snorted.

This was bad.

Very bad, indeed.

At twenty-six, and his father in remarkable health, there was no reason to expect Barry to set aside his bachelor ways and…

and… His face pulled. Good God, he couldn't even complete the thought. Alas, his mother was of an altogether different opinion.

Emilia rested a palm on his shoulder in a gesture of understanding. "Surely you saw that, with me having married, Mother would then turn her sights to you?"

Actually, he should have seen it.

"She's positively mercenary where marriage is concerned," he muttered.

"In fairness, she's positively mercenary where anything is concerned," his sister pointed out.

And just like that, all his hope of time among the plants and wildlife here was shattered. He swiped a wet hand through his hair. So much for peace and solitude and a jolly good time at Berkshire Manor.

"If I may offer some advice?" his brother-in-law put in. "As a future duke myself who also had to contend with a mother determined to see me married off?"

Barry looked up. "Yes?" He'd take all the blasted help he might find.

"You've just two courses of action before you. One, you could marry."

That was not happening. Not anytime soon. "And course two?"

His brother-in-law—the miserable blighter—grinned. "Hide."

"Hide," Barry murmured. For fourteen days, he'd need to avoid a house full of company, and yet, Berkshire Manor was more castle than manor, with places to hide and land to explore. Only, when his parents hosted their gathering, it was all crawling with that which he sought to avoid during the summer—people.

His brother-in-law slapped him on the shoulder. "I've faith in you."

Barry brought his shoulders back. The other man was right.

Yes, it was just fourteen days to stay largely out of sight and avoid determined matchmaking mamas and title-seeking daughters.

How difficult a task could that be?

CHAPTER 4

As Meredith Durant's carriage rolled up the long, graveled drive, then rocked to a slow halt outside the entrance of Berkshire Manor, there was only one absolute certainty—no good could come from being here at the Duke and Duchess of Gayle's country estate.

In short, because no good had *ever* come from her being here.

Seated on the carriage bench, she tugged distractedly at the locket she wore, a gift from her father when he'd still been lucid. The pink-gold piece, which she always touched for comfort, this time failed to provide its usual calm.

She stared out the window at the turrets that reached high into the sky, great peaks heralding the power, wealth, and prestige of the dukes who'd all called this place home. A parade of servants was already filing through the front doors of the impressive manor, the young footmen all strangers to her.

Nay, it wasn't altogether true that no good had come from her being here. There'd been loyal friends and a happy childhood. This place had been a home... until her father was passed over for a newer, younger, more clever man-of-affairs and her heart had been broken, her future unsettled overnight.

Oh, if she had reached out after her father died, they'd likely have offered their support—financial. They'd been incapable of providing any on an emotional level, which in the darkest days of her father's deterioration had been all that she'd required.

And when he'd died and she'd been left alone, and all the funds depleted in her caring for him, Meredith had clung to all that remained—her pride. Then, she'd vowed to never accept anything from anyone and certainly not from the Duke and Duchess of Gayle—because they'd proven they weren't family.

Not in the ways that mattered.

Which was, in fact, why Meredith was here now.

Her entire career had been built upon and was reliant upon the *ton*. Therefore, declining a summons from a duchess was tantamount to signing the writ on one's own demise. And as one who'd come to see how quickly life could be shattered, Meredith had developed a keen appreciation that there was no certainty in life except uncertainty.

So she'd answered the summons. Returned to the place where she'd committed her greatest folly, the mistakes that only she knew of. And were the world to find them out, her career as a respected matchmaker—as a respected *anything*, for that matter—would be destroyed.

Despite her gloves, her palms went moist. That perspiration had nothing to do with the summer's heat and everything to do with the prospect of losing everything she'd built.

There was a light knock at the door, and she jumped. "Just a moment," she called. She gave her head a clearing shake. "I am ready."

The driver drew the door open. "Ma'am," he greeted, stretching a hand inside.

If there had been any doubts that the reason of her visit was anything less than business in nature, they were shattered a moment later as the Duchess of Gayle came sweeping into the foyer with her arms outstretched. "I've been waiting for you. Shall we begin?"

Wrinkled and dusty from her carriage ride from the other end of Dorset, Meredith wished only for a bath and then a bed, not necessarily in that order.

Alas, she'd been serving in her role as matchmaking companion too long. Her own desires and discomforts were secondary to… everything. "Of course, Your Grace." Bowing her head, she sank into a deep curtsy.

The regal woman, showing barely any effects of the passage of time, had already started forward, expecting Meredith to follow.

Straightening, she hurried after the duchess, bypassing room after room in which Meredith had played hide-and-seek as a girl. Or ridden around with Barry atop her back, neighing all the while and attempting to buck her rider loose, as the only thing that had kept him upright had been his fingers tangled in her hair.

She'd suffered a bald spot at the base of her scalp for three years, a credit to his efforts and her devotion.

Barry, whom she'd seen earlier in the Season at the Royal Horticultural Society and then not again.

Which had also been a welcome reprieve and not truly a surprising one at that. Given the direction of his interests, she'd wager her reputation as London's leading matchmaker that he was far from the dutiful son to attend his mother's formal summer party.

"Here we are," the duchess murmured as they reached her offices, as though clarity was needed. As though Meredith did not know the ins and outs of this palatial residence as well as she knew the annoying freckles on her own nose.

A servant held the door open, and the duchess waited until Meredith had entered before sweeping in behind her and taking up a spot at the floral upholstered sofa.

The duchess motioned to the chair beside her, and Meredith perched herself on the edge. "I trust you—"

"I am well—"

"—know the reason I've invited you this summer, Miss Durant."

Not *Are you well?*

And also… Miss Durant.

Miss Durant. At that stiff, direct, and not at all… welcoming greeting, Meredith found herself blinking, uncharacteristically knocked off-balance, and incapable of directing the powerful woman to use Meredith's new name. Why, this was no homecoming. This was no attempt to make amends for the Aberdeens' absence at the end of Albie Durant's life.

Are you truly surprised? They all but sacked your father and sent the pair of you on your way, and not so much as a word had been exchanged between them since.

Bitterness stung her throat and nearly choked her. And here she'd believed herself immune to the pain of that betrayal.

Regaining her equilibrium, Meredith straightened. "I confess to being… mystified by your summons, Your Grace." There could be no doubting now that hers was not a social invitation. Nor could it be a matter of business, however, as Emilia, Meredith's childhood friend, had at last married this past winter. Not that a duke's daughter would ever require assistance in securing a match.

The duchess opened her mouth, but was interrupted a moment later by a scratching at the door. "Enter."

A pair of young servants came forward, one bearing a tray of tea, the other tarts.

Not speaking until the maids had gone and closed the door behind them, Her Grace proceeded to pour first one cup and, not even bothering to ask, poured a second. "As you are aware, Emilia has married at last." There was a palpable relief in her tone that met her eyes. The duchess added a spot of cream and a dollop of sugar.

"I did hear of the happy news, Your Grace," she said as the duchess handed over the porcelain teacup. With her business dependent upon unwed ladies and gentlemen, Meredith made it a habit of reading daily any mention of courtships and marriages. She'd come across news of Emilia's marriage to Lord Heathcliff—a surprising match for the other woman. And if she was being honest, at least with herself, the truth that her friend had married and hadn't sent 'round an invitation had stung.

"It was a surprising match. A superb one." The duchess preened as if she herself were responsible for that feat... and knowing the Duchess of Gayle? No doubt, she was. "Also, more important, Emilia's husband is a noble one... of the noblest ranks." The duchess stirred a silver spoon within her teacup. At Meredith's answering silence, she looked up and clarified, "Because Lord Heath will one day be a duke, of course."

"Of course," she said neatly as the Duchess of Gayle sipped from her tea. Wasn't that what drove all parents? That their children made the most advantageous matches?

I just want you to be happy, my girl. I'd prefer you didn't marry a pauper, but as long as he makes you smile.

Her father's voice pinged around her mind, his voice as real and as clear as if he were there with them now. But as he'd been long ago, and not in those last, darkest months when he'd believed Meredith a stranger and railed at her to stay away.

"You know something of noble matches, do you not, my dear?"

It took a moment to register that the duchess had put a question to her.

"I do." After they'd left Berkshire, her father's sizable pension had gone entirely to his care. When he'd died not even a year and five months later, there'd been nothing left, and Meredith had been forced to craft a career... or starve.

"It is my understanding that you had a hand in the Turnover match." The young lady, nearly on the shelf, had at last found marriage with the Marquess of Roxby.

"I did, Your Grace." Meredith took a sip of her tea.

The older woman's statement had been just that, a statement. There was no praise from the duchess, who was only a smidge below royalty. Compliments were to be *given* to those of her exalted ranks.

"And most recently Miss Saltonstall."

"You've kept abreast of my work." Surprise pulled that remark from her. Why would the duchess, unless she cared—

"I've asked you here on an assignment," Her Grace said bluntly, shattering all foolish illusions.

There it was. The reason for her visit was related to Meredith's work, after all. She curled her toes tight. It was silly to feel disappointment, and yet, there it was. When would she cease being disappointed by this family?

Putting aside her teacup, the duchess lifted the tabletop desk situated beside the tray of untouched desserts. "I am hosting a house party,' she explained as she opened the lid and withdrew several sheets from within. "These are my guests," she explained, handing them over.

Meredith set down her barely touched tea and accepted the pages, and while the duchess spoke, she read the names there. Most were familiar, and the one thing all those families she did know had in common was at least one daughter in the market for a husband.

"They are all ladies of the noblest, highest birthrights."

And yet... Meredith rested the sheets on the table beside her cup. "Your Grace, I'm not certain what you are asking of me."

The duchess blinked slowly and then smiled. "Why, Miss Durant, I'm asking you to matchmake for my son."

Several beats of silence went by.

The duchess's smile quickly withered. "You do recall my son, I trust?"

"Barry?" she asked dumbly, and as soon as the name left her mouth, heat exploded in her cheeks. "Lord Tenwhestle," she hurriedly amended.

"He remains my only son."

Did she imagine the uncharacteristic droll edge to that response?

Surely she did. Because as certain as it rained in England, the Duchess of Gayle was not given to jesting… and certainly not about matters pertaining to spares and heirs and birthright.

"He's nearly twenty-seven, and my husband is not getting any younger. The mantle of responsibility will soon pass to Lord Tenwhestle—the title, the holdings, all of it. As such, he needs to make a match with a woman like him."

In rank and standing. It was there, as real as the request that had been put to her.

"I…" To give her hands something to do, Meredith picked up the sheets once more and looked at them. Play matchmaker for not-so-little Barry Aberdeen: the gentleman who'd tricked her two months ago at the horticultural society and who, with his roguish nature, would give most matrons fits. Everything about the proposed assignment screamed one word: *run*.

She glanced over at the duchess. "I am honored you should think of me for such"—an impossible—"distinguished assignment, Your Grace. However, the clients I serve? They are… they have all been"—and would only ever be—"young ladies."

Her Grace's lips puckered in a frown, no words of disapproval needed.

Meredith continued into the silence, "Either way, I am certain his lordship will not require the services of a matchmaker. He is—" A marquess. A future duke. And a charmer. The latter of which wasn't even necessary to snag the most proper lady, given his title.

The duchess's brows drew together ever so slightly, faintly enough to be almost imperceptible and terrifying for the unspoken warning there. "Are you suggesting that you know my son more than I do, Miss Durant?"

Miss Durant. That formal use had once been affixed to Meredith only when the duchess was displeased with her for some antics or another she'd been up to. Now, that formal usage came as a reminder of the station difference between Meredith and this family.

She bowed her head. "I'd never presume, Your Grace."

"Ah," Her Grace sent a single brow arcing up, "but you just *did*."

"Yes. But no... I..." Meredith sought to order her thoughts.

"Is it yes, or is it no?"

"No," she finished lamely. "I don't presume to know more than you about your son." Blast if the Duchess of Gayle hadn't managed to reduce her to tongue-ties, as she always had with her mere presence alone.

The duchess gave a little toss of her perfectly coiffed silver-tinged strands. "Splendid. As such, since you've agreed that his lordship requires assistance, the assignment is yours."

The assignment?

Feeling like she'd stepped out onto a crowded, unfamiliar London street without the benefit of directions, Meredith accepted again the pages the duchess thrust into her hands. "These are the young ladies. I've kept copious notes on each of them. The second page..."

Hurrying to keep up with the rapid-fire directives, Meredith flipped to the next sheet.

"...details all the areas in which my son will require assistance."

Entirely too amused.

Singing...

Playing pianoforte...

Her lips twitched up, and she fought desperately to repress her first smile since she'd arrived.

The duchess leaned forward. "My son sang at the Duchess of Sutton's winter house party," she explained on a whisper before stealing a quick glance at the doorway. "He was deplorable, Miss Durant. Just deplorable. I'd never dare say as much aloud to him, lest I wound his self-esteem. As you know how men are with their esteem."

"I do," she said, before moving on to the next page.

"He'd be crushed, and therefore refuse to ever again perform," the duchess continued as if Meredith hadn't already agreed with her. "On that page there, I've enumerated all my son's strengths."

Meredith skimmed the list—the rather sparse list.

1.   *Fine smile.*

Yes, given the brief exchange she'd had with the scoundrel at the horticulture society earlier in the Season, Meredith could personally attest to that.

2. *Riding.*
3. *Fencing.*
4. *A knowledge of horseflesh.*
5. *Wagering.*

"Wagering?" Meredith echoed dumbly.

"I didn't say they were necessarily *admirable* or *good* strengths, Miss Durant. Just strengths." She spoke slowly, as if instructing a slow-witted student.

Meredith made quick work of the perfunctory list. According to his mother, Barry Aberdeen possessed the same predictable interests as every other last rake, rogue, and scoundrel from the corner of Cornwall all the way to Cumbria.

"It is all there," the duchess was saying as Meredith reorganized the sheets into a neat little stack. "As such, I've carefully balanced the guest list to include more ladies to gentlemen. No need to spur competition, is there?"

It wasn't really a question. Nonetheless, Meredith agreed—aloud anyway. "Not at all, Your Grace."

"Oh, and I've also this for you…" The duchess withdrew another folded page and handed it over.

Meredith read through the names. It looked like…

"They are the ladies who I believe would make the best match for my son."

It looked like exactly what it was. Meredith read the list of familiar names, all of London's latest and still unwed diamonds. Most of the young ladies on the list were notorious gossips. And the ones who weren't had reputations for being unkind. In short, Meredith would not dare match any of the women with any gentleman… and certainly not Barry, who'd been like a brother to her growing up. Meredith measured her words carefully before she spoke. "Your Grace, that is not how this process generally works…"

The duchess scoffed. "Of course it is." She paused. "For the Aberdeens anyway."

Yes, a ducal family would *never* be held to the same constraints or expectations as… well, anyone. And yet, Meredith had built her business and her name by conducting her work without interference from anyone… not even the hiring families. Carefully choosing her words, Meredith refolded the page. "I appreciate that you've composed a list…" Of diamonds destined to be the future hostesses of Polite Society.

The older, regal woman crossed her arms. "Yes?"

Only a duchess could make a single syllable sound like a threat and a warning. Meredith picked her way even more cautiously through the exchange. "It is just there is a way I go about coordinating unions." The process was far more meticulous and effortful than simply looking at lineage. She composed notes for each potential candidate for her subject and compared the accumulated research.

"And I take it this is not it," the duchess intoned dryly when Meredith added nothing further.

"This is not."

"Ah, but I'm not looking for you to make the decision about my son's wife." Gathering her palms, the duchess lightly crinkled the sheets clutched between them. "I'm asking you to find a way to make my son amenable to the most suitable ones there."

Suitable as decided by Barry Aberdeen's mother and, no doubt, father.

"Lady Ivy Clarence is quite witty and clever."

As beautiful as she was and in possession of a stunning singing voice, the nineteen-year-old lady's reputation preceded her. As did her reputation for being unpleasant with her servants. "She is at that. However—"

"Lady Marina is an exceptional conversant." *Gossip*. She was particularly crafty at ferreting out details a person had no wish to have bandied about. "It is my suggestion that you begin with those two ladies."

Meredith glanced at the list once more. "But, Your Grace—"

The duchess sailed to her feet. "Now if you'll excuse me. Your rooms are readied. Given our family's… connection, I've taken the liberty of having you stay in the family suites."

"Thank you, Your Grace." She murmured the words of gratitude at the unexpected kindness. Even so, she could not stay here. Not and serve in the role of matchmaker for the son of a woman who'd largely seen to the task herself. "But—"

Her Grace waved a dismissive palm. "Think nothing of it."

And here, Meredith had believed she'd meant less to the Aberd—

"Closer proximity to Barry will allow you time to school his lordship sight unseen from the other guests." The other woman was already hurrying to the door.

"Yes, that is a wise idea." Or it would be, if… Meredith jumped up. "However, Your Grace, I'm afraid I cannot—"

The duchess whipped around. "Of course. How could I have forgotten? Three thousand."

Meredith cocked her head. "Beg pardon?"

"Three thousand pounds. Your commission when you see Barry matched."

With that, the duchess left.

Meredith remained rooted to the floor, her mouth agape, the pages in hand.

Three thousand…?

Meredith's legs gave out, and she found herself sinking into the previously abandoned seat.

A fortune. A sum that would take her a lifetime to earn.

And all she would have to do was match her first male client.

Not-so-little Barry.

"Ahem."

She glanced up.

A liveried footman stood at attention in the doorway. "If I may show you to your chambers, Miss Durant?"

Giving her head a clearing shake, Meredith hurriedly stuffed the pages inside her valise. "I have the way," she assured him. After all, despite being a servant, she'd called these halls home, and never, in all her time here, had a servant escorted her about as some special guest.

After he'd bowed and taken himself off like she was, in fact, just that, Meredith resumed packing up her things. All the while, she contemplated Her Grace's directives… and this newest of assignments.

Matchmake… for a man.

It was an unheard-of idea. For Meredith anyway. Never before had she been charged with finding a suitable bride for a bridegroom. It was… unconventional, and Meredith had, as a rule, done nothing outside the bounds of conventional.

And yet… neither was there anything remotely the *same* in this assignment. She'd been invited by a friend of her late father on a request to help their son. A son who, by all rights, would benefit from being guided toward a proper, safe match.

Given the Duke and Duchess of Gayle had all but cast Meredith and her father out, she owed them nothing.

Only… a long-ago memory traipsed in: Meredith weeping in the duke's barn while Barry comforted her.

Nay, she owed his parents nothing. But this was about more than the duke and duchess. For, if Her Grace had her way, Barry would find himself wed to a coldhearted Diamond who'd make the lives of the staff here at Berkshire a misery.

No, that would never do.

Furthermore, Barry was a marquess and a future duke. Far more charming than when he'd been a boy of three demanding to ride her back. As such, how very difficult could her task possibly be?

She stood and reached for her bag.

Outside the doorway, a voice boomed, powerful in its fury and outrage.

A familiar voice.

Barry.

"By God, you had better be there, Mother. I am not—" Barry sailed through the doorway, his stare leveling on the empty desk the duchess had occupied. "Bloody hell," he muttered, glancing around…

And then his gaze landed on her.

He slowed to a halt, and then a wicked and decidedly dangerous grin curved his hard lips up. "Meredith." He pushed the door shut behind him, and she wetted her suddenly dry lips.

She was alone with Barry Aberdeen, the rogue who'd been reading at a horticultural society.

She… knew the *precise* moment she'd been completely forgotten by the rogue.

"Bloody hell," he muttered to himself. "I need a damned brandy. A whole bottle of it. A big, enormous, untouched one. I don't even care if it's the French sort."

Meredith's eyes shot open another fraction as Barry dropped to a knee beside a hutch and jiggled the doors, loosening the ineffective lock. He yanked them open and fished around inside. "Aha," he said to himself. Drawing out a bottle of brandy, he jumped to his feet and held the half-empty bottle aloft with a triumphant lift.

Meredith couldn't sort on whether to be shocked by his

outrageous display… or by the fact that Her Grace had a secret liquor stash.

Removing the stopper with his teeth, he spit it out and then downed a hefty swallow.

In the end, Meredith settled on the former.

After he'd lowered the decanter to his side, Barry scratched at the corner of his mouth. "So," he drawled, stretching out that lone syllable. "It would seem you find yourself an unfortunate guest of my mother's house party." He walked over to her, his boots covered with mud, his trousers wet and clinging to every muscle of his sculpted legs, and stopped before her.

Meredith's pulse thundered in her ears.

She'd been wrong.

It would appear her task was to be a difficult one, after all.

CHAPTER 5

ℐN THE ABSENCE OF A mother to call out, Barry would settle for the next best thing—an ally.

An ally who proved the only welcome guest in this now-damned infernal household, not solely because of the scheme Emilia had alerted him to, but rather, because of the woman's identity.

Meredith.

Miss Meredith Durant, whom he'd had last seen some months ago, as pinch-mouthed as she'd been then and wholly different than the girl who'd plaited her hair and let it flop about her shoulders as she'd raced the hills of Berkshire.

Quiet.

She was also decidedly quieter. Though, if one was being more accurate, she'd never been silent. Garrulous, always laughing. Silence had been as foreign to her as the sun was to the London sky.

"I never thought I'd see the day," he noted, taking another sip from the bottle.

"I... my lord?"

Because of that hesitancy, he wondered for a moment if he'd stumbled upon some other woman who merely resembled Meredith Durant.

"*My lord?*" he teased.

Meredith fiddled with the heart locket at her throat, then catching his stare upon that nervous fidgeting, she let her arm fall to her side. "You are a marquess."

"I assure you," he drawled, "I'm aware of my title." From the moment he'd taken his first breath, he'd had ground into him the undisputable truth: He was first and foremost a future duke, and because of that, every expectation had been laid out for him. Life was nothing more than a mold that he'd been hopelessly stuffed into. Why, they'd even pick his wife. Nay, not *they*. In this case, his damned mother. His mouth tightened. "I'm very aware of my title, indeed."

"Then you know that it's expected I should refer to you so." She gave a snap of her skirts, and a memory traipsed in.

"Why in God's name are you snapping your skirts, Mare?"

"Because that is what ladies do to convey their displeasure. It is a most useful skill. For instance..." Meredith snapped her skirts at her ankles.

A smile pulled at his lips. "Pfft." Barry perched his hip along the back of his mother's sofa. "That will never do," he chided, reaching for a strand of her hair to tug as he'd done as a boy determined to bother her... and finding all those strands perfectly in place. In the end, he settled for cuffing her under the chin. "I daresay first names shall still suffice. I mean..." He leaned forward and lowered his voice. "Given that you were gracious enough to serve as my 'mare' for the first four years of my—"

Meredith dissolved into a paroxysm, her previously pale cheeks going red, adding an endearing color to her slightly long face. "M-my lord..." she choked out, whipping her gaze about as if she feared she'd be discovered committing some great scandal.

"Barry," he corrected. "Or were you praying?"

She choked once more. "The p-proper form of a-address. I was referring t-to your title."

For the passage of time that had elapsed, one constant remained: It was enjoyable as hell teasing the minx. "Ah, pity that." He lifted his mother's hidden bottle and took another drink. "I see you received the summons." Given that Meredith had been born at Berkshire and given her connection to the Aberdeens, it had been a summons long overdue. Though one he'd never envy a person for. "My apologies."

"My lord?"

There it was again, hesitant... and formal.

He lifted a brow.

Meredith wetted her lips, darting her tongue out, trailing their narrow seam. And it was only because a rogue's blood flowed in his veins that he was riveted by that subtle movement. "*Barry*," she conceded. Her voice, a shade lower, added a husky depth that only further fired his awareness.

"Generally, my mother's summer house party is my least-loathed event." He gave her a look. "You do remember, I trust? The fair where my father allows the gypsies…"

Her features grew stricken. "I remember," she said quietly.

The flash of sadness was gone as soon as it came, so that it might have merely been a trick of the light.

There were several beats of silence, and to fill the void, Barry lifted the bottle to his mouth for another drink. "My mother has plans for me." He held out his mother's brandy.

Meredith ignored the offering. "Oh?" she asked, seating herself.

"Matchmaking." He strangled on the syllables, waving his spare hand about. "Finding me a bride. A suitable one. An *illustrious* one."

Something glinted in her eyes. "I… see." Something he could not make sense of… and yet, it intrigued him all the further.

"Goodness, you're a good deal quieter than… ever."

"I'm a good deal many more things than I was," she murmured, and were she any other woman who refused to be flirted with, he'd have taken her response as a deliberate attempt at being coy.

Yes, she was more restrained. Reserved. And… completely unlike her once-boisterous self. The Meredith of old would have had some commiserative—mayhap even choice words—and only after she'd grabbed the bottle of brandy and downed a swallow.

She'd changed… in so many ways. Even this version of Meredith Durant was a more somber version than the woman he'd run into at the Royal Horticultural Society—a woman whose eyes had been on him while he'd read.

And he quite despised it. Because propriety rotted a nobleman's soul and dulled his excitement, but now time had proven it had the same effects on young women… like Meredith.

Restless, he quit his place on the back of the sofa and moved around, finding the place beside her.

Meredith stiffened, her spine going ramrod straight, and then she inched closer to the arm of the sofa.

Now, this was interesting, indeed. At what point did a girl who'd set out to tease and torment him become so very skittish?

Regardless, none would dare confuse Barry as one who set about to make ladies uncomfortable. He stopped his approach. "I thought you of all people would have something to say on it," he admonished, dropping his legs atop the rose-inlaid table alongside his mother's tabletop desk.

"On what?"

He gave her a look.

Meredith yanked her gaze from his legs, and a bright blush stained her cheeks. Well, this was even more interesting. "Oh," she blurted. "You referred to your upcoming marriage."

Upcoming marriage. "That is certainly the way my mother would refer to it," he muttered. Never Meredith Durant.

She scooted closer, and he felt a lightness that they could simply be around each other as they'd been. "And… why do you expect I should have something to say about your marital affairs?"

Barry tossed an arm out, looping it around the place on the back of the sofa where Meredith's shoulders would have been—had she not been sitting painfully erect. "Because it is *you* of all people."

A small frown turned her already tense mouth down at the corners. She fought with herself. Old Meredith would have spit out the question and ten others behind it. This new, more measured version of herself tried to hold on to propriety above all else. In the end, the Meredith of old won out. "And what is *that* supposed to mean?"

"You remember, do you not?" Barry leaned in all the more and placed his lips against her ear. "You ladies and your desire for a duke. What of the love and laughter of an honorable man?"

Meredith gasped and whipped her head around so quick her forehead slammed into his nose.

With a curse, he pressed a palm against the wounded appendage. "Bloody hell. I think you broke it," he muttered, checking his fingers for blood.

"You *heard* us?" she whispered. "And it's not broken. You're not even bleeding. Though I should break it."

Even through the pain, he grinned. This was the Meredith he recalled. "Oh, I not only heard you ladies that day, but I remembered it and committed it to memory."

Meredith gasped. "How dare you?"

"Oh, I dared quite regularly." Alas, if he'd been a more polite gent, he'd have taken mercy. Fire, however, lit her eyes, spurring him shamelessly on. "What was it that you and my sister and her friends were plotting? Hmm?" He made a show of tapping a contemplative finger against his chin. "I have it! You were plotting ways to win the heart of a duke."

A bright blush flooded her cheeks again, rather transforming her into someone quite… pretty. When was the last time he'd so enjoyed himself? "You are a scoundrel still, Barry Aberdeen."

He pressed a palm to his chest. "Unapologetically so. I will say, however, it was rather shortsighted of you to have failed to consider there was at least one future duke in your mid—*oomph*." He grunted as Meredith let a sharp elbow slide into his ribs.

Good God, by the time they were through here, she was going to have broken or bloodied some part of him. Nonetheless… "That is better."

She puzzled her brow. "What is?"

"You're showing hints of your former"—more spirited—"self. I could really benefit from having an ally through… through… this," he settled for, unable to make himself utter anything about the demise of his bachelorhood.

"Generally, if one is in the market for an ally, they don't go about needling and making a pest of oneself to the ally in question," Meredith said dryly.

"Fair point," he conceded. "Perhaps we can begin again?" He dropped his stained boots to the floor, splattering mud upon the Aubusson carpet. Meredith winced, eyeing the mess. Oh, bloody hell. Need of an ally or not, it was just too irresistible. *She* was just too irresistible. Barry leaned close, placing his lips near the shell of her ear. Only… the hint of jasmine that clung to her proved distracting. Heady. A fragrant intoxication, sweet and alluring. All earlier teasing fled as Barry drew in a deep breath, inhaling the summery scent of her.

The long column of Meredith's throat worked, the muscles moving in a rhythmic display as she angled her neck the slightest amount, and yet, close as they were, he saw her body's reflexive opening, an invitation. Odd that he knew so very much about Meredith Durant, and yet, the feel of her skin, the taste of it escaped him. A moth to the flame, Barry angled his mouth closer to at last have an answer to the question he'd not known he needed an answer to—until now. "Mayhap, we might even return to that day at the Royal Horticultural Society when you were admiring my recitation of poetry," he suggested on a whisper.

Meredith was awash with an inexplicable and dangerous awareness of the most unlikely of men, so it took a moment for Barry's words to penetrate.

When they did, they pulled another gasp from her lips. "You are incorrigible, and we are done here, my lord," she said tightly, reverting back to the use of his proper title. A lifetime of knowing each other be damned.

She made to jump up.

And she would have.

If the muscles in her legs were not already fatigued from her twelve-hour journey from London. If she hadn't already been more than slightly weak-kneed from the sough of his breath upon her skin.

But she was both of those things.

Meredith lost her balance and came down hard, landing squarely on Barry's lap.

"Whoa, love." His hands caught her by the waist, righting her so she didn't tumble backward onto the floor.

The earth stilled in the most peculiar way.

"You *were* admiring me," he pointed out, as though it were the most natural thing in the world to cradle her on his lap and converse about that past moment in the public garden she'd not allowed herself to think on.

"I most certainly was *not* admiring you."

Alas, such as a rebuttal could never be convincing when it emerged on a whispery exhalation that was more sigh than speech. And no convincing rebuttal could ever be given when perched atop Barry's lap.

A perch that admirably displayed the muscle he'd added to his form in their time apart. Meredith swallowed hard.

She really needed to storm off. Such was the suitable, ladylike response.

And she would have, if he'd teased her further. Only he didn't. He angled her body closer, bringing their chests in perfect alignment, and she remained there, her chest pressed to his, keenly aware of every ripple of muscle when he moved. "Do you know what I believe, Meredith?"

Meredith.

Not *Mare.*

Not *Miss Durant.*

Husked on a whisper laced with a promise.

The dampness of his trousers penetrating her skirts did little to stifle the warmth fluttering low in her belly.

Stop, you're no virginal miss. And she was certainly not so… so… imprudent to be enraptured by little Barry Aberdeen.

Liar. Aside from the half grin he'd always perfectly affected, she couldn't even find a hint of the boy of her past. She made her head move in a semblance of a shake. "I… don't…" Even recall the last question he'd asked. Had it even been a question?

His mouth moved close to hers, and her breath hitched in her lungs. "I believe you *were* admiring me that day." He winked.

It was that slight flutter of his impossibly long golden lashes that managed to break whatever momentary madness had held her under its snare.

With a gasp, she scrambled from his lap. Her skirts—her now-damp skirts—tangled about her legs.

Meredith came down hard on the floor. She groaned as pain radiated from her buttocks up her back, and she resisted the urge to massage the wounded area.

Barry leaned over, an entirely too amused grin on his lips. "May I…?" He stretched a hand out.

"I-I most certainly do not require any help," she stammered, rising with as much grace as one could who'd fallen first in his lap and then at his feet and now had mud-spattered skirts for her efforts.

"Oh, come, Mare, I was teasing," he called as she grabbed her bag. The floorboards groaned as he rushed over and placed himself in her path, blocking her slow retreat. "I came looking for support."

"You want *my* support." Meredith switched her increasingly heavy bag to her other hand.

"Emilia is otherwise occupied by her newish husband. My mother and father only have one plan for me."

"And you've identified me as your only friend in this place?"

she drawled.

"Among a houseful of marriage-minded ladies? Indeed, I have." His smile widened, dimpling his left cheek and doing odd things to her heart's natural rhythm.

She'd used to pinch that dimple when he'd been a boy with pudgy cheeks. How very different that mark was in his chiseled features.

Disgusted with herself, she struggled with her bag. "We haven't seen each other in years, Barry."

He relieved her of her bag, holding on to it with an infuriating ease. "Two months."

"That isn't the same," she insisted. Furthermore, she'd been alone these past years, looking after herself and her belongings, and that wouldn't change now that she'd returned to the Aberdeen residence. She rescued her valise, her shoulders slumping slightly under the added weight, and then she made herself straighten them.

"I was merely teasing before, Meredith," he said quietly, with the first seriousness she'd heard in his voice since he'd stormed the room, searching for the duchess and her bottle of brandy.

Of course he'd only been teasing. Barry had ever been teasing. His accidental confiding in her about his efforts to subvert his mother's matchmaking—or, more accurately, Meredith's matchmaking—had proved both distracting... and far more useful.

But entirely less pleasurable. Sighing, she set her bag at her feet and faced him. "I'm listening."

His lips twitched, and he perched himself on the back of the sofa once more. "Though slightly better, that's hardly a vast improvement in the renewal of our childhood friendship."

Meredith gave him a look. "You're incapable of being serious." She turned to go.

"My mother and father are trying to marry me off," he called after her, freezing her in her tracks. "There you have it. You've been invited to attend the summer house party where they attempt to maneuver me into a match with an estimably suitable young lady."

He didn't know why she'd been invited here. As she turned slowly back, she thrust back the niggling part of her that said that remaining here under the guise of not knowing was shamefully underhanded. "And you don't wish to marry?"

"Egad. Me?" He grimaced. "No."

"Why?" she asked quietly, and by the way he opened and closed his mouth several times, her question had taken him by surprise. "Why?"

Meredith drifted over to him. "What are you in search of, Barry?"

"I… I…" He gave his head a bemused shake, dislodging several droplets of water. A lone bit of moisture hit her cheek.

Meredith brushed it away and stopped so the tips of her travel-worn boots brushed his mud-splattered ones. "What is it you enjoy?" she asked quietly. Meredith merely asked to gather information to help her in her work here. Except, as the next question left her, why did it feel as though she wished to know more about this very tall, very muscular version of the Barry she'd once known?

"I…" His gaze grew distant, and he glanced down at the bottle in his hand. Instead of slogging another swallow, however, he studied the decanter before setting it on the console table behind the sofa. "What would you say, Meredith Durant," he began on a quiet murmur, "if I told you it doesn't matter because my purpose is singular: I'm an heir to a dukedom and not much more."

This was a more serious and solemn side of Barry. Her chest tightened at the deviation from his usual carefree self. "I would say," she ventured slowly, "I don't believe you. And that you should let more than your title and future title define you and your future, Barry."

He smiled, this one a small sad expression that briefly ghosted his lips. "Alas, one cannot truly be separated from the other."

She'd never envied Emilia or Barry their birthrights… until she'd gone off on her own to make a future and living for herself, without the benefits and protections enjoyed by those of the peerage. Reflexively, she touched a hand to his chest. "I'm not suggesting that you separate yourself from it, Barry, but rather, recognize that you are first and foremost a man."

Tension crackled in the air. And his gaze dipped slowly to her hand.

She quickly dropped her arm. Meredith cleared her throat. "Let us say you were being forced into a match—"

"Which I won't be."

"But if you were, what interests do you have that you'd hope your future bride would also enjoy?"

Barry eyed her suspiciously for a moment, and in his eyes, she saw the battle he fought with himself. And she knew he didn't know whether he wished to carry on this real conversation between them in which he would share parts of himself. Or whether he wanted to give some flippant reply.

"I'd want a woman who can understand plants."

She let out a sound of frustration. How utterly foolish to believe him capable of delivering a serious answer. "Good day, Barry," she said, infusing that with an air of finality as she grabbed her bag.

Except... he called after her, his next five words bringing her up short.

"You believe I'm funning you? That I was at the Royal Horticultural Society for what purpose? Mayhap to seduce some widow among the rhododendron dell? Hmm."

Her cheeks fired as an image flitted forward of Barry, quickly leading a lady down those trails, losing themselves in a maze of greenery. Only, it wasn't some other woman she saw with him... but herself.

Meredith swallowed a groan of disgust. *You blasted ninny.* She made herself face him, praying he'd not note the blush heating her cheeks. "As you pointed out, I've known you many years. I've never known you to have an interest in plants."

"Why would you?" he asked curiously. "Were you paying attention to me when I was a young lad?"

"Yes." He winged a brow up. "No," she said quickly. "Not in *that* way."

"And what way is that, Meredith?" he purred, sending her pulse skittering.

"H-hush," she admonished, the slight tremble destroying her bid to be the stern matchmaker. "I was merely noticing you as a younger brother getting yourself into trouble." An entirely different way than she'd thought of him since their run-in several months ago.

"Ah," he murmured, taking slow, languid steps forward. "So I must be lying to you now, then? Because who I was as a boy doesn't match with the man I've become?"

No, no, it didn't. He didn't fit at all with the image of the boy he'd been.

"Should I provide you a lesson in all the things you don't know, love?"

Oh, God. Meredith's knees went weak as he stopped so close before her that she had to tip her head back to meet his hooded gaze. "I…"

"About how the honey produced from the nectar of certain types of rhododendron can make a man mad?"

She didn't blink for several moments. It took a moment for her mind to slog through the desire to find the other side of clarity. Had he said…?

Barry did a small, slow circle about her. "Or how an invading Greek army was accidentally poisoned by harvesting and eating the local Asia Minor honey?"

"How do you know that?"

"Because it's so hard to believe that a future duke should be in possession of any information aside from the running of one's estates, horseflesh, *ton* events, and fencing and shooting, of course?"

He compiled that list as one who spoke routinely about the expectations enumerated for him. And then through the wave of humiliation at her mind having wandered a path of wickedness while he'd been speaking from a place of genuine knowledge came something else—shame. For having failed to consider that Barry Aberdeen might have a real interest in plant life. She'd simply taken him as the roguish heir to a future dukedom. "I… didn't know."

"And why should you?" He lifted his shoulders in a shrug that on the surface anyone would have taken for blasé. But she was looking closely at him, had known him too well as a child. "Troublesome Barry and then roguish Barry. You saw what you would." Had there been recrimination there, it would have been easier for her than his matter-of-factness. "What I allowed the world to see," he murmured, almost to himself. And then, as if he'd realized he'd spoken aloud, an endearing crimson color splotched Barry's cheeks. He lifted the brandy bottle. "Either way, my interests, Meredith, extend to plant life."

As he started for the door, Meredith stared after him. *Let him go.* It hardly mattered… and yet, for research purposes it did. "And… what else?" she asked as he took another step toward the door. She didn't want him to leave. Except, as he turned back to rejoin her, why did it feel as if she lied to herself? Why did it feel as though genuine curiosity gripped her about the secrets Barry Aberdeen carried?

"What else?" he repeated back, more slowly.

Feeling his gaze on her, she dropped her arm to her lap and straightened. *Work. Keep focused on the work Her Grace has put to you.* "If you had to spend all your days with one woman—"

"Egad, horrifying stuff."

She fiddled with her necklace. "What interests would you hope she shared of yours?"

"All of a sudden, you're besieged by a fascination with my pastimes, are you, Meredith?" His words were spoken in another of those silken whispers that brushed over her like a physical caress.

"Y-yes." *For my research. For my work here.*

Liar.

He wound his way back toward her and then stopped, his chest brushing her back as he dipped his mouth close to her neck. Her eyes slid closed, and she swore she felt his lips brush a kiss upon that sensitive skin. "Alas, I'm afraid you'll have to find out during your time here," he said cheerfully, his amused tones sobering. "Until later, Mare." With a wink, he spun on his heel and just like that... was gone.

The ormolu clock ticking, Meredith stared at the empty doorway and then forced herself to breathe.

Why did she, of a sudden, feel that in accepting the duchess's assignment she had wandered down a perilous path?

CHAPTER 6

ℬARRY WAS GOING TO GOUGE his eyes out.

The act would undoubtedly prove agonizing, and yet, it would still be a good deal preferable to suffering through any more of old Lady Glassmere prancing around, blindfolded, and grabbing for a nearby gentleman.

As it was, the only reason he'd taken part in this evening's festivities had been so that he could spend the night loosening Meredith Durant's too-tight chignon.

The stubborn chit would have proven contrary even in this. After dining and adjourning with the other ladies, she hadn't rejoined the party, and Barry had been left alone with a stubborn memory of her... and the words she'd leveled at him.

What are you in search of, Barry?

Even now, the softness of that query lingered and echoed in his mind.

It was a question he'd never been asked, or even thought. Everyone simply assumed, given his reputation, that they knew what he wanted out of life: a bottle of spirits, a scandalous woman on his arm and then in his bed. And... not much more.

In fairness, Barry had never shared that he was anything more. Meredith, a friend of his past, asking that question of him, however, had made it surprisingly easy to share.

Only now that he had? He felt uncomfortably... *exposed*. His gaze slid involuntarily over to the urns overflowing with flowers and greenery.

"A microscope? What do you want with a microscope?"

Barry looked over at his tutor, who hung his head, avoiding his eyes. Barry opened his mouth to explain to his papa, but his father interrupted him. "Boys do not worry themselves with flower terminology, and they certainly do not worry themselves with flowers."

And with that, a nine-year-old's hopes of a future in botany had been dashed with the sacking of the tutor who'd indulged him. A new one replaced him, with a ducal curriculum suiting the heir.

"You're not a botanist. You're first and foremost a duke. Everything else comes second to that."

That had been the lesson ingrained into him by his every subsequent, *esteemed* tutor: ducal responsibilities. Math matters as they pertained to the ledgers. It was always and only about the title he'd one day inherit. As such, there'd not been a place for the scholarly pursuits that fell outside of those responsibilities.

From then on, Barry had accepted that those dreams were foolish, the ones that all children invariably had to put behind them as they accepted the practicality that came with life. In his case, the discovery of life's expectations for him had come sooner than for the other young men at Eton and Oxford. And yet, if he'd accepted his present for what it was, why had he mentioned those interests to Meredith Durant? Interests he'd deliberately hidden from... everyone since those early days.

Over the years, his resentment had faded, and he'd simply hidden his research. It was accepted that lords indulged in botany as a hobby. It was the exception, however, for those gentlemen to pursue it as a field of study. Yes, Barry had accepted his life for what it was... and for what it would be.

Damned tedious and predictable.

Until Meredith had arrived.

Mayhap it was the familiarity of the face of a friend from his past that had dragged out not only that remembrance, but also that admission. And yet, for whatever reason, he'd shared that personal part of himself...

Laughter went up around the parlor, briefly breaking into his reverie.

Lady Glassmere grabbed Lord Afton by the arm and rubbed her enormous, fleshy bosom against his arm. "Squee, I've found you, you sly devil."

Barry cringed. Mayhap some soap in his eyes would help, to either scrub them clean or blind him to the sight of her shameless groping.

Out of the corner of his gaze, he caught Emilia winding her way through the guests as a young lady assisted the old matron out of her blindfold. "I'll see to that," Lady Glassmere barked when her young goddaughter attempted to blindfold Afton. She snapped at the poor girl's fingers and then snagged Lord Afton by the back of his jacket and proceeded to cover his eyes.

"My God, she's positively aggressive." Emilia spoke in hushed tones as she took up a spot alongside Barry.

"I was going to go with offensive," he said from the corner of his mouth. As it to emphasize that very point, Lady Glassmere pinched Lord Afton, none too subtly, on his buttock. "But your choice of words is also entirely suitable."

"Yes, yes, well, I believe *both* descriptors suffice."

There was no wonder, however, as to why their mother had invited the woman, who was chaperone to the only daughter of the late Marquess and Marchioness of Halliwell.

"You've done an impressive job of staying out of the fray," his sister remarked.

"Have a care, or you'll give me away."

Emilia winked.

They fell silent, watching the festivities from their corner of the parlor. Laughter and squeals went up around the room as Lord Afton, with his arms outstretched, wove around the room.

"You are... aware that Meredith has come," Emilia said, breaking the quiet.

It didn't escape his notice that it wasn't a question. Rather, she spoke as one in possession of more knowledge than any sibling wanted one's sister to have.

So that was why she'd abandoned her husband for Barry's company.

Oh, bloody hell.

For one horrifying moment, he believed she knew. Because blast and damn if it weren't the way of elder sisters to know—or figure out—everything. "I..." He resisted the urge to yank at his cravat and kept his gaze on the parlor game. "I... am aware," he said, having to settle for something and opting for vagueness. Oh, good

God. Perhaps the women, who'd been as close as sisters, had picked up precisely where their friendship had left off, and Meredith had exposed his less-than-subtle attempted seduction of her earlier. "I was in Mother's offices when we ran into one another. Meredith, that is," he said quickly, rambling on. "Not Mother. I mean, I've run into Mother there, too. But not this time."

His sister shot him a peculiar look. "Are you... all right?"

"Fine," he croaked. She was probing. Wasn't she? "Just fine. Why wouldn't I be?" *Would you stop running your mouth like a ton gossip?* Tensing, Barry stole a sideways glance at his sister, searching for a sign that he should make a swift exit.

A troubled glimmer lit her eyes. "As I was saying, it has been years since we've seen her."

"Two months." It had been two months since he'd run into the now-proper minx.

His sister's interested gaze came whipping up. "*You* saw her?"

Barry silently cursed yet another blunder. Only... this time Emilia's eyes didn't reflect a general older-sister suspicion about the roguish game he'd played two times with Meredith, but rather an interest in the other young woman's whereabouts these past years. "At... some event or another in London, we ran into one another," he allowed. The day Emilia would have with him if she learned he'd been at a botanical garden.

"Hmm," Emilia said noncommittally. "It was unpardonable."

That he'd yearned to take, and nearly had taken, the daughter of his family's loyal, late man-of-affairs into his arms? Absolutely it was. "I'm aware of that," he said tightly, adjusting his cravat. In fairness, what had started out as teasing Meredith Durant had shifted, and sometime during their exchanges, he'd been captivated by the woman.

"You aren't responsible for this, Barry."

"It surely isn't Miss Durant who is," he muttered, still too much a coward to meet his sister's eyes and opting instead for the hideous sight of Lady Glassmere jumping in front of the latest blindfolded gentleman.

"Of course it's not her fault," Emilia scolded. "It's mine."

That brought his attention whipping over. "*Yours?*"

Emilia worried at her lower lip. "Renaud."

Oh, good God, Barry *really* should have been paying closer

attention. What in blazes did Emilia's former betrothed, a bloke who'd broken it off more than ten years ago, have to do with Meredith Durant? "I'm afraid I don't follow."

His sister released a beleaguered sigh. "A gentleman wouldn't. You see, when I made my debut, I was so enamored of the Duke of Renaud and being in love that I forgot all those friends dearest to me. All my time became centered on that gentleman, and the ones who truly mattered I let slip from my life."

"Gentlemen don't jilt ladies at the altar," he gritted out with the familiar fury at his sister having been thrown over. "You were better off. Your husband is a far—"

His sister swatted him on the arm. "I do appreciate your devotedness, but do focus. I quite know that my heart wasn't engaged, but the important thing is, at the time, I thought it was, and because of that, I cut out Rowena and Constance and Meredith. And then after… after I was jilted? I didn't want to see anyone. I went my way and… Meredith went hers."

Where had she been? More… what had her life been like since she'd gone? It was one way to go through life a lady with family… but after her father's passing, Meredith had been alone, making her own way in the world. The Aberdeens had failed her, and all that was left were questions as to what accounted for the solemnity that hung over her once-cheerful self. His chest tightened uncomfortably, and he resisted the urge to rub at the peculiar ache there. They'd make it right. Meredith had always belonged in their fold.

"She is here now," he said, awkwardly patting his sister on the back.

Once more his sister looked at him strangely. "Given everything, you seem incredibly tolerant."

Given everything? What in hell did she take him for? A pompous lord who cared far more about his own pleasures than the well-being of others? He bristled. "And why should I not?" He'd never had any issues with Meredith. Nothing that had been abnormal where a teasing older sister-like-figure was concerned. "I'm not an ogre." Yes, he'd gone out of his way to tease Meredith and bait her as a boy, but they were adults now.

"Of course I don't think you're an ogre, Barry," Emilia said. "I just expected that given the reason Mother's summoned her, you strike me as one who'd be far less… welcoming."

Warning bells tinkled at the back of his head. The slight pause in his sister's words bespoke of a greater knowing. He sharpened his gaze on Emilia's face.

A look passed between them. *No.* And then she gave a slow nod, confirming he'd spoken aloud.

Taking her lightly by the arm, he drew her deeper into the corner. "Are you suggesting what I think you are?" he clipped out.

"Precisely that."

He cursed, the sound swallowed by another round of laughter that went up around the parlor. Of course, his mother was determined to see him married off. But this…? It was impossible. It fit not at all with the woman who'd given him life, a woman who placed rank in Society at a greater importance than even the air she breathed. "You expect me to believe that Mother— our mother—is attempting to maneuver me into a marriage with Meredith?" Only, that utterance hadn't even fully left him before an image slipped in of him tugging free the pins of Meredith's too-tight chignon and spreading her dark curls about her shoulders.

His sister looked at him as if he'd sprung a second head, and for one horrifying moment he believed she knew he stood before her, lusting after her best friend. "What are you *talking* about?"

He blinked slowly. "What are *you* talking about?"

"Mother hasn't invited Meredith here as your bride."

Then…?

His sister leaned in. "Do you even know what Meredith has been doing since she left?"

"She's a companion." Which, in and of itself, was a travesty. A woman who'd been raised in a duke's household, the cherished daughter of the duke's best friend and man-of-affairs, deserved far more than employment looking after unappreciative, tittering misses.

Emilia cocked her head. "She isn't a companion."

He opened his mouth and then closed it. Barry knew he'd run into her with a young lady at her side. One who'd not been a relation because, well, Meredith didn't have any. Therefore, he'd not considered just what else her role *could* have been. "Then what is she?"

"She's a matchmaker."

There were several beats of silence as he attempted to muddle through that revelation. In the end, he managed but one word: "What?"

Emilia stole a glance about, and then when she returned her focus to him, she spoke so quietly he strained to hear. "She's a matchmaker, and well, we know why Mother invited her here."

"Meredith is a... matchmaker," he repeated dumbly, his mind slow to process that revelation. Because then it would mean... Horror filled him. "*For me?*"

Emilia rolled her eyes. "Of course, *you*, silly."

He rocked on his heels.

Meredith Durant, the woman he'd nearly kissed and been dreaming of embracing since she'd toppled onto his lap, all rounded buttocks and curved hips, had returned to Berkshire... only to coordinate his match with one of the ladies even now prancing about the room.

What is it you enjoy? She'd asked as though she cared. And she'd not been a woman after his title or interested in his marital state. She'd been a woman he'd known as a child and considered a friend, but all the while she'd been gathering information to help her in her task.

Her task which was, in fact... him.

"Barry?" Concern wreathed his sister's voice.

And yet, Barry was unable to formulate a response.

Fire sparked to life and quickly sizzled through his veins. A growl built in his chest and climbed into his throat. Ignoring his sister as she called after him, he quit the parlor and went in search of the little traitor.

CHAPTER 7

If Meredith were being honest with herself following the duchess's formal dinner, when the party had begun to gather for the evening's games of blind man's bluff, she'd wanted to join in the fun.

She'd wanted to enter that same room where she'd played that same game a lifetime ago. She'd wanted to wander around, a silk cloth draped over her eyes, breathless with excitement and anticipation.

She'd of course made her excuses.

Because servants didn't take part in those festivities.

Spinsters also didn't take part in those games, not without earning looks of censure or pity.

But she'd wanted to.

Lying in a bed she'd slept in so many times, her hands clasped atop her chest, Meredith opened and closed the locket at her throat.

Click-click-click-click.

When was the last time she'd taken part in any frivolous activity? When was the last time she'd felt breathlessly excited about… anything or anyone? Or smiled or laughed?

Click-click-click.

Meredith abruptly stopped.

She let her necklace fall.

Why, she could not call forth a single moment after she'd departed Berkshire. For not long after they'd gone, she'd discovered that her father was sick. His had been an illness in his mind that had progressed in a way that had required her to devote the whole of her days to care for him. Then, after that, she'd immediately begun the process of finding employment and building her business. There'd been no time for anything but work.

So the happiest memories she carried were of this place.

She braced for the memory of Patrin to traipse in and, along with it, the old familiar hurt that had dulled but lingered.

And, this time, it did not come.

For… she *had been* breathless… and not so very long ago. Recently, in fact.

Whoa, love…

Her breath grew shallow at the memory of Barry's husky laugh and the sough of his breath. Her hand reflexively went back to the chain at her throat.

"Stop it." She whispered the command into the quiet, to make it more real. She'd been a fool where another man was concerned and had been wise to never trust another thereafter.

Lusting after Barry as she did now? Was pure folly that jeopardized the stability his parents had proffered, all of which hung contingent upon Meredith securing a bride for Barry.

A bride selected from the ladies who were engaging in the games that Meredith wished to be part of.

There were no games for people like Meredith, however, because… well, in short, there was no time for anything else. As such, she'd believed herself incapable of enjoying the childish pursuits. Barry wouldn't. Barry, prone to smile and laugh, would never make apologies for taking his pleasure where and when he would.

Barry, who was also playing blind man's bluff with some entirely suitable-for-him young lady.

An unexpected frisson wound its way through her, sharp and green and biting and feeling very much like—

Her bedroom door exploded open, and she shrieked. The panel hit the wall with such force it bounced back and nearly caught Barry in the face. And it would have if he hadn't slammed his foot out to keep it from closing.

"B-Barry?" Meredith burrowed under her blankets. With a dangerous silence made more volatile by the still-thrumming echo of the slammed door, he slipped inside.

"Hullo, Meredith," he purred on a silken whisper somehow more terrifying than the violent entry he'd made.

"Leave my rooms a-at once," she ordered in a more measured whisper, even if it emerged more squeak than anything. She was mindful that any guest or family member or servant might happen by, and her reputation would be shattered, along with her career. Even if it was just... Barry.

"Oh, do you know, Miss Durant? I don't believe I shall."

"Y-you should not be here, Barry," she whispered, scrambling to her knees and clutching the coverlet close to her pounding heart.

That managed the seemingly impossible: He stopped his forward approach. "Ohhh," he said almost conversationally, as if they conversed over tea and biscuits and not in the middle of her bedchambers with Meredith attired in nothing more than her nightgown. "And where should I be?" Barry dipped his brows menacingly. "Below stairs with my mother's distinguished guests?"

She nodded. "Precisely."

"Forgive me." He sketched a bow. "I should return, then."

"At least you're now being reasonable."

And then, his gaze burning into her, he reached back and turned the lock with a decisive click that sealed them away together.

"You were being sarcastic," she blurted, clutching her coverlet all the tighter.

"I was."

Barry started forward. The candlelight played off his sharp, chiseled features. When had he become this... beautiful?

"You've gone silent, Meredith Durant. Feeling guilty, perhaps?"

"I've nothing to feel guilty about." Aside from this breathless fascination with him, her best friend's younger brother who also happened to be her charge. Her heart hammered erratically in her chest.

It was solely from fear for his reputation and her own. That was all it was.

Why, as he stalked forward with sleek, pantherlike strides, did that feel like the greatest of lies?

"Do you have anything to say to me, madam?" he purred, completing the image in her mind of the great Bengal tiger she'd observed alongside one of her charges at the Royal Menagerie.

Meredith darted her tongue out, wetting suddenly dry lips.

Barry's gaze sharpened on her mouth, increasing the beat of her heart.

"Th-this is hardly the kind of visit f-from a childhood friend."

"Ah, but then, does a friendship truly remain if one friend betrays the other?" He dropped a knee on her mattress, and Meredith, hugging her blankets close to her modest nightdress, scrambled back. She became tangled in her covers and fell back on her haunches.

"Th-there's been no betrayal," she denied, breathless as she feinted left.

Barry matched her movements. "No?"

Meredith moved right, but he immediately anticipated and followed suit. "Of course not."

"Are you here with the intent of finding me a *suitable* wife?"

Meredith stilled. "Oh. That." He *would* be one of those lofty lords who'd fight the parson's trap.

His brows dipped. "Oh. *That?*" he repeated slowly, and she'd have to be stupid to fail to hear the satiny warning there.

Her foot snagged the underside of her hem, and with a shriek, Meredith tumbled backward.

Barry was immediately there. In one fluid movement, he'd scrambled across the bed and caught her with her head and back dipped precariously over the side. He guided her back onto the mattress and remained there, effectively framing her between his elbows, trapping her. He lowered his brow to hers.

Meredith's heart beat erratically.

At her near fall? Or his body's nearness?

The safer answer was the former. She secretly feared, however, it was the latter.

Alas, with the dangerous narrowing of his gaze that he now worked over her face, that awareness remained entirely one-sided. "I am not pleased with you, madam."

Her chest rose and fell at the press of his body against hers.

"I can see that," she whispered. "And g-given that, I'd expect you would have let me happily fall," she said in a bid to be blasé, the tremble in her voice making a mockery of her efforts.

Barry lowered his face closer. "Ah," he murmured, closer still, his breath warm against her lips, a satiny soft caress.

Her lashes fluttered. *He is going to kiss me.* And she'd not been kissed in so long. The kisses she'd received had been hasty and sloppy, but something in Barry's embrace said his mouth would teach her all the reasons some ladies traded their reputations for sin. Meredith tipped her head back to receive that kiss.

"But that is the difference," he murmured. "I'm not the ogre, madam."

The... ogre.

The cool admonishment had the same effect as the cold water he'd managed to cajole the serving maids into substituting in Meredith's bath some fifteen years earlier. "Are you calling me an ogre?"

"No." He paused. "I already called you one."

Meredith pushed against his chest. Lusting after him, indeed. "Get off me at once, Barry Aberdeen."

Alas, it was hard to muster the chilling matchmaker tones she'd used on improper gentlemen approaching her charges, when one's night shift was rucked about her thighs while a man held one trapped.

"Or what? You'll scream for help? That would certainly ruin your plans, as well as my mother's."

Oh, she'd had quite enough of this. Meredith brought her knee up and caught Barry hard between the legs. Groaning, he collapsed atop her and muttered something that sounded very close to "ogre" in her ear.

Meredith grunted, struggling to draw air into her lungs.

Or rather, they both struggled to draw breath.

Meredith bucked her hips until he rolled off of her onto his side. "Furthermore," she carried on, slightly winded, "I'll have you know that the proper term for a female ogre is, in fact, ogress."

<hr />

Barry didn't know whether he wished to lambaste the chit for the violent blow and tart tongue or kiss her.

With her delicate cheeks awash with color and her plaited hair draped over an exposed shoulder, she bore no hint of the straitlaced woman he'd reconnected with that morn.

Even still writhing from her well-placed knee, this spirited, fearless version of her earlier self proved captivating. "Very apt moniker for you," he muttered through the pain.

Meredith swung her legs over the bed, and her white skirts fluttered about her ankles, but not before he caught a delectable flash of long legs and lush thighs perfect for a man to sink his fingers into.

He swallowed a groan and rolled onto his back, forcing his gaze up to the cherubs silently jeering him with their knowing smiles for the devil he was.

"Furthermore," Meredith was saying as she sprinted across the room, her gold chain whipping about as she did, "you are being unreasonable."

That brought him upright. "*I'm* unreasonable?"

She grabbed her wrapper from the back of the chair at her vanity and shrugged into it. "Yes. Un-reas-on-able." She broke the word up into five syllables. "You are nearly thirty."

"I'm twenty-six."

"A ducal heir."

"Am I? I didn't know," he said, sarcasm dripping from his voice.

"You're responsible for carrying on one of the oldest titles in the realm. You have families dependent upon you, including your own, for their security and safety. And as such, it makes entirely perfect sense that you'd marry." On a huff, she belted her wrapper at the waist.

The rub of it was, the infuriating woman was correct—on all scores and all points. Only… "How very cold you've become, Meredith," Barry murmured. He stood and started a slow cross over to her.

Meredith stiffened and followed his approach with wary eyes. "I'm not cold. I'm realistic, Barry."

What accounted for that wariness that had not been there before? It served as another reminder, to his sister's point, that Meredith Durant, raised like a daughter in this household, had been forgotten, and her life since remained a mystery.

He stopped before her. That wariness deepened in her eyes, and suspicion wreathed her delicate features. "Is that all I am, then? Hmm?" Unable to resist exploring the texture of her skin, he dusted his knuckles along her cheek. Satin. Pure, unblemished satin. Smooth and warm to the touch. "A title?"

"Of course not."

Did he imagine the threadbare quality of her whisper-soft response?

"And yet, you've a single purpose in being here. Finding me a suitable bride." Barry placed his lips close to hers, and her breath caught audibly. He thrilled at the hint of her desire. "Rather mercenary of you, Meredith."

She brought her palms up and pressed them against his chest, and his heartbeat accelerated under her light touch. "Th-there can be more."

There can be more… For the whisper of a moment, he believed she spoke… of them.

But then…

"I'm not here to see that you only wed for rank, but rather with genuine affection for the woman whom you marry."

It all came rushing back. The fury that had sent him flying from the parlor and storming her chambers. His lips peeled back in an involuntary sneer. "Do not present your being here as though it is some generous bid of kindness on your part, some quest to see me happy."

Coupled with the rage swirling in his chest were shades of hurt he didn't wish to feel. Long ago, he'd realized—and then accepted—that all the world saw nothing more in him than his future title. But Meredith Durant, the girl who'd been like a big sister, had never been among those numbers.

Surprise lit her pretty brown eyes. "But I do wish to see you happy," she said softly.

How very convincing she sounded, as though she believed that very lie. "Ah, yes. And that is why you wished to know about my pastimes, is it not, madam?" He'd shared with her a passion he'd kept from all, content to give the world the image they craved of him. "Because you genuinely cared?" God, what a fool he was for confiding anything in her. Giving his head a disgusted shake, he stepped around her and made for the door.

"Barry, I did ask because I wished to know," she called, a strident edge there that rang with shades of truth. Shades of truth he'd be a fool to believe. "That is… at first, you are correct. I was thinking that I might gather information." His shoulders tensed. "But only because I thought to help you make a match with someone who you might enjoy spending the remainder of your days with."

She'd given him the truth. "Good evening, Miss Durant," he said coolly, striding for the door.

There was the faint rustle of cotton skirts, and with an alacrity he'd forgotten her capable of, and admired her for as a child, she beat him to the door and placed herself against the panel.

He folded his arms. "Step out of the way, Miss Durant."

"No." Meredith lifted her chin. "Not until you hear me out. I did seek information earlier for the reasons I gave. But only partly, Barry. I…" She laid her hands against the door. "I wanted to know who you've become." She paused. "Other than a rogue, that is." Her gaze met his with a directness so very different than the sly slide-away glances of the women who'd sought his favor. "I don't believe that is all you've been or become."

She was wrong. And because of his foolish pride, he couldn't bring himself to admit as much. "Why?" he asked instead.

"Because…" Some emotion glittered in her eyes.

Did she recall the night she'd wept in his arms? When he'd just held her and then said goodbye?

In the end, Meredith offered a casual shrug. "Because… I knew you."

Neither of them truly knew each other. Not any longer.

But he wanted to find out. For some maddening, inexplicable reason, he yearned to loosen her plait and find the secrets she, too, carried.

"Very well."

Meredith didn't blink for several moments, then her eyes went saucer wide. "What?" she blurted, displaying shades of the unrestrained imp she'd been.

He repressed a smile. "If I'm going to allow you to select my bride…"

She gasped and touched a hand to her mouth in a belated bid to stifle that exhalation. "You're going to let me serve as matchmaker for you?"

"If," he went on dryly. "I said if." He didn't know whether to be further entranced by the happiness softening her features or wholly insulted by what had brought it about. "If I allow you to pick my bride, there will be terms."

"Of course," she said, frantically nodding. "Of course. However, I'm not *selecting* your bride. I'm helping you *find* a suitable match."

"Meredith," he said warningly.

"Yes, yes! Right, then." Meredith darted around him, and muttering to herself, she found her way to her valise.

He stared on, bemused, as she dug out a notepad and pencil and remained perched on her haunches.

She cleared her throat. "Very well. As you were."

This time, he didn't fight it. Barry laughed, his shoulders shaking with amusement, until tears leaked from his eyes.

"Hush," she whispered. "Someone will hear you."

He couldn't care if the King of England himself had requested his presence with his arrival. "What in God's name is th-that?" Through his vision blurred with tears, he caught the endearingly confused look as Meredith searched the room. He pointed.

Meredith followed his gesture. "My notepad?" she asked slowly.

His laughter redoubled. "God, you are positively m-mercenary, after all," he guffawed. "Keeping"—it was too much— "noooooootes." Barry clutched his side. "Oomph."

That effectively quelled his humor, and in the silence that echoed, it was hard to say who was more surprised by the book he'd taken square to the chest.

As one, they looked to the small volume lying on its now-bruised spine. "Why, did you throw your notepad at me?"

"No," she exclaimed, sprinting over, her bare feet peeking out as she raced.

Nimble as she might be, Barry beat her to it. He scooped up the pad. "I'm fair certain you did." Oh, this was going to be a good deal more fun than he'd anticipated.

Her chest rose and fell. "Give me my book, Barry."

"Do you know, I don't believe I shall."

"Barry," she warned.

"Given that you threw it at me and all." Angling away from her to prevent her from grabbing at the leather tome, he flipped through, scanning the pages.

"Lady Lydia prefers a man who can race and hunt. Hmm," he mused aloud, lifting Meredith's notes higher out of her reach when she went up on tiptoes. "You should have advised her to find a dog, in that case. That would have saved the lady from a lifetime of misery in marriage to dull Lord Plummer."

"Stop it this instant."

He merely flipped the pages, pausing again. "Miss Hartland prefers the pianoforte. A music instructor would save the girl a good deal more misery than a husband."

Meredith ceased giving in to his very deliberate baiting. She folded her arms at her chest and went absolutely silent, donning the façade of staid matchmaker... but it was too late. She'd already revealed herself to be the same spirited, defiant minx who'd go toe-to-toe with him. And now that she'd revealed as much, it was a secret she couldn't call back.

Holding her gaze, Barry slowly licked the tip of his finger and snapped a page, turning it noisily. "Continuing on," he goaded.

And then, he did. Except...

His eyes flared slightly on the page.

Barry lifted his gaze briefly. "Well, now *this* is interesting."

Meredith stamped her foot in an angry staccato that grew increasingly frantic, along with the furious color climbing high in her cheeks.

"Aren't you going to ask me what I find interesting?" As a girl, she would have. As a woman, she had far more restraint. It was that restraint he wanted to shake her free of.

"No," she said simply, tapping away with that foot, hard.

"No?"

At last, she stopped the frenetic movement. "No, because to do so feeds whatever game you play, and as I learned as a child, it is always best to not indulge you in a game, Barry. My answer remains no."

So, she'd liken him to his childhood days, when they'd played alongside each other in the nursery. Very well... two could play at that game. Holding the book out, he wandered off, presenting her with his back and making a small circle around her chambers. "Barry Aberdeen, the Marquess of Tenwhestle," he murmured slowly, reading his name in her notes.

Meredith gasped and abandoned all earlier pretense of indifference. She flew over and planted herself in front of him. "Give that to me, *now*."

Not taking his eyes off the page, he stepped around her. "His smile is pure magic... when it is not dangerous."

This time, he allowed himself to pick his head up. "Interesting that I'm the only one who's granted the familiarity of a first name." He flashed a half grin. "Makes the compliment all the more personal."

She set her teeth hard enough that they clicked loudly. "I merely used your first name because I know you."

Yes, he didn't doubt that. But ribbing her over it was entirely more fun.

He curved his lips up in another smile. "Is this the one? The purely magical smile?"

Meredith choked. "No," she strangled out between great gasps for air. She slashed her hands toward the floor. "It is, in fact, neither."

Barry tapped the book against his leg, teasingly. "Which begs the question…"

She wanted to ask him to clarify. He saw the question in the three little lines furrowing her brow. And yet, she fought herself.

Knowing her as he did, he knew she'd ultimately give in to curiosity, because that impishness, even with the passage of time and life, could not be stamped out of her.

"What?" she gritted between clenched teeth.

"How many other of my smiles have you noted?"

"None," she squeaked, her cheeks firing crimson. "I've noted none."

"Tsk-tsk. Do you know, Meredith," he whispered, leaning in, "I find I don't believe you." With a wink, he lifted the book once more and read on. "He possesses a quick wit." Barry waggled his brows. "Witty, am I?"

She made a grab for her book, but he turned, retaining his hold.

Meredith sank back on her heels and settled her hands on her hips. "Infuriating, Barry Aberdeen. You are utterly infuriating and exasperating and obnoxious and—"

"Do you know," he murmured, making a show of scanning the pages, "I'm not finding that information in here, love."

"It is for your match," she said weakly.

His smile slipped as her reminder ushered in the same sharp sting from when his sister had revealed the reason Meredith was, in fact, here. And there it was… written as item three on her *list*. An item he'd never shared with anyone else, that she'd reduced to just two words on her page. "Enjoys flowers." He forced himself to turn another grin on her, but this one felt strained to his own muscles. "How very tedious you make it sound." How very tedious she made *him* sound.

She grabbed her book, and this time, he made no attempt to intercept her efforts. "Not at all."

He waited for her to say something else about him... but she didn't. Meredith simply closed those damning pages and held the pad close, as if it held some other secrets she feared he'd uncover. She eyed him warily and then finally spoke. "I trust you're going to make this impossible for me, Barry."

Yes, that was the safest of assumptions. He dropped his hip atop her desk. "My, I'd say you have a low opinion of me," he said quietly, and her eyes darkened. "*If* I hadn't read all those otherwise glowing words you'd written there." He followed that with another teasing wink.

Meredith tapped her left foot so quickly it was a wonder she hadn't drilled through the hardwood floor. This time, she didn't take the bait.

Pity, that.

"There's nothing wrong with marriage, Barry," she began.

Oh, good God, surely she didn't intend to make a case for—

"In fact, it is the natural and inevitable state for any—"

"Ah-ah," he cut in, raising a hand to stymie the unnecessary defense of matrimony. "I'm well aware what a proper union forged between powerful peers is." One of duty, with social expectations and future ducal responsibilities taking precedence. One where people were reduced to pawns.

Meredith set her book on the desk, bringing his gaze to an unnoted-until-now etching of initials there.

MD and...

What looked like a heart and...? He narrowed his eyes. Who was the boy whose name she'd marked on that mahogany surface?

"Why don't we cease playing games, Barry?" she asked crisply, bringing his gaze away from those partially obscured letters beside hers. "Based on your reaction to my role and your ill opinion about marriage, there is no way you'll allow me to fulfill my responsibilities here."

The wheels in his mind spun happily on. "On the contrary."

The lady sprang forward. "Beg pardon?"

It was endearing how her entire body arched toward him and the answers she sought.

"If you are to play matchmaker for me, I expect you'll allow me to play matchmaker for you."

She shook her head slowly. In denial? In confusion? Or mayhap both.

Smiling, Barry tapped a fingertip on the top of her book. She followed his hand... and promptly sputtered. "Wh-*what*? *Absolutely* not..."

Barry winged an eyebrow.

Clearing her throat, Meredith gave a toss of her plait, and the dark braid bounced at her shoulder. "Not that there is anything *wrong* with matchmaking. It is simply that I neither want nor require a husband."

He made to pounce on the hypocrisy of that very statement, but his ears snagged and lingered upon the faintest thread of emotion that slightly husked her voice. "I... see." Meredith would disavow marriage. She had her secrets, then. Intrigue stirred, a desire to know them. "Either way," he went on, "I'm not looking to matchmake you with a husband."

Meredith tipped her head, an endearing befuddlement reflecting in her previously shuttered expression. "But you said..."

"That I intend to play matchmaker for you, as well... which I do." As he spoke, Barry slid closer to her. "You, Meredith Durant, have forgotten how to enjoy yourself and life." He braced for her denial. Yet, that she didn't dispute that point spoke more volumes than the entire collection in his family's libraries. "As such, I'm determined to play matchmaker between you and some activity to occupy you."

Her mouth moved several times before she got words out. "I have an activity—"

"Other than your work," he whispered, catching her plait to give it a small tug. Only, now that he had those tightly plaited strands in his fingers, instead of teasing, he found himself stroking the end of her braid between his thumb and forefinger. Soft as silk, with shades of fire woven in the auburn strands.

Meredith's lips parted, and her lashes fluttered.

Barry brought his mouth close to hers. Desire rolled off her in seductive waves that threatened to take him under in this game he played. A game that had shifted into a moment of something more. "I'm going to help you find pleasure"—her breath hitched—"in life again, Miss Durant." And it took a force the weight of Atlas's strength to step away from her.

The breathless minx didn't blink for several moments. Confusion clouded her eyes. "What?"

Did he imagine the disappointment in her hoarse voice? He thought not.

"A deal. I'll allow you to serve in your role as matchmaker, and you are to allow me to help you find again what brings you happiness."

"No," she said on a rush, her previous defensive, stern-faced edge back up. "I'm not agreeing to this."

"Then I'm afraid the deal is off, Miss Durant." He sketched a bow and made for the door.

"Wait," she called after him. He continued forward, drawing out the moment. "Wait, Barry," she repeated, a greater stridency in her voice. Her cotton skirts whirred slightly in the quiet as she raced over to join him. "I'll... allow it if, and only if, your plans for me are scheduled for first thing in the mornings."

Plans for her. He proved as wicked as the reputation he'd built, for her words conjured a host of images he'd dearly love to bring to life, all of which ended with Meredith Durant in his bed, in his arms. "Scheduled plans?" he drawled. "I do say that rather defies the whole purpose of fun."

"Barry," she said warningly.

"First thing," he allowed.

She tipped her chin. "Six o'clock."

Ah, the poor chit thought she knew him so well. She expected that he was still the same boy who'd despised rolling out of bed and who'd slept until the afternoon sun crept into the sky. He nodded slowly. "I... suppose I might allow it."

"No. Mm-mm." She shook her head. "These are the terms."

Barry made a show of releasing a long sigh. "Very well, but I only reluctantly agree to the hour. The terrace gardens at six o'clock."

The chit had no idea he was already ten steps ahead of her.

"And during those times, we'll discuss possible brides."

"No," he said instantly. That was where he drew the bloody line. "My time is not for work, but rather, play."

"Play." As if he'd uttered a black curse from the streets of the Dials, Meredith pulled a distasteful grimace. "We do not have much time, Barry."

"Ah, but you, love, are the best. Are you not?" This time, he did tweak her braid and managed to let the alluring strands go.

"That is neither here nor there."

"I'll allow your questions and discussions about my future bride, but only during the planned activities my mother has. That is your window."

"Fine," Meredith muttered. "Now, go." She gave him a slight shove in the way of Meredith of old. "But don't use the front door."

"Oh, I know." He made for the one that linked her chambers to Emilia's girlhood rooms.

"You know! Which means…" She gasped. "You weren't leaving. You were bluffing."

"Indeed," he drawled, not so much as glancing back as he slipped from the room.

The moment he'd shut the panel, he let the triumphant grin tip his lips.

Poor Meredith Durant. She had no idea she'd just been had. Barry had no intention of finding a wife anytime soon and every intention of teaching the young woman how to have a good time.

CHAPTER 8

SIX O'CLOCK IN THE MORNING had been a disastrous idea.

Meredith had not always been an early riser. However, as she'd become a self-made woman, she'd fashioned a strict schedule for herself and had adhered to it with a religiosity. And never before had she struggled to rouse herself.

But none of those times had she had to contend with a night of tossing and turning, pacing and counting sheep. It had all proven futile. Until she'd abandoned all hope of trying and made herself take copious notes on the very person who'd robbed her of sleep—Barry.

She'd been besieged over and over by the memory of a wickedly grinning, grown Barry Aberdeen.

She made her way to the terrace gardens.

He stood, a hip perched against the stone railing as he whistled a cheerful tune, looking very well rested. While his attention was directed out, she used the moment to study him unobserved. Attired in a dark green wool tailcoat and a pair of buff trousers, he was a study in elegance, set apart from every last man who donned black or sapphire. He commanded colors as easily as he had Meredith's dreams.

Barry abruptly stopped whistling, and she made her feet move just as he turned.

The moment his gaze landed on her, Barry grinned widely, and her heart sped up, for she could almost believe that smile was for her. "At last! I thought you'd reneged on our terms."

At last…

Because she was, for the first time in her career… late.

"Forgive me, my lord, I'd urgent matters to attend first," she lied, praying he wouldn't focus on her bloodshot eyes or the circles lining them that gave her the appearance of a racoon.

"An agreement is an agreement." Barry straightened. "I'll expect those minutes to be made up in the evening hours, Miss Durant."

Miss Durant. It was the first time he'd referred to her in that formal way since their run-in months earlier. And given that she'd been insisting he honor Society's rules on proper form of address, there was a peculiar twinge at the absence of her name as it had previously fallen from his lips.

Arriving late. Lying. Lamenting the proper use of her surname. It was decided: She'd been corrupted.

He'd corrupted her.

He held an arm out. "Shall we?"

For the first time since she'd entered the gardens, Meredith noted the equipment resting against the wall. "What is this?" she blurted.

"Bah, I know it's been awhile, Meredith, but with the way you once fished, I trust you've not forgotten what a rod is?"

Actually, she hadn't… She just hadn't thought of fishing since she'd left Berkshire… In London, there were no lush hills to race over, and the only ponds were artificial ones meant for following one's charge around. Wistful, she drifted over and touched her fingertips to the fishing rod. When was the last time she had fished? She'd been gone so long from this place, but even before she'd left, she'd become more focused on rushing off to meet a man who'd been exciting in the moment.

How much safer all would have been had she fished instead.

Feeling Barry's piercing gaze on her, Meredith drew her hand back. "I'm not entirely certain I even remember how to fish," she said gruffly. "Nor have I ever seen a… rod like that."

"Ah, but then, that is the purpose of this venture." He collected the rods in one hand, then offered her his spare arm. "Is it not?"

Automatically, she placed her palm along his sleeve. His muscles were coiled and defined under her arms, straining at the constraints of his wool tailcoat.

Meredith curled her fingers, reflexively gripping him.

Yes, corrupted her, indeed.

Whether he noted her appreciation of his form, he gave no indication. He led the way through his family's gardens onto the paths they'd traveled many times before, usually with him calling after her and Emilia to wait up as he struggled to match their strides. The overgrown brush and trees glistened with the morning dew drops, those beads shining like crystal under the sun's rays. Every step she took drew her deeper and deeper into the lush landscape, and Meredith briefly closed her eyes and allowed Barry to lead her onward.

She inhaled deeply of the crisp, clean scent of the pristine Berkshire air. When she opened her eyes, she found Barry's stare upon her.

She felt her cheeks pinken under his scrutiny. "I'd quite forgotten the smell of the country."

His eyes lingered on her lips, which were too thin to ever appeal to any man. "Beautiful," he murmured. And her heart quickened, for she could almost believe he'd spoken in that hushed murmur, his eyes still riveted on her mouth, about her.

Not another word passed between them as they made the remainder of the trek to the stream.

Barry set down the basket and poles and then proceeded to unfasten the buttons of his jacket.

"Wh-what are you doing?"

"Nothing improper, Mare," he drawled as he shrugged out of the emerald article. "Unless you want me to, of course."

"No," she said quickly. Meredith caught the glimmer in his eyes. "You're teasing."

"Only if you want me to be," he murmured, and this time she shivered with an awareness of the promise there.

He set the garment on a stone boulder marked by red paint that had been faded by age and the earth's elements.

Despite the fact that she was even now alone with one of Society's notorious rogues—in fact, a client who was disrobing—she was drawn forward. As Barry removed his boots, Meredith sank to a knee and touched her fingertips hesitantly to the rough outline of a heart on the boulder. The initials contained within were faded but for the hint of the M in her name. How very appropriate for that naïve time in her life.

"You are next, love?"

Meredith jumped and glanced up. "What?"

Barry motioned to her foot. "Your footwear, madam."

"You want me to... to... disrobe?" She finished on a scandalized whisper, stealing a search around. Alas, only the occasional song of a morning bird and the soft cascade of the flowing stream served as their company.

Barry dropped his hands atop his knees and leaned forward. "Oh, well, I certainly wouldn't mind if you were to do so," he whispered.

She swatted him, the chastisement ruined by the faint tremble his words had elicited.

"But rather, I'd have you remove your boots so we might fish."

Meredith sank back on her buttocks and glared up at him. "You're funning me. You forget, Barry, I've fished before."

"This is a different type of fishing, love."

Her protestations immediately died, replaced by curiosity. "Indeed?"

"Fly-fishing will require us to wade out into the water."

"In the water," she said dumbly.

"That is generally what wading 'out into the water' refers to."

And just like that, propriety took precedence over her earlier intrigue. "I... I cannot." Not when her entire existence depended upon her being above reproach. As it was, being alone with Barry threatened all that.

He held a hand out, waving his palm. "Ah, but you've agreed to the terms, love."

Staring at those long digits, Meredith warred with herself. Every last thing she knew about Barry Aberdeen as a boy, and even more terrifyingly as a grown rogue, said to quit the copse. To turn on her heel and return to the manor and sort through the whole matchmaking a gentleman who didn't wish to be matchmade. Only, something held her there. Not the agreement she'd struck with his mother. Not the three thousand pounds. Or even the deal she'd agreed to with him.

But rather, it was the challenge in his eyes that compelled her. The one that said he didn't believe for one moment that she intended to take part.

It was then that she knew that if he'd insisted they fly-fish in the buff, she would have stripped down to the state she'd been born in and demanded the rod. Holding his eyes, she lifted her chin mutinously and then shoved her skirts up a fraction and removed first one boot and then the next. Barefoot... and yet...

"Look away," she ordered.

Surprisingly, he complied, presenting her with his back.

The moment he was faced away from her, Meredith shoved her skirts up and made quick work of rolling her stockings down.

The air slapped at her skin, cool and soothing, the bliss of that forgotten until now. She came to her feet. "Very well, Barry. On with your lesson."

Barry turned and froze.

His gaze went not to her, but rather, her stockings neatly resting upon her boots, and then he looked at her toes.

Her bare toes. Meredith curled them into the soft earth.

He slowly lifted his eyes, and when they met hers, she was knocked back, the words she might have said ripped from her by the heat of his stare.

"Come with me," he urged, his silken baritone surely the same as that affected by the Devil who'd led Eve to sin. Meredith at last understood the reason for that fall.

She quickened over to him, and then with the basket and rods in hand, he guided them over to the shore.

Barry set the items down and wandered into the water with one rod. "Your skirts, madam," he called, as if he'd forgotten Meredith's presence until that moment.

"What of them?"

"They'll get wet. Hitch them..." Muttering something under his breath, he returned to the shore. Setting down the rod, he gathered Meredith's hem.

"B-Barry," she squeaked as he lifted the fabric, hiking it to her waist.

"Spread your legs," he said, all business, and one would have believed he'd asked her for a report on the weather and not something so scandalous she'd have been ruined forevermore. But it was, however, that matter-of-fact ordering that had her complying.

In quick order, Barry had her skirts up around her waist, using the fabric itself to form a makeshift belt. "There, that should help some." With that, he grabbed his rod and waded into the water.

Meredith hesitated. It had been so long since she'd done... anything at all improper. And there could be no doubting that fishing alone with a gentleman, bare of her boots and stockings, with her skirts up and her undergarments revealed, was anything but.

And yet, there was also... a thrill in being more than the staid, dull matchmaker the world had come to expect.

She stepped out into the water and promptly cursed. "Bloody hell," she cried, dancing backward. "That is freezing."

He wandered farther out as if he were in a warm spring. "You curse still," he said, cheer in his tones. "That is encouraging."

A blush would have burned her skin if it weren't for her frozen feet. "You are mad," she mumbled and forced her feet forward until she reached his side. "Now what?"

"Hush. Don't go rushing it along. That's hardly a way to enjoy yourself. Take the rod." He held it over, and Meredith gripped the reed in her fingers.

"First, you'll want to high-stick it," he murmured. "Like so." Moving into position behind her so that her back was pressed against his chest, Barry guided her arm up and through the movement.

Had she really believed the water cold? Her body's temperature had climbed. It had thickened her blood, which now pumped slowly through her veins.

"Lift it slowly, a bit higher," he counseled, his tone all business and wholly unaffected. How was he unaffected? "So that just your lead is showing."

Her eyes slid closed.

I cannot fish. I cannot think of a trout. Not with him behind me...

Still, she had to say something. "Like so?" she asked, her voice shaking, that tremor having little to do with the cold and everything to do with the way the muscles of his belly and chest rippled as he moved.

"A bit higher," he murmured. Blessedly, he gave no indication that he was aware of the battle raging within her.

Meredith forced her eyes open. Made herself attend his lesson. All the while, wickedly wanting another more scandalous one.

"Having it elevated as you do here, you'll then want to trace the undercurrent." Barry steered her through those movements.

"This will eliminate most of the drag and help represent the natural movement of the fly." They remained that way, their bodies motionless against each other, arms aloft. Waiting.

Even when her limbs began to tire and tingle from the time they stood there, unmoving, she wanted it to go on forever. And she didn't want to think about why. Or think about the fact that Barry was... Barry, her best friend's younger brother and now the man she was playing matchmaker for. Now, he was simply a man who held her so easily and cared so much about her again being exhilarated by something other than her work.

Only... she chewed at her lower lip. That wasn't quite right. Her work didn't thrill her. It was functional and purposeful and even meaningful, but it wasn't something that filled her with joy.

"What are you thinking about?" he whispered against her ear. This time, her arms did waver, for reasons that had nothing to do with fatigue and everything to do with the sough of his breath.

You.

"How wonderful this feels," she said softly, offering him the truth in that.

Meredith felt the tug on the line, and the moment was shattered. "I've got one!"

"Easy," he coaxed. "Patient."

Together, they followed the trout as it hooked itself, and then they reeled him closer, all while he fought for his freedom.

Dropping to his haunches, Barry gently disentangled the hook from the creature's mouth. How easily he handled the ensnared trout. In his palms, even this creature was malleable. Meredith fell to a knee beside him. "I've done it," she exclaimed with a breathless laugh.

"You always had a way with fish. You just lost your way."

Lost your way.

"I've not really been lost," she said softly. "We"—were cast out—"left." Only, as that clarification slipped from her, she recognized the inherent lie in it, for neither statement proved mutually exclusive. *Both* held true: She'd been lost... and she'd left. Because they'd had to. Which had come first?

Barry's piercing blue eyes moved over her face. "Why did you go?" he asked quietly, as if he'd plucked her very thoughts from her head.

And then it hit her. "You don't know?" The startled exhalation slipped out before she could call it back. Only, why would he have? The boy who'd come upon her, weeping, in the stables had been just that, a boy. He'd never have been privy to his family's decisions. Not then.

His body straightened. "Know what?" When she didn't immediately respond, he repeated with greater insistence, "Know what?"

Meredith picked her way around in search of the right words. For the ease she knew with Barry, the truth remained: Meredith was an outsider, employed by his parents. And a servant to a duke did not go about casting aspersions upon that family. Even if that family was in the wrong.

"My father was getting on and needed to turn the role of man-of-affairs over to someone younger," Meredith murmured, her gaze trained on the grey trout. "Your father provided a sizable pension." She was unable to keep a trace of bitterness from creeping in. For what she'd needed most in those days had been support through the slow, agonizing death her father had suffered. The duke had seen long before Meredith all the ways in which her father's mind had begun to fail.

"Not sizable enough to see you cared for," Barry said tersely, and at the fury humming in his voice, she glanced over. He'd direct that outrage at his family?

"The care my father required was extensive. No one could have anticipated just how ill he'd fall." Her throat worked. "He died not long after we left."

"Meredith," he said somberly. "I'm so..."

She shook her head, not wanting his apologies. Not now. None of that would erase those hellish moments her past.

"It is fine." Now, it was. She'd put away her resentment and moved on with her life.

Until she'd been called back to this place and all those most-painful memories.

"My family should have been there, Meredith."

Somewhere along the way, little Barry had grown up. He'd become a man who saw entirely too much.

Yes, they should have been. The fault, however, was not his. "You were there, Barry," she softly reminded him. He'd been the lone friend in a moment when she'd needed one. When she'd thought of Barry and the rest of the Aberdeens, she'd wondered if he remembered their exchange.

His eyes darkened. "After that night."

He had recalled it, then. And there was a spiraling warmth in her chest. She'd been alone for so long that something as simple as knowing he'd remembered her brought with it... peace. "You couldn't always be there, though," she reminded, her eyes locked on the fish he held, tender in that touch. "Emilia moved on with her life, and you..." *Will one day marry and become a duke.* "And you did the same. Either way, it is in the past, Barry." She didn't want her father's dismissal or death or Patrin's betrayal or any of those memories of her youth to intrude on this moment. Because they didn't belong in it. Not when she was here, happy.

Barry released the trout, and the creature fell with a splash before weaving off, catching the stream, and disappearing. "Why did you do that?" she asked, this topic safer, less volatile than her reasons for having fled Berkshire.

He stared off at the rippling stream, his gaze locked on the direction the fish had taken. "Because as we'd caught him, I thought it unfair that he be captured."

"Unfair?" She laughed softly. "That is the purpose of fishing, Barry," she reminded, skimming her fingertips along the cold surface of the water, breaking a curtain. "To catch, cook, and eat."

"Ah, for you and I, perhaps?" he agreed, glancing over with a grin. "But he didn't want that fate."

"There would have been good to his having... been caught," she reminded him gently.

"Being devoured by people who didn't give a thought to where he came from or anything more than the sustenance he provides." Barry held her gaze. "His freedom should belong to him, Meredith, and no one else should decide his fate. Certainly not you." He paused. "Or I." He added those two words almost as an afterthought.

Meredith's heart stilled in her chest for several moments, and then it resumed a slow, painful thud as Barry's meaning became clear...

He spoke of himself.

"This is why you brought me, then," she said quietly, hating herself because she'd enjoyed these moments with him when all along he'd intended only to teach her a lesson related to her assignment here.

"Not at all." He spoke with such a quick assurance that there could be no doubting the veracity of that reply. He grinned. "It just occurred to me as we caught him." He stood and stretched a hand out.

Meredith placed her palm in his, allowing him to help her to her feet.

Except, as she stood there with her fingers in his, she could not draw them back. Nor did she want to. Nor did he. He folded his palm over hers, and her breath quickened.

I should pull my hand back. I should step away.

There were a million things she should do, and yet, as he drew her closer, giving her time to pull away, there was only one thing she wanted.

He covered her mouth with his. Heat shot through her, and Meredith leaned into his chest as she met his kiss. His lips moved over hers, and there was nothing hasty or sloppy about his hard lips on hers. This was nothing at all like the only kisses she'd known. This was the embrace she'd dreamed of as a girl, and then as a woman, and had come to believe was the stuff of pretend. Only it wasn't. It was real. Barry was real.

Moaning, she let the rod slip from her fingers and gripped the front of his lawn shirt, pulling herself closer. Wanting this embrace to continue on even as a yearning, almost painful in its ferocity, stirred low in her belly. Their kiss took on an increasing desperation as he slanted his mouth over hers. Again and again, and then she parted her lips, allowing him entry.

Barry swept his tongue inside. The bold lash of that hot flesh against hers, steel and heat, a brand that marked, would leave her marked forever from the sear of it.

She tangled her tongue with his. With their mouths, they swirled and danced a primitive waltz as old as time.

Groaning, Barry slid his hands over her exploratively, running them down her waist, the curve of her hips. And then he filled his hands with her buttocks, sinking his fingertips into the flesh, and she cried out, her breathless exclamation of desire sending a flurry of blackbirds from their perches, screeching noisily.

Rasping for breath, Meredith jerked herself from Barry's arms. The blood bounded in her ears, muffling the sound of the stream and the cries of the birds overhead. And the only stabilizing part of this moment was the like confusion reflected in Barry's dazed eyes.

Barry, the rogue who'd given her yet another lesson.

Choking on embarrassment, Meredith spun and stalked off. At some point during her embrace with Barry, Meredith's skirts had tumbled about her ankles, and they dragged heavily as she marched from the water.

"Meredith," Barry called after her hoarsely. The splash of water as he trod after her marked his quick path.

She damned the cumbersome garments that slowed her.

"Meredith," he repeated with more insistence.

She made herself stop. Unable to look at him. Not wanting to see that this had been another one of his games. A rogue's game... just like his fishing tutorial.

His knuckles brushed her chin, and she resisted, but he forced her gaze to his. "I... this wasn't..." He scraped a hand through his golden curls. "I didn't mean to kiss you."

Meredith couldn't help it—she winced.

"That isn't what I meant," he finished lamely. "I'm... usually better at this..."

"Rogue's business?"

"Yes." His brows shot up, and a flush stained his cheeks. "No." His color deepened. "That isn't what I meant. Bloody hell... I'm butchering this. I want you to know that I didn't bring you here to seduce you, but rather to show you a good time."

Meredith flinched again. "Well, consider yourself successful, then," she clipped out, and with all the grace she could muster, she strode out of the stream, over to her garments. Gathering up her things, she fled.

Fearing he'd follow her.

Fearing that she wanted him to.

And fearing the disappointment that swept through her when he did not.

CHAPTER 9

THROUGH DINNER AND AFTER, MEREDITH resumed the role she'd so perfectly affected as the starchy matchmaker: reserved, measured, distantly polite.

In fact, Barry might as well have imagined the woman who'd come undone in his arms at the stream.

Nay, there could be no doubting that moment had been real. At the stream, their bodies had layered against each other's... She'd been breathless, first from the thrill of fishing and then from the embrace they'd shared.

Though that wasn't altogether true.

His gaze found her, lingering in the corner of the parlor. At some point since the party had adjourned to the parlor, she'd plastered herself to the wall, having managed the impossible feat of making herself an extension of the silk wallpaper. Failing to realize that, with the curve of her hips and the natural pout of her lips, she attempted an impossible feat.

From the moment he'd wrapped his arms about Meredith and guided her through the motions of fly-fishing, he'd felt the undercurrents of her desire, greater than the movement of the stream they'd stood within. The shaky timbre to her voice as she'd spoken. The way she'd leaned against him.

And then, the moment they'd kissed. In his arms, she'd revealed the depth of the passion that still simmered under the surface. Heat sizzled through him again, a rush of the desire that had compelled him to take her into his arms that morn.

For all her show of proper matchmaker, in that hideous gown and sporting a painfully tight coiffure, Meredith remained the same passionate, spirited woman she'd always been.

Only... he'd not known her as a woman. Not as she was now. When she'd gone off, leaving Berkshire behind, she'd been just twenty or so. His last memories of Meredith were her sobbing in his arms. She'd reemerged this... woman, still with sad eyes, clinging tight to her past like the secret it was. And he was a man besieged, filled with a gripping need to know everything there was to know about her. When he'd never before had a desire to have any manner of connection with a woman outside of the physical.

As if she felt his stare, Meredith glanced over.

Her cheeks pinkened, but she did not look away. There was a boldness to her stare, which was devoid of any coquetry. And that directness proved more compelling than any carefully fluttered lashes.

Hers was the gaze of a self-possessed woman who was confident in herself and the business that she did.

She might as well be the only woman in the room, for she was all that he saw.

Amidst the hum of the guests chatting and the occasional trill of laughter, the air crackled and hummed with an energy that came from the connection between them.

Barry bowed his head, the first to break their impasse. "Hello," he mouthed.

Then, with all the regal bearing of a princess, Meredith tipped her chin up, an unspoken admonishment that not a single one of Barry's hopeless tutors or university instructors could have managed. She looked away then, directing her attention to the inanity of the mingling guests.

His fingers curved into reflexive fists as annoyance killed the inexplicable hungering for Meredith Durant.

She believed he'd merely toyed with her. She assumed that the whole reason he'd taken her in his arms and covered his mouth with hers, explored the lush contours of her body, had been some intent at revenge.

And it grated. It grated that her opinion of him could be so low... given the length of the time they'd known each other.

That charge she'd hurled before flying off had stung in the

moment. Coupled with this, her palpable disapproval, he didn't know whether he wanted to lecture the chit or kiss her senseless—again.

Meredith darted a tongue out, trailing it over her lips. It was a nervous gesture, a distracted one even, and yet, also the greatest taunt she no doubt didn't realize she doled out.

He tamped down a groan.

The latter.

It was absolutely the latter. Kissing her mindless.

"You are being rude." The sharp whisper effectively doused all hint of his previous ardor, and there could be no doubting that, with the current company he kept, it would remain firmly squelched.

"Mother," he drawled. His mother, ever the consummate duchess, glowered at him in return. "And here I thought it would be enough that I've joined this evening's festivities." Instead of running off as he had last night, straight for Meredith's chambers, where she'd been in her bed, and he'd been over her and... His neck heated. He'd been wrong. He could lust after Meredith Durant in even the most miserable of circumstances.

His mother pinched his arm. "It isn't."

"It isn't what?"

She pinched him again, and he cursed. "Good God, stop pinching me."

"Enough," she went on and gave his arm another sharp squeeze.

"And what was *that* for?" he clipped out, rubbing at the bruised flesh.

"Because you're not paying attention. You said your joining the festivities was enough, and I'm telling you it is not. I've every expectation that you'll take part in the actual events, Barry."

He glanced around the room where guests still noisily conversed. "But there are no events." Not yet.

"There are *guests*." She lifted a finger. "And young ladies whom at the very least you should be respectful enough to engage in polite discourse."

Unbidden, his gaze drifted over to Meredith. Meredith who was even now tapping her serviceable shoe on the floor in a one-two-three beat. *Stop noticing even the most trivial details about the minx.* One-two-three. As bored as he himself w—

"Ouch," he exclaimed.

His mother lowered her pinching hand. "Pay—"

"Attention. I know, I know," he muttered. "And which lady are you expecting me to give my attention to?"

With that, Barry managed what he'd otherwise believed impossible until now—he'd ruffled the duchess. "What?" she squawked.

Ah, she feared he'd caught on to her using Meredith Durant as his matchmaker. He delighted in having the unaccustomed upper hand. "Come, Mother, did you think I shouldn't have gathered your... intentions?"

Were she any other woman, the duchess would have revealed a modicum of chagrin or embarrassment. A blush. Downcast eyes. Alas, she was a duchess through and through. "You've no one but yourself to blame for the situation."

Situation. So that was what they were calling Meredith's role here.

"And this I must hear," he said from the corner of his mouth, his gaze on the guests.

"Several months ago, when you stormed our townhouse and demanded to see your father and me, you truly highlighted all number of concerns we'd neglected to properly note. In that moment, it could have been"—his mother's already hushed voice dropped to a barely discernable whisper—"any number of scandals in which you'd found yourself."

Horror crept in. "And so you determined...?"

"That the only thing to ensure you'd settle down was for you to..." She gave a toss of her head. "Well, settle down."

He didn't know whether to laugh, groan, or cry. Good God, he'd put his oblivious parents' focus on him. "And I trust you've handpicked my bride, too?"

His mother trilled a laugh, and when she reached a hand out, he flinched away from the attack... that didn't come. She patted his arm, almost affectionately. The way she had when he'd been a child. "Never! I'm not so old-fashioned that I'd make *that* manner of decision for you."

He couldn't help the snort from escaping him at her slight emphasis on that particular word. "No, you'd just hire a matchmaker to do it for you." Not just any matchmaker. Meredith. A woman he'd become hopelessly enraptured by since he'd come upon her at the horticultural society.

"Your father and I are both aware you'd likely react as you have."

"Have I reacted?" he asked dryly.

"You are displeased," she pointed out.

"And with good reason."

"Everyone requires a bit of incentive…"

He stiffened. She was a master chess player. Only, her board was the world of Polite Society, and all the people upon it, her pawns. "Go on."

"You want the land for your flower gardens."

"Experimental gardens," he automatically corrected, all his nerves on alert.

His mother beamed. "And your father would be amenable to providing that gift…"

His stomach sank. "If I wed."

Her smile deepened. "You always were a clever boy."

Checkmate.

"Either way"—she clapped her hands—"I don't care who it is you speak to as long as you're speaking to someone. It won't do for Society to believe my boy is impolite."

"Imagine the scandal," he said crisply. "Ouch," he exclaimed when she attacked him again with that too-quick thumb and forefinger.

"Socialize." With that, she swept off, her arms extended. "Lady Sutton," she called warmly as she joined her closest friend in the world.

After she'd gone, Barry gave his head a shake and turned his stare on the bustling parlor. Socialize, she'd ordered. Take part in the evening's fun. Mingle with the guests. And now, she'd add another command: marry. And what was worse was she'd managed to attach the one thing he desired, the pursuit that brought him joy. And that temptation she'd dangled before him only stirred the bitter resentment in his chest.

From where she stood conversing with Lady Sutton, his mother caught his eye. "Socialize," she mouthed and then shifted all her focus to the other duchess.

Barry gnashed his teeth. The evening had soured, indeed, and he'd no interest in engaging the ladies here. Every last one of them had been assembled, handpicked by his mother with marriage in mind. That was, of course, with the exception of just one—

His gaze homed in on the lone figure in the corner.

Tap-tap-tap. Tap-tap. Stop. *Tap-tap-tap.*

She stole a glance in his direction and immediately ceased that endearing tapping. The immobile matchmaker mask was back in place. And he'd no doubt, after their lakeside interlude, that it was anything but a mask. All earlier boredom lifted.

With a grin, he started across the room.

Since she'd fled the stream that morn, Meredith had gone out of her way to avoid Barry.

At dinner, she'd kept her eyes entirely away from him, an altogether easy feat given his placement toward the front of the table and hers? Well, hers at the end, afforded one of her less exalted station.

That hadn't meant, however, that she hadn't felt his stare. Had known it was on her.

Just as she knew at this very moment that the purposeful set to his steps put him on a trajectory to her. Despite the room full of younger, bright-cheeked, glowing young ladies, he sought out Meredith.

It's merely because he's playing yet another game with you. Just as he did at the stream.

She knew that. She was jaded enough by her experience with men—her first love and the gentlemen of Polite Society she worked amongst—to know the manner of perverse pleasures that brought him joy.

Still, knowing that and reminding herself of that very thing couldn't slow the steadily accelerating beat of her heart.

And then he was there.

"Meredith," he greeted, not with a bow but with a smile.

A lady of his station would have merited a bow. She found herself preferring that unaffected grin. "Barry," she said, diverting her focus forward and gathering all the strength it would take to keep her stare on the room—and not on the impressive figure beside her. "Is there something I may help you with?"

"Not at all."

It was futile. She abandoned her earlier attempts and looked over at him. "And?"

"My mother tasked me with socializing."

"And so you chose me?"

He lifted his head. "And so I chose you."

He was a flirt. His reputation had been cemented among Society. He'd crafted the skill as a boy in the nursery, wheedling weak-willed nursemaids who'd been helpless around his cherubic smile. Even knowing that as she did, she couldn't stop the spread of warmth at the suggestive nature of those words… that met his eyes. "I hardly think this is what your mother had in mind with that order." In fact, she knew it. For there could be no doubting that, from the duchess, it would have been anything but an order.

"Oh, she didn't specify, and as such"—he smoothed his lapels—"I'm merely following the wishes as she set them out."

Meredith snorted. "And of a sudden, following your mother's requests is of paramount importance? If that was the case, I'd expect you to pick a bride among the ladies assembled." What accounted for the peculiar twinge that accompanied her own retort? That odd pulling sensation in her chest?

"My, how improper of you, Miss Durant the matchmaker," he murmured, angling his head lower so that his whisper caressed her skin. "Snorting and then calling out your hostess's son? Whatever would Polite Society say?"

"I didn't call out the hostess's son. I called you out." She *had* snorted. She'd not, however, concede that.

He arched a brow. "And?"

"And?" she asked primly, refusing to indulge him.

"Well…" He dropped an elbow against the wall, nearly shielding her—shielding *them*—from Society's prying eyes. "It is simply that if I'm not 'the hostess's son' or 'your assignment,' what does that make me?"

Her heart knocked wildly. It was merely because of the potential scandal that his intimate positioning could herald. It had absolutely nothing to do with his languid pose, or the heat spilling from his words, or the ripple of his biceps as he shifted his shoulder.

Lying. I am lying, and poorly, even to myself.

"Hmm?" he prodded on a silken murmur. "Who am I, if not simply the future duke you'll marry off?"

"Barry," she said, her voice breathy to her own ears. "You are just... Barry."

Her response managed to shatter the teasing façade that this charming, affable gentleman presented to the world.

"Just Barry," he murmured.

"That's what you've always been." Through the haze of her own longing, her words served as a reminder of why she was here now. "And it is as a friend that I wish to help you, Barry."

"How... very touching." He spoke in his usual drawl, but this time, it was laced with cynicism.

She ignored it.

She ignored him.

After all, if she paid him no notice and didn't rise to his ribbing, he'd continue on his way so he could go about fulfilling his mother's expectations, his responsibilities, and... well, her own responsibilities for him.

Of course, he'd never allow that silence.

"I saw your tapping," he said conversationally, all earlier vestiges of bitterness gone.

"My tapping?"

"I saw your feet," he whispered.

Butterflies danced in her belly. He'd been watching her that closely? And why did it matter so much that he had? "I don't know what you're talking about," she forced out with a casualness she no longer felt around Barry Aberdeen.

"Yes, you do." His rebuttal put her as an all-out liar, and he owned that pronouncement with all the factuality of one who knew. "And now I can't help but be curious about what had you tapping those painfully severe boots."

Imagined music. Dances she'd never danced. Waltzes she'd never had. Music she played in her mind through the tedium of events that she was part of but never really included in. No one had noticed because, in short, no one had noticed her. There'd been no reason to.

"Music," he murmured, shifting his body closer. Scandalously close.

Meredith's pulse pounded. She tried to make herself look about for prying eyes, but couldn't bring herself to look... or care. Care about anything more than the words whispered from his lips.

"What?"

"Knowing the girl I once knew, you were imagining a song in your head and secretly dancing yourself through that set." His gaze smoldered, and it was like being kissed by a flame. This man bore little trace to the underfoot boy of her youth.

Her breath hitched. "How—?"

"Because, as I said…" He dipped his head so that all she need do was tilt hers a fraction, and their mouths would meet. "I know you."

I know you.

Sadness tugged her lips up in smile. "You don't know me. Not truly." Nor did he have a need to. And yet, at every turn, he sought answers about her and her past and her life. That regard didn't fit at all with the rogue he'd become.

"No," he said quietly. "But I suspect no one knows you, Meredith. Not anymore. Because the same girl who would have once sung a ditty and danced around this parlor is now determined to hide in a corner, just dreaming of dancing."

Her pulse thundered, and she hated him in that moment for having gleaned those secrets, just as much as she hated herself for having thought those very thoughts. From the moment her father had fallen ill, to the moment of his death and the years beyond, she'd ceased to be a girl and had instead become a woman with but one purpose and focus: her work. She'd believed herself content with what her life had become, only to have Barry prove the lie there.

He peered at her with a far-too-knowing stare, one that saw too much. More than she wished. "The Meredith of old is still there enough that I know what you're dreaming of, even if you're hiding the truth from yourself."

It was too much. "What I wish for or don't wish for out of life doesn't matter," she said, finding her legs once more.

"Ah, yes." Barry abandoned his casual repose. "The terms of our arrangement." He inclined his head. "I like to fish."

He liked to fish… That reminder conjured memories of that morn, wading through the water, casting their rods… and him taking her in his arms. Her breath hitched.

Barry gave her a peculiar look.

Good Lord in heaven, what in blazes is the matter with you? Agog over Barry Aberdeen. "Fishing," she echoed belatedly, needing to say something to ground her in her purpose here. She dove for the pencil and notepad tucked in her pocket, but Barry stayed her attempts, pressing a palm against hers.

"No writing."

"But—"

He dusted the back of his palm lightly over her mouth, and her heart skittered out of control at that faintest and swiftest of caresses. "Only listening, love."

Meredith stole a glance about the crowded parlor. She, however, remained blessedly invisible to the more important lords and ladies present, who'd never spare a look for one of her station. "But I need to record—"

"Uh-uh. Those are the rules."

But she recorded everything. Such was the entire purpose of her being here and the deal they'd struck related to her discovering his interests and finding him the ideal match. As such, Meredith dug her heels in. "No, those are not the terms we agreed to." They were also the rules she needed in place... the ones that would keep Barry Aberdeen as business and not the fascinating figure he proved himself to be with every wicked encounter.

He quirked his lips up in a half grin. "They are now."

Their eyes locked in a silent battle, and Meredith was the one to relent. "Very well," she allowed. "I'll abide by your ever-changing rules." Not because she craved the secret parts of this grown-up Barry. Rather, she was required to know everything there was to know about him, for the work the duchess had hired Meredith to do.

Liar.

As he lowered his mouth close to her ear, her breath again caught, but was muffled by the hammering of her pulse and the din of the crowd. "I love being outside," he murmured, his words a secret intended only for her discovery. "Not London. But here. Amongst nature where the air is pure and the sky clear. *That* is why I took you fishing, Meredith."

Had he whispered forbidden words to her, Meredith couldn't have been more captivated, sucked into whatever maddening spell he now wove.

Gentlemen didn't prefer anything outside their clubs and their brandy and their billiards and horseflesh.

"You look surprised, Mare," he said dryly. Only, a wariness underscored his tone. One that she might have missed had she not been so very attuned to everything about this man. But she was listening, and she noted it.

"In my experience, gentlemen tend to have singular interests… ones vastly different than matters of nature." And solely channeled on nothing more than material pleasures. Why, even the man she'd given her heart to years earlier hadn't been born to those elevated ranks, but had still been largely absorbed in horseflesh.

Barry smiled, this one a different smile than any of the previous he'd turned on her. There was a faint trace of sadness to it. "I fear I must disappoint you, then, with my more scientific interests."

"I'm not disappointed," she blurted before she could call the words back.

Neither of them moved. Both going completely motionless with that admission.

At that faintly breathless appreciation she'd revealed, Meredith prayed for the floor to open or rescue from above. "Not that it matters," she said.

His brows came together in a line she didn't know how to interpret. "That is," she amended, "it does matter as it pertains to how it might help me find you the ideal wife."

Unlike his previous reaction, there could be no doubting the annoyed frown that marred his otherwise perfectly formed lips. He was displeased. *And why shouldn't he be? You've reduced him and his future to a job his mother hired you on for.* "Not because of the assignment," she said. *Stop talking.* Alas, her tongue failed her. "That is, not because of the assignment. Not entirely anyway." In the end, rescue came from the unlikeliest of places.

"Meredith!"

Or rather, people.

She and Barry turned as one and faced the unexpected intruder. Only… she wasn't an interloper. Not truly.

"Emilia," she said dumbly as the recently married marchioness came to a stop before them. On the heels of that informality, Meredith's cheeks burned up. "Forgive me." She sank into a deep curtsy, and when she straightened, it was hard to determine whose glower was greater: Barry's or Emilia's.

"Don't be ridiculous." Emilia spoke at the same time that Barry said, "There'll be none of that."

Her friend, Barry's sister, looked over to her younger sibling and then nodded approvingly. "Precisely. There'll be none of that. We're friends."

Was that what they were? "Friends," she murmured, testing that word. They certainly had been. But friends were also there for each other through the darkest moments. Friends shared each other's lives.

Emilia smiled so wide her cheeks dimpled. "Indeed." How easily she stated her words as fact. In more than ten years, what had she and Emilia shared? "Isn't that right, Barry?"

And yet, for Emilia's insistence, a lifetime had passed. A lifetime ago, she and Emilia certainly had been the closest of friends. Nay, they'd been like sisters, their bond forged in all but blood. Did friendship simply... resume as though years hadn't passed, filled with a lifetime of hurts and moments missed, moments they'd never shared? "Thank you," she said.

As Emilia slid her arm through Meredith's, she joined them in a way that angled Barry out.

He bowed his head. "I'll leave you two to your company."

An appeal for him to remain sprang to her lips, but remained unspoken. With Barry, there was an ease and comfort that she didn't know with... anyone.

She searched for some hint of regret layered within his deep baritone. But his tonality, along with his chiseled features, was carefully masked.

How singularly odd that he'd once been the underfoot, bothersome younger brother whom she and Emilia had gone out of their way to avoid... and now it was his company Meredith craved.

She resisted the urge to shift back and forth on her feet, feeling like a stranger for the first time in the company of the woman before her. Alas, Meredith was a matchmaker. A grown woman, well-versed on conversing... with anyone.

They spoke at the same time.

"You've been w—"

"Meredith, I—"

Emilia cleared her throat. "I've been very well. Though, that hasn't always been the case since…" Since they'd last spoken? Since the other woman had neatly cut Meredith from her life? Her pretty blue eyes drifted briefly toward the floor. "I fear I've not been the best of friends," Emilia murmured. "In fact, I fear I've not been even a remotely good one."

No. The tale of Emilia's broken betrothal and subsequent broken heart should have come from her friend, and instead, Meredith had been reduced to reading those details in the scandal sheets. All the while, she'd been caring for her dying father.

And yet…

"I could have reached out, as well," she said softly. It was an acknowledgment she'd not made before this moment, even to herself. It hadn't been Emilia's or Barry's fault that the duke and duchess had turned out Meredith's father. But it had been Meredith's fault for resenting the friends she'd grown up with, when she could have reached out. "We both could have been more." And with the secrets Meredith had retained and the parts of herself she'd withheld, Meredith now saw she also hadn't been the best of friends. "We grew up as children do," Meredith said gently. "We went on with lives of our own. It is the way of life," she added, that reminder for the bitter person she'd been when she'd come here.

"It is not the right way," Emilia said, looking at her squarely. "Not in real friendships."

"Perhaps not," she allowed. "But it does explain how two people"—as close as sisters—"drift apart." Long ago, Meredith had been besieged with resentment at how easily she'd been snipped from the fabric of the Aberdeen family. Now, she accepted the change that time invariably wrought on all.

"How unchanged you are." Emilia's murmurings held a wistful quality.

How wrong her friend proved in this. Meredith had been changed in every way. She wasn't at all the girl she'd been. *Except, when you were with Barry, he remembered all the joy you found before your heart was broken and work became your purpose.* "I'm not the same woman I was," she said softly. No matter what Emilia saw, or thought she saw, a heart twice broken—first by love and then by the loss of a father—left a person irrevocably altered. "Time changes us all."

"Yes. It does."

They fell to a comfortable silence, both looking out at the guests mingling about the room. And Meredith found herself missing the company of another. Odd that as a child she'd gone out of her way to avoid Barry Aberdeen, and now she wanted nothing more than to slip from Emilia's side and...

What are you thinking?

Barry was the subject of her work here. Any fascination with him and his attentions was folly.

And then she found him. Several inches taller than most guests, he and his tousled ash–gold curls towered over the crowd.

As if he felt her stare, Barry quirked his lips up, setting her heart to dancing. And every reminder she'd just given herself rapidly faded. For this was not Barry's magical smile that he turned on her. This was the rogue's one. The dangerous one.

Heat formed low in her belly.

He winked.

Meredith flared her eyes. Why, the scoundrel. He well knew the effect he was having on her. *And here you stand, ogling him like—*

"Are you well, Meredith?"

"No," she muttered. She was not well. She was... She whipped her focus back to Emilia. "Why would I not be?" she squeaked. "I was just..." And then she took in her friend's cocked head, and it hit her. Emilia hadn't been speaking of this moment. "Oh," she blurted. "You didn't mean in this instance. You meant *overall*." And with every incoherent prattling, Emilia's brow grew increasingly befuddled. "Since we've been apart."

If her friend angled her head any more, it was going to be touching her shoulder. "Are you... unwell *now*?" her childhood friend ventured.

"No!" Her voice emerged high-pitched to her own ears. "Why would I be?" *Stop!* Drawing on the reserve that had built her reputation, Meredith gave her throat a slight clearing. "I've been... well." For it was true. For so long, Meredith hadn't been. She'd had her heart broken, and then on the heels of that she'd lost her father. She'd since picked up the pieces, which was why she was able to now give the assurance she did. Of course, *well* and *happy* were altogether different matters.

Emilia covered Meredith's right palm with her own. "We should not let time or life separate us again. I want us to be friends once more."

She opened her mouth to remind her that they'd always been friends, but her friend cut in.

"I mean friends who are there for one another and share their dreams and hopes and happiness." There was a slight pause. "And the heartbreaks, too," she said softly. "I'd have us return to the way we were."

A ball of emotion lodged in her throat, and she struggled to speak around it. How alone she'd been. For so long. "I'd like that very much." And then proving just how little Emilia had, in fact, changed, even with the title of marchioness affixed to her name, there, amidst a room full of Society's most prominent members, Emilia hugged Meredith.

She let her arms hang by her sides for a moment and then returned the embrace. "I've missed you," she whispered, her voice cracking.

"I've missed you, too."

Meredith briefly closed her eyes. She had been so consumed by her resentment of the Aberdeens and lost in her work that she'd allowed herself to think the friendships she'd once had weren't of importance. Now she realized she'd been lying to herself. She'd convinced herself she was fine enough without Emilia and Rowena and Constance, but ultimately she had missed them all.

And Barry. You missed him, too.

The rapidly increasing noise about the room penetrated the reunion she'd thought would never be, recalling her to the present. And her role and reputation. For being reunited in friendship with Emilia meant nothing for the work she did or the clients who'd hire her.

Meredith stepped out of her friend's arms.

"I've noted the time you've been spending with Barry," the other woman said without preamble.

Had Emilia have yanked the Aubusson carpet out from under Meredith's feet and sent her toppling, she couldn't have been more thrown off-balance. "What?" she croaked, glancing frantically about. But the guests remained immersed in other exchanges of far greater interest than an old, unmarried matchmaker and the married marchioness she spoke to. If Emilia had noted that, it was likely that other people had as well. All her muscles tensed at the thought that the stolen moments she'd had with Barry had not been so very private, after all.

Emilia's gaze remained trained on her family's guests, and when she spoke, she did so through lips that barely moved. "That is, I observed you both speaking a short while ago." Some of the tension left Meredith. "And unless I was wrong in my assumptions this morn when Barry was missing from his usual early morn breakfast, he was, in fact, with you."

Just like that, all her muscles went taut once again. Her friend had noted much. Too much.

"I..." She had no idea what to say. She had not one single coherent response to explain that she'd been off fishing... and kissing... not-so-little Barry Aberdeen.

Emilia glanced over. "Of course, I'm well aware of why my mother has asked you here."

"You are?" A wave of giddy relief swept her. Her friend hadn't been wondering after Meredith's dangerous fascination—and even more dangerous agreement—with Barry but rather, she spoke of Meredith's work with the young marquess.

Emilia gave a flounce of her curls. "Come, it's been a long while, but surely you'd neither forget nor underestimate my ability to ferret out my mother's plans."

"No." The burgeoning relief brought her lips up in a smile. "I've not forgotten."

"And though I'm generally not of a like opinion as my mother in, well"—Emilia's nose scrunched up—"anything, I do happen to agree with her intentions for Barry."

The duchess's intentions, which were, in fact... marriage.

It was a sobering reminder, when it shouldn't be, of the ultimate expected outcome for Barry at the end of Meredith's time here.

Her friend went on, wholly unaware of the tumult wrought by that reminder.

"I'm not sure if you've been aware of the reputation Barry has earned?"

"I..." A memory traipsed in of the rogue in the floral gardens reading from Byron. Meredith was well aware of Barry's effect on women. Not even she, a straitlaced, proper matchmaker and companion, was immune to his charm. "I've not really had any interactions with him since we were younger," she lied.

Taking her by the arm, Emilia steered them deeper into the corner, and for one horrifying moment, she believed her friend intended to call her out as the liar she was. "It's not good, Meredith," her friend said bluntly. "It is not good at all. He is… a rogue."

The other woman looked at Meredith as though she expected some grand reaction or response to that revelation. "Surely not," she allowed.

"Indeed." Emilia dropped her voice to the faintest of scandalized whispers. "He visits his clubs and rides. And enjoys spirits. His interests are quite singular, really."

Only, they weren't. The world—and not long ago, Meredith— believed that to be the case about Barry. "I'm sure that isn't all there is to him," she said quietly, unable to stifle the defense of him even in the name of self-preservation. Even if she revealed more than she should.

"There isn't," Emilia countered, her tone a blend of confidence and frustration, and that only stirred the latter sentiment in Meredith. "What the world sees of my brother is, in fact, exactly what he is."

How singularly unfair that the same world that had shamed Barry Aberdeen for his fascination of plant life and gardening should now condemn him for living the life they expected of him.

"My brother would greatly benefit from a happy marriage," Emilia remarked, all older-sister-like in her pronouncement. "And there's no one I'd trust more to help him find a wife suitable for him than you."

Just like the duchess, Emilia thought Meredith would be the one to help maneuver Barry into a respectable union. "I'm honored," she murmured. Or she should be. Given the time they'd been apart and the strangers they'd grown into, it was a remarkable display of trust from Emilia for the work Meredith did, and she should take it as the greatest of compliments. Instead, she found herself focusing on just one aspect of her friend's assumption: the idea of Barry married. "I'd not just see him wed anyone for the sake of marriage." And certainly not to some ruthless Diamond more intent on a title than a happy union.

Her friend drew back like she'd been struck. "Never," she said, her voice aghast. "But you can help him find someone that would make him happy."

Her belly twisted in uncomfortable knots that made as little sense as her response to Emilia's praise.

More than half fearing her friend would prove perceptive and see things that Meredith didn't want seen, she looked out.

And found him.

Barry stood alongside Lady Agatha Clarence. The woman was a spinster, firmly on the shelf, here at the duchess's party as a companion for her younger, more beautiful sister. And yet, despite all that, Barry didn't seek out the lovelier Lady Ivy, but the older sister. Whatever it was he now said to the lady earned a boisterous laugh.

The woman had not been at the top of the duchess's list for her son. She'd not been even at the bottom of it. And yet, known for her charitable work and effortless work running her family's estates, she was unlike any of the simpering debutantes and, therefore, would make Barry a good future duchess.

For some unexplainable reason, Meredith was filled with the urge to cry.

"My mother is motioning to me," Emilia muttered, thankfully drawing Meredith's focus from Barry and over to the duchess.

Only, it wasn't solely the duchess with a gaze on Emilia. "As is your husband," she said gently. The other woman's features instantly softened. Warmth lit her eyes, and just like that, the tall, dark-haired marquess across the room transformed Emilia into the bright-eyed girl she'd once been. "Go," she urged gently.

Emilia tugged her hand. "Come with me."

"I…"

The duchess clapped her hands, immediately compelling the room to silence.

"The games are commencing," Emilia persisted. "You always enjoyed blind man's bluff."

Yes, when she'd been a girl. Just as she'd enjoyed fishing.

She'd simply forgotten how much joy she'd found in those simple activities. Lady Agatha was being called to the center of the floor.

Lady Agatha, who just then said something to those around her that set laughter up amongst the group… Barry Aberdeen included.

Meredith fisted her palms tight at her sides. "Go," she urged. "I am going to retire for the night."

Her friend looked as though she might protest, but glanced over to the still-waiting marquess.

Seeing the other woman wavering, Meredith offered a smile. "We will speak again later," she promised. "I'm here for the remainder of the house party." All twelve days remaining, where she'd serve in the role of matchmaker to Barry and—

A blindfolded Lady Agatha lunged and nearly caught Barry.

Envy—vicious, green, unpleasant, and unwelcome—coiled tenaciously inside her chest.

"If you're sure," Emilia said.

She was entirely sure she wished to leave now. "I am."

Thankfully, Emilia took herself off, hurrying across the room, sidestepping the furniture that had been shoved out of the way and the guests dancing to escape Lady Agatha's outstretched arms.

Just then, the young lady feinted left and caught Barry with an exuberant laugh.

Barry reached up to help the young woman out of the makeshift blindfold, and those tendrils of jealousy wound all the tighter inside Meredith.

She forced herself to study the pair of them. She made herself look with an objective eye at Barry and the potential bride before him. That was how she'd built a career and a reputation— by carefully noting one's subject and then inevitably recording everything that might help her successfully maneuver her client into a prosperous marriage.

Only, why, watching the dark-haired spinster and Barry, could she not bring herself to focus on her work?

Instead, she remained attuned to just one detail about the gentleman: his lips. They would tell her everything there was to know about his thoughts about Lady Agatha Clarence. The occupants of the room and the din that crowd created faded into a muffled hum of noise in her ears.

And then he smiled.

This was not the rogue's smile. Or the dangerous one. But rather, the magical one.

With that, Meredith quit the rooms. The laughter of the duchess's guests echoed from the parlor, dogging her footsteps as she went.

Meredith reached the crystal doors that led to the duchess's prized rose gardens and let herself outside.

The whisper of cool hung on the night air, and she welcomed it. The air proved invigorating. It cleared her head and restored her.

Tomorrow, when she and Barry resumed their meetings, she'd do well to remember the purpose of her presence here. She resolved that there'd no longer be any confusion about her role… or about Barry Aberdeen's fate once she was gone.

CHAPTER 10

AFTER THREE ROUNDS OF BLIND man's bluff, himself once in the role of blind man, Barry managed to make his escape.

His footfalls echoed along the darkened corridors, softly marking the path he'd taken.

Generally, he'd not found the games at his mother's parties agonizing. Had even enjoyed them, an admission he'd never make to a soul and would take to his grave.

Only, this time, this night, he'd found himself restless, eager to quit the rooms and the festivities and games. There'd only ever been one place that brought him a sense of calm. A place he'd stumbled upon during discourse between his father and mother, the duke lamenting his son's peculiar interests. After that, Barry had stolen away only when the world wasn't looking.

As Barry reached the double doors leading to the duchess's prized gardens, however, he did not delude himself into believing his desire to escape had anything to do with his unnatural fascination with botany or the tedium of the evening's festivities.

Rather, he'd retired for the evening because he'd been consumed with thoughts of one person. The one guest who'd not been present.

Or rather, in this case, the one woman.

The very woman who was here even now.

Barry remained frozen, his fingers on the door handle.

With her back to him, Meredith sat on a small, wrought-iron bench that, despite the rust that had begun to chip at the once-neat white paint, retained a place in the duchess's gardens. The tips of her toes brushed the first row of his mother's prized tulips.

She would be here.

There was an odd sense of rightness to her presence—not just in this place, but at Berkshire Manor—a rightness that went back to Meredith's connection with Barry's family. She'd been gone entirely too long. Slowly depressing the handle, Barry opened the door and slipped outside. She gave no indication she'd heard him.

With her unaware of his presence, Barry drank in the sight of her. The moon cast a soft, natural light around her, wreathing her head with a pale halo that played off her dark tresses. Those dark strands stood in stark contrast to her cream-white skin, which had been satiny soft to his touch. His fingers curled reflexively around the handle as the memory of Meredith in his arms, and the sudden need to again know her in that way, took hold.

You pathetic wretch. What manner of rogue are you? Lusting after Meredith Durant… a woman who'd been raised alongside him like another sister. His father's late friend's only child.

There were a thousand and one reasons to quit his silent, appreciative study of her. So why did the task prove so bloody difficult? What was it about this woman that compelled him?

Somewhere in the distance, a night heron called, cutting into the disquiet wrought over his inexplicable fascination. The bird's muted cries were met with the immediate chitters of its mate.

Quietly, Barry pushed the door closed behind him. "Miss Durant. How very unexpected seeing you here," he said quietly. And it was. The gardens had never been a place he'd found her as a girl. But then, generally, she'd always been off with Emilia, and Barry had been the forgotten afterthought of a brother.

Meredith's narrow shoulders went taut, and she climbed to her feet so quickly that she sent gravel skittering into the tulip garden.

"Barry," she greeted.

He smiled. "Not surprised to see me, Meredith?" he asked, drifting over. He stopped on the opposite end of the graveled path, directly across from her.

She leaned forward, far enough to keep distance between them, but close enough that he easily spied the mischief dancing in her eyes. "I heard you."

He scoffed. "Impossible."

"You were never the quietest child, Barry."

"Untrue. I was eminently good at it. Need I remind you of your heart-of-a-duke pledge I overheard?"

Bright crimson circles filled her cheeks. "Hush."

"Or your plans to steal your first kiss?"

Meredith gasped and slapped her palms over those ever-brightening cheeks. "Barry!" She stole a frantic glance about.

When was the last time he'd so enjoyed himself? "Forgive me." He grinned. "To steal *two* kisses from two men... so you had basis of comparison..."

Meredith groaned, muttering something into her hands that sounded a good deal like a threat upon his life and manhood. Then, suddenly, she let her arms drop to her sides, brought her chin up, and was once more very much the driven matchmaker who'd schooled him on all the reasons she should let him fulfill her task here. "I'll have you know, I was a girl then."

"Yes." He brushed his knuckles briefly along the high arch of her cheek. "You were a good deal of fun."

Sadness crept into her pretty brown eyes, and with it came a desire to call back the words that had ushered in that reaction. "Yes," she said. "Yes, well, you are correct on that score."

"And you don't allow yourself to find enjoyment in life anymore."

It wasn't a question, and yet, she answered it anyway. "I do," she said, her chin tipping up at a defiant angle.

Barry crossed his arms. "Do you? Name one thing..."

She made to speak.

"That isn't work," he interrupted.

Meredith folded her arms, matching his pose. "It *is* possible to enjoy one's work."

"Indeed, but it's still just that." He tweaked her nose. "Work. Is that why you snuck away from the parlor after just one game of blind man's bluff?"

She stilled. "How—" Her cupid's bow lips formed a neat, tight line as she cut off the remainder of her words.

Barry grazed his index finger along the dainty point of her chin. "Yes, I noted your leaving, Meredith," he murmured. He'd known the very moment she'd slipped away from the gathering and had wanted to follow along after her. "Well?"

"I..." She closed her mouth and then tried again. "I..."

He gave her a pointed look.

"Very well," she said tightly. "I'll allow that I might not—"

"*Do not.*"

"—find enjoyment in those things I did as a girl of seventeen or eighteen." Her voice took on a wistful quality. "But it is far better that way."

She sought to convince herself, he thought. "Better?" he asked, taking a step closer. "How could it be better?"

"Safer," she allowed.

All his nerves went on alert.

She'd been hurt. *Someone* had hurt her.

Questions fairly burned his tongue with the urgency they demanded he ask them, an exigent need for the name of the person responsible for the change that had befallen her. So Barry might ruin the one who'd left a lasting legacy of hurt. "What happened after you left?"

There was a palpable pause.

"And don't feed me half stories and words meant to protect my parents."

She started.

"Of course I knew with the little you said before, Meredith."

Meredith wandered off, the same path she'd skipped along as a child and young woman. How measured she was in everything: her speech, her steps. And how much he thrilled at the moments where she faltered and revealed hints of who she'd been. That woman still existed within her. Somewhere. She'd kept her hidden, but she was there, buried under responsibility.

"Would you?" he pressed. "Would you have swum or fished?" Or done any of the other things he'd so admired about her when she'd lived here at Berkshire Manor?

At last, Meredith stopped and glanced back. An errant breeze toyed with the hem of her skirt, whipping it lightly against her legs, the fabric contouring to her long limbs. "Too much happened in my life." Her father. "There wasn't a time for laughter and joy, and then after…" Her gaze grew distant. *After my father died.* "Then there wasn't a reason for it."

I wish I'd been there. I wish in those hardest of times that I had been close so she'd not have gone through all she had… alone.

Because he cared about her… He always had.

Not like this. Not with this all-consuming emotion that robbed him of sleep and had him thinking only of her.

That realization threw his mind into tumult.

For this, this desire to be with another person, with her happiness mattering more than his own or anyone else's was wholly foreign. As unexpected as a bolt of lightning in a snowstorm.

He wanted her to smile... but he wanted to be the one responsible for the delicate upturn of her lips.

And standing there, staring at Meredith Durant, the irony was not lost on him: He, an avowed *rogue* who'd no intentions of marrying any respectable lady, found himself wanting the one who'd been gravely hurt by his family.

The temperature had long dropped and left the earth cold, and yet, there was something so very invigorating in it. There always had been. Meredith tipped her head up toward the star-studded night sky and inhaled deeply.

"How I've missed the smells of this place," she murmured. Pure, not clogged by coal and dirt, the Berkshire country air was so crisp it filled her lungs and cleared away the concerns that filled her mind.

Feeling Barry's gaze upon her, Meredith glanced over.

He studied her through thick, golden lashes, his expression inscrutable, and even so, her belly quickened.

She cleared her throat. "I'm sure I've bored you with talk of my past."

He joined her so they stood with their arms brushing. "Never." He paused. "Now, fifteen years ago, my answer would have been decidedly different," he teased, raising a smile to her lips that was effortless, when she'd believed those muscles incapable of such movements.

Meredith nudged him in the side with her elbow. "You would have been twelve and more likely to have put ink in the flask I'd snuck from your father."

He smirked, entirely smug at her reminder of when he'd outed her and Emilia for pilfering the duke's brandy. "This is true."

Several clouds passed overhead, blocking the moon and bathing the earth in shadows.

She shivered and rubbed at the gooseflesh on her arms. *I should go…*

Those were the words she should speak, as a woman alone with a bachelor and certainly as a matchmaker responsible for coordinating a union for that very bachelor. With the passage of time, the years they'd known each other might as well have never been.

"Here," Barry murmured. Shrugging out of his jacket, he whipped the black garment around her shoulders.

The soft woolen article hung large upon her frame, and she drew the fabric closer, burrowing deeper into its folds. The smell of sandalwood clung to the garment, the slightly woody, masculine scent so very perfect for the man he'd grown into. "When did you grow up, Barry Aberdeen?"

"When you still lived here." Clasping his arms behind him, he stared out at the gardens. "You just failed to note as much."

"Yes," she murmured softly, as he wandered away from her. Only, she'd failed to note *so* much where he was concerned. She'd only ever seen Barry as Emilia's bothersome brother. How much she'd missed. And how wrong she'd been about him.

His gaze remained fixed on the stretch of gardens that continued on for as far as the eye could see, both at nightfall and during the heart of day.

How very serious he also was. Intent. In ways she'd never before seen in him.

But then, as he'd pointed out, she'd not really paid enough attention to notice those details about him.

Was it that he was as aware of her as she was of him? His kiss earlier that morning, and his very presence here, spoke of one who was. And yet, having long ago surrendered her virginity, she was not one who'd be deluded into thinking there was necessarily more to a rogue's physical response.

Wordlessly, Barry turned and faced her. That slight movement drew his white lawn shirt tight along his arms, accentuating beautifully defined muscles better suited to a man-of-work than a powerful marquess. And then he began to walk toward Meredith.

Slow.

Pantherlike.

His steps were sleek and predatory in a sexual way that sent her belly into a mad fluttering, and she recognized the lie she'd sold to the world so successfully. She'd come to believe it herself: Meredith was no proper miss. Only, she well knew, with a woman's intuition and from the hint of passion she'd experienced in Barry's arms, that making love with him would prove magical.

And I want to know that passion. She wanted to know more than the faint stirrings she'd experienced as a girl and feel herself come alive in all her body's splendor.

He stopped before her.

Meredith's breath came hard and fast, the respirations shuddery and telling. And with that same unhurriedness that had marked his steps, Barry stretched a hand close.

"B-Barry," she whispered, her voice throaty and wanton to her ears. Her lashes fluttered as he slipped a hand inside her jacket.

His jacket.

As she struggled to draw air into her lungs, she proved very much the wanton she'd been as a girl, for she wanted his hands on her.

Only, *he* proved not so very much the rogue the world purported him to be.

"Here it is," he said triumphantly, as if he'd been searching through a greenhouse drawer and not inside her—his—jacket. He withdrew a small iron pair of...

"*Scissors?*" Meredith blinked slowly. *That* was what had earned that devoted glimmer in his rogue's gaze?

Barry gave her a look like she'd kicked his dog. "I'll have you know these are not scissors."

She gave thanks for the cloud cover that hid the moon's glow and, with it, her burning cheeks. "They *look* like scissors."

He slid his fingers into the handle. "They are secateurs." Barry weighed the peculiar object in his palm, a tenderness to his touch as he handled the inanimate scrap of metal with far greater longing than he'd shown her moments ago. "Cutting plants dates to the antiquity in Europe. Why, since ancient times, the Chinese have had specialized scissors they used for penjing and its offshoots."

As he wandered off into the gardens, she cringed. Envying an inanimate scrap of metal? "You are pathetic, Meredith Durant," she mouthed after his retreating form. For his were not the steps of a scoundrel that begged a lady to follow. But mayhap that was the magic in them, for Meredith's legs moved with a will of their own, carrying her after the gentleman. "What is a penjing?"

As if he'd just recalled her presence, Barry paused and cast a glance back. He eyed her suspiciously. "That doesn't seem like a question to benefit you in coordinating a match for me, Meredith."

No, it wasn't. And yet, nearly all the questions she'd put to him, even the ones about him and his passions, hadn't been asked with the thought of a match at the forefront of her mind. The realization sent terror ricocheting inside her chest. "Is it so hard to believe that I should simply be curious about what you're speaking on?" she rejoined.

There was another beat of silence. "It is the ancient Chinese art of depicting artistically formed trees, other plants, and landscapes in miniature. Not entirely dissimilar to our topiaries." He motioned to one of the meticulous boxwoods as he continued walking. "Scissors used for gardening are not an altogether new concept. A French aristocrat, a fellow by the name of de Molleville, craftily designed the things," he explained. "These, in fact, are one of the original pairs he constructed."

His smile. His masculine physique. His teasing charm. All of it paled when compared with this animated version of Barry Aberdeen as he spoke about botany.

As if he felt her stare, Barry looked over, and the moonlight played off the sharp planes of his cheeks, highlighting the endearing color there. "I'm sure this is entirely more than you wished to know."

"No," she said on a rush. "Not at all." She ran her fingers over the petals of one closed pink bloom. "I confess I've not truly given thought of flowers beyond admiring them." Leaning forward, Meredith closed her eyes and drew in a deep breath, filling her nose with the sweet fragrance. When she opened them, she stared wistfully at the bud. "I don't know that I've ever felt about anything the way you do about botany."

Feeling his gaze burning into her, Meredith looked up, embarrassment stinging her cheeks. "I trust it is a sad commentary on my life." A life that she'd thought was otherwise complete.

"How so?" he murmured, drifting closer.

Meredith palmed the silken flower and clenched tight. "I've not allowed myself to find or feel joy."

Had it been a punishment? Had she simply been lost in work?

Or had it been a combination of both?

"That's not true, Mare."

She frowned, and her annoyance had nothing to do with that moniker and everything to do with his bold assumption. "You don't know that, Barry."

"I saw you fishing today. And more?" He took a step closer, and the gravel churned loudly under his boots until he stopped beside her. "And I knew you when you wore the same smile while swimming naked in the heart of summer," he murmured.

She gasped.

Only, he continued on with words that were not teasing, but solemn in their deliverance. "I saw you when you were speaking with the horses."

The peace she'd found in the stables had come long before Patrin and her girlish excitement to seek out her sweetheart.

"You loved the stables." Again, he spoke with the ease of one who knew her. And by everything he'd seen and gathered about how she'd lived then, and how she lived now, he knew her better than she mayhap knew herself.

Meredith burrowed deeper into Barry's jacket as she wandered down the graveled path. "I did." She'd loved the duke's horses and the barn cats. That shared interest was how she'd come to first notice Patrin. She pushed thoughts of him back, not allowing him to intrude on this moment with Barry.

She felt Barry move into position behind her. Felt him leaning close, his breath caressing the sensitive shell of her ear as he spoke. "I recall you racing through the countryside—"

"Barefoot," she chimed in, angling her head back to meet his eyes.

"—barefoot."

They shared a smile.

Then his lips returned to their previous, serious line as Barry took her lightly by the shoulders, bringing her so close their bodies touched.

Meredith tipped her head back to meet his blazing eyes.

"You may have forgotten what it is to enjoy life, but never doubt that you once did so unapologetically," he said quietly. His baritone wound about her senses, wreaking havoc. "And you can... and will do so again." Those words proved even more quixotic.

His thick, golden lashes swept low did little to conceal the glint of desire in his eyes.

Her heart continued to dance a maddening rhythm, and she was certain it would never resume its regular safe cadence.

Then Barry lowered his head. And the whisper of brandy on his breath, softened by a trace of mint, proved headier than any of the glorious smells in the duchess's gardens.

He is going to kiss me.

He eased his jacket from her shoulders, the cool night air proved to be a balm upon her heated skin.

He is going to kiss me, and I want that… and more from him.

In this moment, unlike the others that had come before, there was no guilt. There was just the glorious thrill of being in his arms and being alive and simply feeling. She tipped her head back farther to receive his kiss, but there was to be no embrace.

Why did he not kiss me?

She'd wager her soul on Sunday that, by the smile ghosting his lips, he knew precisely the scandalous path of her thoughts.

Barry tweaked her nose.

Tweaked her nose? Just like she'd flicked his as a girl. "What are your plans for me, Miss *Duranseau?*"

Miss… Duranseau? Who?

The use of her falsified name had the same effect as water being tossed over her heated body, effectively cooling her. "What?"

Barry gave her an odd look. "Morning meetings are mine. Evening sessions are yours," he reminded, casually shrugging into his midnight-black jacket.

Her role as matchmaker. His need of a bride. He spoke of their arrangement.

"We shall meet in the library."

His thick lashes swept down. Had he gathered those barriers she'd sought to resurrect between them? "Until then, *love.*"

And with that, he left.

Meredith stared after him, and after he'd closed the door and gone, her entire body sagged.

"What in blazes has come over you?" she exclaimed into the quiet, needing to hear that chastisement from someone… even if it was herself. Her entire purpose in being here was to coordinate a union between Barry and some noble-born lady.

She'd do well to remember that before she did something foolish... like fall in love with a man destined to wed another.

CHAPTER 11

ꟄEVERAL HOURS LATER, ꟄARRY STEPPED into the library and promptly burst into laughter.

As anticipated, Meredith was there.

Just not as he'd expected her.

A desk better suited to a schoolroom had been brought into the room and positioned at the center, a shell-back chair alongside it. And there, seated like a stern headmistress, was a very stern, very composed, and by the frown between her brows, a very much displeased Meredith Durant.

"*What?*" Meredith asked, a defensive edge to her voice.

Barry only laughed all the harder. "What in blazes is *this?*" he managed to strangle out.

Sailing to her feet, Meredith folded her arms at her chest. "As I explained to your mother when agreeing to the post, there is a... way I conduct my business."

He pushed the door closed behind him and pressed the lock. "Said business being me?" When he turned back, he matched her positioning, folding his arms in a like manner.

"Said business being our arrangement together."

"You're splitting hairs." Looping his right palm in a circle, he motioned her on. "Well, on with it. I am ever eager to hear this one, love."

Meredith tugged a page from her desk and brandished the list of names. "The entire purpose of my being here is to coordinate a match between you and one of the ladies present."

"Yes," he said, perching his hip on the edge of a side table. "As if I could forget." Except, with their every exchange, he had. He'd simply enjoyed being with her. There was no obsequious fawning because he was a future duke. There were no aspirations for his title because of the wealth and influence a marriage to him would bring. Barry eyed the stack of notepads, the inkwell and pen, the row of pencils. He gave his head a rueful shake. "Does it ever occur to you that yours is an austere approach to marriages and love?"

She bristled. "I beg your pardon?"

He straightened and joined her at the neat workstation she'd had arranged. "You are certainly *not* forgiven."

On a huff, Meredith let her arms fall to her sides. "I was certainly *not* apologizing, my lord." There it was. The use of his title. As though, with the proper form of address, she sought to remind them both of the divide between them. "There is nothing *austere* in what I do."

He picked up a notebook and waved it under her nose. "Isn't there?"

Meredith swiped the leather pad from his fingers. "Give me that." Muttering under her breath, she set to work reorganizing her pile. "Do you have any idea how many matches I've helped coordinate over the past eight and a half years?"

She'd been doing this for eight and a half years, then. And their paths had never crossed. How close they'd been to each other, and yet, they'd moved throughout London as strangers. That idea left him oddly melancholy. "I trust you'll tell—"

"Thirty-seven."

That gave him pause. It was a testament to the amount of work she'd done and the success she'd had. "Thirty-seven happy marriages," he drawled. "The number of unions you've coordinated, however, does not happiness make."

"All the marriages I've coordinated have been happy ones." She proceeded to tick off on her fingers. "The Earl and Countess of Marbury, so in love they…"

"Left London," he murmured. He'd heard tale of the former rake who'd wed the spinster bluestocking.

Meredith lifted another ink-stained digit. "There is Lord Aster, who loved to travel, and the now Lady Aster, who dreamed of touring the globe, but would have never been able to do so under her family's constraints."

The Asters were rumored to be one of Society's greatest love matches, and Meredith had paired them together. Despite himself and his views on the mercenary role she served, he found himself wholly impressed.

"Shall I continue?" she asked smugly.

"I trust you intend to anyw—"

"The Viscount and Viscountess of Tenderly."

He whistled. "Lord and Lady Tenderness." As the couple was affectionately referred to amongst the *ton*. The viscount had been a beast of a man with a perpetual snarl—Society had avoided him at all costs—and yet, since his marriage, none recognized any hint of the beast in the grinning, besotted husband he'd become.

Meredith spread her arms wide, as though presenting a delicious offering. "And I can do the same for you, my lord."

"You mean you can change me." That was what the world had been doing where Barry was concerned since... well, since he'd come into the damned world.

Frowning, Meredith let her slender limbs fall atop the table. "Of course not. I don't *change* or seek to change anyone. Rather, I..." She paused, her brow wrinkling as she considered her words. "Find the interests each young lady carries and help pair her with a gentleman of like pursuits. Invariably, sharing those passions brings together men and women whom the world would not have otherwise thought to bring together."

Hearing her practice laid out gave him pause. Hers wasn't the ruthless plotting he'd expected for... well, any matchmaker— either for hire or born to the peerage. She spoke of mutual interests and shared affections, and those alone set her apart from... well, every woman he knew.

As if she sensed his weakening, Meredith smiled again and gestured to the chair nearest to him.

He narrowed his eyes, watching the minx between the thin slits. With the ease she'd gone about divesting him of the opinion he'd carried for her and her work, he'd be wise to be wary. Wordlessly, he tugged out the chair and seated himself.

An entirely too-pleased-with-herself smile on her lips, Meredith dragged the chair on the opposite side of the desk so that they were seated across from each other, two players upon a battlefield.

In a way, that was what they were. "Now, shall we begin?"

"Given I've already seated myself, I trust that was the general plan?"

"It was a rhetorical question."

Clasping his hands behind him, Barry kicked back on the legs of his chair. "I'm awaiting your magic, Mare."

"Miss *Duranseau*. When we are working, I'm Miss Duranseau, and you are my lord."

"I'm waiting for you, then, Miss *Duranseau*." God, she was delightful to tease. He could almost forget that the minx sat there with a ruthless intent to marry him off to one of his mother's houseguests.

Meredith glanced about, and when she returned her focus to him, she dropped her voice to a whisper. "There is a secret to finding a spouse."

His lips twitched. Righting his chair, he lowered his elbows atop the table and leaned forward. "Surely not."

"I'm going to ignore your sarcasm, Barry. And when you finally find yourself paired with a lady who makes you so deliriously happy that you can't remember your name, I'm going to take great delight in reminding you of this moment."

Never. That moment would never come. Not with the sea of debutantes salivating for a title and caring not at all about the man.

"You don't believe me." Meredith smirked. "That is fine. Your eventual happiness will be thanks enough."

"And your two thousand pounds, I trust," he said drolly.

She blushed. "Three."

"I was merely searching. She's paying even more than I expected." The sizable fortune would see Meredith comfortable for life, and despite his earlier anger at her duplicitous role in aiding his mother, he could not begrudge her taking on the *assignment*. "By that sum, she is *very* determined to see me wedded off."

The color in her cheeks deepened. "I'll have you know it isn't about the money."

Barry gave her a look. "Some of it is," he felt inclined to point out.

"Yes. Because most of us don't have land and fortunes awaiting us, Barry. In fact, most of us need to use our wits and skills in order to have the security that you've been afforded since birth."

Just like that, he found himself properly chastised. Shame smarted in his chest. "Meredith," he said softly.

She snorted. "I'm not giving you a woe-is-me tale, Barry," she said pragmatically. "I'm merely speaking on a matter of fact." How confident, how strong she was, when any other woman would have crumpled. And God help him, he fell a little bit in love with her in that moment. "Now, where were we?" she asked.

"You were realizing that there's no way I'm going to agree to a match with any lady handpicked by my mother."

Her lips twitched. "That was not it."

Leaning forward, he whispered, "I know." He followed that with another wink.

"You're incorrigible. As I was explaining, there is a secret to finding the spouse with whom you long to spend forever." She paused, and despite his earlier baiting, something in her tone compelled him forward. "It is to simply be yourself."

He cocked his head. "What?"

She nodded. "Be yourself, and only be with someone who doesn't put up pretenses around you. Those are the couples who invariably marry... and remain happy," she quickly added.

You. I'm able to be myself with you.

The staggering realization knocked him off-balance and sent his heart climbing into his throat. From terror. Confusion. And he forced it back.

"Tell me this, Meredith," he murmured, resting his forearms on the table. "If you've discovered the secret to love, then how is it you yourself are still unwed?" he asked without inflection.

"Because I was already in love, and it did not work out for me."

Of any answer she could have given, that was the last one he'd expected.

His body went simultaneously hot and cold with a whole torrent of emotions roiling through him, making it impossible to discern all of it but one: rage. Red-hot and palpable.

All business, she gathered the top notepad, drew it over to her side of the desk, and opened it. "Now, continuing on," she said, flipping through a quarter of the filled pages before Barry managed to move.

He shot a hand out, staying her in midturn.

Meredith looked up.

"Surely you don't expect to say that and nothing more."

"What else is there to say? I fell in love, I had my heart broken, but good came of it. I was able to see the dangers of making the wrong match."

"And yet, you're completely capable of determining what is best for others?" he asked slowly.

"Precisely."

He shook his head. "I don't understand."

"How to explain it?" Meredith chewed at the end of her pencil. Suddenly, she stopped. "I have crooked teeth."

Barry's mouth moved, and words were slow to follow. When they emerged, they came out wrapped in confusion. "I don't understand."

"My teeth." Pulling back her lips in a stretched smile, she revealed pearl-white teeth, the bottom row flawlessly even and the top nearly so but for the exception of the front two. A smidgeon too close, they angled in toward each other.

They were endearingly perfect.

"It's these," she clarified, tapping a nail against the area in question. "I was teased mercilessly by several of the village boys."

He scowled. "Who? And how was I not aware of this?" He'd have bloodied the little bastards' noses.

"Because you were four when I was eight and… do pay attention. My father would forever praise my smile. It was one to rival an angel's, he'd say."

And it was… odd that his captivation didn't rouse a greater sense of panic. Mayhap it was because the minx was thoroughly confounding.

"But he couldn't see the reality, because he was too close to me."

He processed that logic. "And so… you're too close to matters of your own heart."

She pointed at him. "Exactly. I can step back and look objectively at other women and the men who might be deserving of their hearts. I'm not as proficient at knowing what is best for me in matters of the heart." With an air of finality, Meredith licked the tip of her index finger and turned to the next page in her notepad.

"*That* was what you took away from your foray into love?" he asked incredulously.

Meredith shrugged. "I'm not sure there is a more important

piece to take away from it."

"Because you chose wrong once, it means the man whom you were meant to be with is still out there, and you are at risk of missing out on a lifetime of love for yourself because you're too afraid of committing the same mistake twice."

He braced for her expected outburst. His words hovered in the air for a long while.

The tension eased from her face, softening her features. "Barry Aberdeen, are you a romantic?"

"Yes. I like flowers. I enjoy poetry. And I hate hunting because I despise the idea of senselessly slaughtering any creature just for sport. You spoke of being honest in who I am, so there it is. Now it is your turn."

Her lips parted, and he tried to make sense of the glimmer in her eyes. But then she blinked several times, clearing whatever emotion was there, and dove for her pencil.

She proceeded to scribble frantically on her open pages.

About me.

She was recording the interests he'd shared. He yanked the book away.

She cried out, "Barry."

"You, Miss Durant, or Miss *Duranseau*, are a hypocrite."

Meredith glared at him. "I beg your pardon?"

"This time, *you are* not forgiven. Do you know what I believe?" He didn't allow her to get in a word edgewise. "You'd speak to me of love and happiness to be found in marriage. You'd speak to me about simply being myself and sharing every part of myself with you. And you can't even bring yourself to talk about… any part of yourself, really."

Frustration broiled in him. Because he wanted to know about her and the man who'd hurt her—and all her hurts—for reasons he couldn't bring himself to analyze in this moment.

"Very well." Meredith let one shoulder rise and fall in a casual shrug belied by the tension emanating from her frame. "I was young. I was reckless in my actions and vowed to live my life in a way that is safe."

How careful she was even with the details she provided in her telling. That ambiguity only ushered in further questions and an ever greater need to know. "Who was the bounder?"

She hesitated. "It doesn't matter."

It mattered very much. "It matters because you matter," he said quietly. Rage pumped through him. Questions swirled around the identity of that unknown bastard. Or worse... was it someone he did, in fact, know? Who? "What happened?" he made himself ask instead.

Even in the dimly lit library, he caught the way her fingers twisted and clenched at the fabric of her pale-yellow dress. "I fell in love where I shouldn't have. I trusted a man who said he'd love me forever, and he went on to fight Boney's forces"—she gave another one of those little shrugs—"and returned with another. That is all. There's nothing grand to the story, Barry. I was just any other girl with a broken heart."

He forced his features into a mask to keep from revealing the riot of emotions that even now tore through him. There could be no doubting... she'd fallen for a rake. Had he been a guest his family had entertained? A gentleman who'd broken her heart and left her hurting. His stomach churned.

She said there was *nothing grand to the story.*

The story lay in her heartbreak.

She'd loved... and someone had violated that gift.

His chest was squeezed in a viselike grip—at her hurt. At the idea that some bounder had been the recipient of her affection and had brought her pain.

Barry was staggered by the intensity with which he wanted to drive away the memories of that other man and replace them with new ones that only left her smiling.

She had told him.

Meredith had confided in Barry about Patrin and his betrayal. Only her father had known and had carried it with him to the grave.

Why had she told Barry?

He set her notepad before her.

Unable to meet his eyes, she fiddled with turning to a clean page in her book. Meredith cleared her throat. "We should begin."

"Haven't we already begun?"

Just like that, Barry restored them to the ease that had been there before any talk of Patrin and broken hearts.

"We had, but you continue to distract, which I'm not altogether convinced isn't a ploy," she said with a smile.

He waggled his eyebrows, startling a laugh from her.

"As we were, then." Chewing at the end of her pencil, Meredith reexamined some of the notes she'd recorded on Barry's interests, and then flipped back to the empty sheet. "You enjoy poetry and botany, and you care for animals."

At his silence, she looked up. Red splotched his cheeks. "You aren't divulging that."

It wasn't a question.

"I gather the better question is, you are keeping this information a secret?"

Except, by the muscle ticking at the corner of his eye, that was precisely what he intended.

"Why is it a secret?"

He shifted in his chair. "Because it doesn't matter."

"It matters if you wish to find a person who can love the real you and not the image you've crafted to fill whatever expectation you think Society has for you."

Barry scoffed. "Do you believe the women here desire anything more than landing a future duke and themselves a title of someday duchess? Do you truly believe any of the women invited by my esteemed mother truly want me as I am?"

I do...

The reply hovered at the end of her tongue, words she kept at bay.

"I believe there are women who would appreciate who you truly are, Barry"—she held his gaze—"if you revealed more than the image you've crafted for the world."

A sound of frustration escaped him, and he jumped up with such speed, his chair scraped noisily over the floor. "If you believe that, you are naïve, Meredith Durant. We shared a schoolroom for several years, and then you resided here as my parents sacked tutor after tutor. Because first comes the dukedom, and any pursuits are secondary to it."

"They stifled your studies," she said softly.

He shrugged. "Dukes cannot be botanists. Dukes cannot be anything other than dukes, Meredith." He spoke in a rote manner, words that had surely been delivered to him.

Her resentment for Barry's parents blazed to life with an even greater intensity. For reasons that had nothing to do with their careless disregard for her and her father's future and everything to do with the fact that they'd seen Barry first as an heir and second as a son.

She slowly came to her feet so that she stood positioned directly across from him. "Do you believe that?"

He hesitated.

"You don't," she said softly. "It's why you still visit horticultural societies and carry gardening shears. And you don't have to hide away parts of yourself, Barry. I'd have you marry a woman who appreciates who you truly are."

An image slipped in. Of Barry with some faceless, nameless woman. A woman who'd be the recipient of his teasing and clever schoolings on botany.

Then the image shifted, and the lady wasn't faceless, but rather, one of the flawlessly beautiful women his mother had assembled.

Meredith was filled with the ugly urge to cry.

He stepped around the desk. "Do you believe there is such a person, Meredith?" he murmured, coming closer. Ever closer. And then he was there, before her. Standing so close she had to tip her head back to meet his eyes. And then she found herself promptly burned by the heat blazing from their depths. Barry stroked the backs of his knuckles along the curve of her jaw, his touch weighting her eyes closed. "Hmm?"

She struggled through the quixotic caress to recall his question and then realized her answer: *I am that person.*

And yet… she couldn't be. Meredith forced her eyes open.

"I do," she at last replied, her voice throaty to her own ears. She smoothed her palms down the lapels of his jacket. The muscles of his chest jumped under her hands, defined, coiled muscles better suited to a man who worked in labor rather than one destined for a dukedom. "I believe there is a woman for you, Barry." *One who cannot be me… and I will hate her until I draw my last breath for having that which I want.*

His eyes darkened, and for one agonizing and horrifying moment, she believed he'd seen the truth of that realization. That glint gave way to raw desire, the kind of passion that a younger, proper, innocent woman would have failed to recognize for what it was. But Meredith saw and, in that moment, selfishly wanted to take.

With an animalistic groan, Barry lowered his head.

Meredith was already going up on tiptoes to meet his lips.

There was nothing tender about their joining. His lips slashed over hers again and again. As if he wanted to devour her.

Heat pooled in her belly, for she wanted to be devoured by him.

Meredith parted her lips and eagerly lashed her tongue against his. They dueled in a passionate battle she was all too content to lose.

Her legs weakened under her, and Barry filled his hands with her buttocks and guided her back. Never breaking contact with her mouth, he shoved the fabric of her skirts high, exposing her hot skin.

She moaned into his mouth just one word, all she was capable of. "Barry."

In response, Barry sank his fingertips into her thigh and lifted it about his waist, bringing her flush to his body. Her modest undergarments proved a thin barrier to the length of his hardened shaft that pressed against her core.

Dropping her head back, she arched into him.

"You are so beautiful," he rasped out, moving his hips against hers, simulating the rhythm of lovemaking.

And then the whole world was moving.

Nay… it was just them.

Slipping off the table, Meredith and Barry came crashing down hard.

Pain shot into her hip and lower back as Barry's larger frame crushed hers, slamming her against the floor.

She grunted.

"Oh, bloody hell," he whispered, his voice ragged. He immediately shoved himself up onto his elbows. "As you can see, I'm not as good at this as I've been credited," he muttered.

Meredith's frame shook, and then Barry's scowl dissolved as he joined in, laughing.

Lying on the floor, wrapped in Barry's arms, her work scattered about them, she acknowledged the truth to herself.

I love him…

Oh, good God in heaven. It was a prayer. For this mistake... this folly was far greater than any error she'd made with Patrin.

For Barry could never be hers... and yet—

"Come." In one fluid motion, he jumped up and helped her to her feet.

They set to work tidying her workstation.

She'd have to turn him over to another. It was what she was here to do.

And yet, before she did, she intended to steal every moment of joy she could, and then the memory of them together would be enough.

It would have to be.

CHAPTER 12

THREE DAYS.

Three days was how long it had taken Barry to restore Meredith Durant to the spirited minx who'd once reveled in games and laughter.

Three days in which she'd driven him absolutely and utterly mad.

"You were entirely too gentle before. This time harder, Barry. But not so fast."

Hell. I'm going to hell, and of course it would be Meredith, the minx who tortured me in my past, to send me on my way.

Before a gathering of his mother and father's guests, no less.

"It matters how you stroke it. I'd expect you would know that, Barry."

Barry briefly closed his eyes. Pall-mall had always been torturous, but this? This was a torture of a different sort, no less agonizing, just in different ways.

Giving his head a slight shake, Barry opened his eyes and made a show of taking a practice swing with his mallet.

Meredith slid closer to him. "Are you listening?" she whispered, her lyrical voice a siren's song.

"I am," he said hoarsely. He'd been listening entirely *too* closely to the forbidden words rolling from her lips. "I'll have you know, I've a reputation for being the best of those who've played here."

Meredith snorted. "That certainly remains to be seen."

Yes, yes, it did. Alas, it was just one more lie crafted by Society about the future Duke of Gayle. Yet again, Meredith was the only one to see through it. To actually look at him. And it only fueled his hunger for her and—

"Is everything all right?"

If anything were to sober a gent in the midst of wicked musings, it would be an annoyed call from one's sister, who was with his brother-in-law. The pair stared down the length of the graveled path at Meredith and Barry.

Meredith waved a gloved palm. "His lordship requires just *one* more lesson."

That pronouncement carried around the grounds and was met with a flurry of giggles and chuckles from the other guests in the middle of their own pall-mall games.

He winced. "You're shredding my reputation, love." Devoting his attention to the ground, he brought back his mallet and smacked the ball.

It bounced two jumps before gliding to a slow halt five paces ahead.

Another round of laughter went up.

Meredith sighed. "I confess to caring a good deal more about this particular point." She jabbed a finger off to where Emilia and her husband prepared for their next shot. "And not at all about your wounded pall-mall pride."

With that, Meredith started after their ball.

It was his rogue's pride. Of all the humiliations, that was the greatest blow he'd been dealt. Meredith Durant's absolute lack of awareness of the effects she and her words and her very presence alone were having on him.

"Now," the young woman was saying when it was her turn to hit. "Your focus is on your strokes. Keeping them smooth and slow," she murmured and brought her mallet back and landed a perfect strike. The ball sailed ten paces forward in a perfectly straight line.

Emilia waved back at them. "You've still some distance to make up," she called out gleefully and then went back to assessing her and her husband's latest shot.

"She's always been smug with pall-mall," Meredith mumbled. "Let us not focus on that. She's merely trying to distract you."

His mother's guests could have simultaneously caught fire, and Barry would have been hard-pressed to pay note to anyone aside from the woman with whom he'd been partnered. "Now," Meredith whispered. "You need to put it in the hole this time."

For the thousandth time, at least, since he'd partnered with Meredith Durant, wicked musings went traipsing through his head.

He swallowed a groan.

Meredith gave him another light tap with her mallet.

He grunted. "What in blazes was *that* for?"

"With all that groaning, you're hardly invoking any manner of confidence, Barry." Shoving back the enormous brim of the hideous bonnet she'd insisted on wearing, Meredith lifted a palm over her eyes and assessed the couple ahead of them. "I'd do better to find another partner. One who knows precisely where to put that ball."

He strangled on a laugh.

Had she been any other woman, he'd have believed her entirely deliberate in her seduction.

Alas…

"You're going to cost us this round, Barry," Meredith muttered, the chastisement for his ears alone.

"God forbid," he said dryly.

Folding her arms, Meredith let her mallet dangle awkwardly in her grip. "I do require that you focus," she said. All the while, she tapped her scuffed boot in a quick beat upon the graveled path, churning up dirt and rock. "We're not all that far away."

"I forgot how positively mercenary you are when it comes to pall-mall."

She knocked her mallet discreetly against the right side of his boot.

"You're making my point for me, love."

"At least one of us is making points… my lord." She tacked on his title as an afterthought. That acknowledgment of his rank, however, had come less and less with the time they spent together. And the admonishment over his endearment… came not at all.

In short, in their time together, Meredith had changed.

He let fly his next shot.

Meredith rushed ahead several steps, her gaze trained on that projectile, her entire body tense as she leaned forward, gesturing at the ball as if she could will movement into it with frantic waves of her arm.

He smiled wistfully.

Nay, Meredith had not truly changed. She'd always been this woman. The one who thrilled at games and alternated between ruthlessly competitive and endearingly excited with each stroke of her mallet.

She let out an exultant cry that faded to a groan as the ball just missed its mark.

Meredith sank back on her heels and spun to face him. A wide smile wreathed her lips, dimpling her cheeks and doing odd things to his heart.

"Given I fell short, I expected I'd have to wield this"—he held his mallet aloft—"as a means of warding off your blows."

"Of course not! That was much improved. How could I find fault with that shot?"

"Mind if an old duke joins in?"

Barry and Meredith looked down the graveled path.

His father ambled down the path.

"Your father is playing… pall-mall."

Barry shielded his eyes. "It certainly *appears* that way." The whole world well knew that, aside from taking part in the hunts, the duke preferred sleeping as his next and closest activity of choice.

Slightly out of breath, the duke stopped before them.

"Your Grace," Meredith greeted, falling into a curtsy.

"Meredith," he returned with a smile. "Mind if I partner with my son for this next round?"

"Not at all, Your Grace," she said, turning over her mallet.

Barry frowned at how easily she'd relinquish her time with him. It was… a foreign state to find himself in. And here, with the only woman who'd ever mattered to him.

After Meredith rushed off, his father didn't waste any time. "Your mother is not happy with you," he said as Barry gathered the ball and then started down to the beginning of the pall-mall path.

"Given the frequency in which she is disappointed with me, I'd dare ask what is so different this time that she'd have you roused from a nap and force you to play in the hot summer sun?" he drawled.

"It's about the ladies present."

That gave Barry pause. "Ah, of course. My future brides."

His father's bushy white brows came together. "Not all of them.

They can't all be your brides, but one of them."

"I've no interest," he said tersely.

Pall-mall had been restored to its previously miserable state. Nay, this surpassed all previous moments of pall-mall miseries.

"But you do have interest in your experiment gardens."

"Experimental," he corrected. "You'd have me whore myself for property I'll one day inherit anyway."

"Ah, but by then the horticultural society will have already chosen some other lord's grounds." And that which Barry sought would be lost. Nay, not lost, just… somewhere else. A place he'd have to travel to if he wished to visit. Whereas this? This was here and his, and… all he'd have to do was marry a woman of his family's choosing. It wasn't a foreign concept. In fact, given societal expectations, which were drilled into the peerage at birth, it was more foreign for a lord or lady to protest as strenuously as Barry had. And yet—inadvertently his gaze sought and found the one woman not upon any approved-by-the-Duchess-of-Gayle list.

Meredith.

His father followed his stare and frowned. "It's your turn."

Barry brought his mallet back and hit the ball hard enough that it jumped and went flying. "What became of the Durants?" he asked after the projectile slid to a stop.

His father paled, and then color climbed his cheeks. Barry would have to be blind to miss the guilty flush. "I'm not sure what you're asking. Meredith is here now."

He put a hand on his father's arm, slowing his march to the ball.

"Yes, but she wasn't here for ten," *Almost eleven.* "years." When she'd been such an important part of the Aberdeen family.

The duke's throat moved, and he looked away. When he again faced Barry, his features were guarded. "Albert became clumsy with his work. Worse. He'd begun to make sizable mistakes. Costly ones."

His gut churned. Oh, good God. "You *sacked* him?" he asked on a furious whisper.

The duke doffed his hat and beat it against his side. "I didn't sack him. I retired him."

Barry swiped his spare hand over his face. "You retire a damned horse, not your best friend."

By the guilt-stricken glint in his father's eyes, the other man knew as much.

"It's your turn, Barry," Emilia called from her place thirty paces ahead.

Barely sparing the ball a look, Barry tapped it several feet, allowing them some distance between Emilia and Heath.

"You did that on purpose," his father muttered.

"Yes."

The duke sighed. "I thought we were doing the right thing, and I still believe we were."

"For *you*." Barry seethed. Ultimately, it was always about what his parents deemed best for themselves.

"For both of us," his father said insistently. "I gave him a sizable fortune."

"And sent them away. And then what of after they left? You didn't think to reach out?" Instead, Meredith had been alone through the loss of her father.

"There was your sister's broken betrothal. She was brokenhearted, as was your mother. Life interrupted, Barry. And when it was finally righted, time had lapsed and…"

"And?"

"I didn't send him away," his father blurted. His father opened his mouth and then closed it. "I asked him to retire, but I didn't ask him to leave. Albert was the one who insisted that he and Meredith leave. He said they could not remain. He was adamant."

And yet…

That didn't fit with what Meredith had shared. And if what his father said was to be believed, then what did that mean? Why had the pair left, then?

There were so many questions. Ones he was determined to get to the bottom of.

Barry truly was a miserable pall-mall player.

And standing on the sidelines as he periodically knocked the ball a handful of feet, Meredith couldn't have been more rapt.

She'd believed herself immune to feeling this emotion again. She'd believed herself immune to feeling anything.

All these years, she'd kept secret the story of her broken heart and the folly she'd made in giving her love to one who'd never truly wanted her. Kept secret those parts of herself she'd been content to trap away, buried and forgotten.

Only, they hadn't been either buried or forgotten.

She saw that now.

Telling herself she'd forgotten those old hurts and actually moving on from them were two very different things. She'd let the folly of her youth shape the whole of her life. And just as Barry had rightfully accused, she'd prevented herself from truly feeling anything. Because she didn't wish to hurt anymore. She'd lost her best friend to time and distance. She'd lost her father to death. She'd lost her lover to another. And because of all those hurts, she'd built up walls to keep herself safe.

Safe, however, was not living.

She'd been so guarded that she'd not allowed herself to simply enjoy being alive.

"You are to be commended, Miss Durant."

Startling, Meredith spun to face the owner of those regal tones. The duchess glided down the graveled path, a young maid close at her heels and a parasol aloft to ward off the sun's rays.

Barry's mother.

My employer.

The duchess.

And Meredith, who'd built a career and her security upon her perfect understanding and execution of propriety, sank into a belated curtsy. "Your Grace," she greeted as the duchess stopped beside her. "There was hardly anything to it. Bar—" The duchess's eyebrows came together even as the young maid's went shooting to her hairline. "Barely anything to it, at all," she neatly substituted, and both women's brows resumed their normal lines. "It merely took him several rounds to find the proper motions."

The duchess looked at her as if she'd gone mad. Collecting the parasol from her maid, the Duchess of Gayle gave a flick of her fingers, and her maid promptly scurried off. "What are you talking about, Miss Durant?"

The better question was: What was the duchess speaking about? "His lordship's pall-mall game."

"I referred to my son's participation in the festivities, Miss Durant," the duchess clarified, her expression deadpan.

Meredith blinked rapidly. "Oh. Yes. Yes. Well, that makes the most sense. Our arrangement." The one she'd not given a thought to in three days. Except to reflect upon all the ways in which the duchess had invited the absolute worst-possible ladies as potential brides for her son.

Barry required a woman who was clever and didn't wilt in the sun, but relished nature in all its glory.

Not like the row of proper misses even now shielding their cream-white complexions with bonnets and parasols like they feared the sun might melt them.

"Walk with me, Miss Durant."

It wasn't a question.

Then, nothing from this woman ever had been. As close to royalty as one could be outside the ranks of prince and princess, king and queen, she issued only statements and orders from her lips.

She quickened to catch up to Barry's mother, easily falling into step alongside the duchess's careful, slow, gliding steps.

"My son is taking part, and yet, my guests are not happy…" She discreetly motioned to the row of ladies on the sidelines, all staring on at the games of pall-mall underway.

Meredith took in the rabid glimmer in their eyes and fisted her hands at her sides. Nay, they didn't give a jot about pall-mall. Like Meredith, they were hopelessly fixed on just one person—Barry.

"And do you know why that is?" the duchess asked.

Startled back to the moment, she jerked her gaze back over to the duchess. "I couldn't even begin to presume, Your Grace."

"Because he is not entertaining the guests, and do you know why that is?" the other woman shot back.

"I couldn't—"

"Because he's spending all of his time with you," she said matter-of-factly.

Oh, God. Meredith's mind blanked and stalled and then resumed quickly, spinning out of control.

"Now, I understand I tasked you with the role of discovering more about my son and determining which of the ladies present might make him the best match. However, he cannot connect with anyone if he is *only* with you." She held Meredith's gaze, and Meredith felt panic knocking away as she tried to decipher the meaning behind the look leveled on her. "Am I being clear?"

Meredith wetted her lips. "You are." She wasn't. Meredith couldn't tell what the woman saw or didn't see. Or whether there was some subtle warning being issued, or just a general duchesslike reminder of the task at hand. None of it.

"We're running out of time, Miss Durant," Barry's mother went on. "I expect a match to be made before you leave." With that, her parasol aloft and a maid rushing to her side, the duchess stalked off.

With a casualness she didn't feel, Meredith looked out at the pall-mall courts. To where Barry had barely made any progress alongside his father.

Barry glanced in Meredith's direction.

A smile formed on his lips, slightly crooked, boyish, and... real, sending a giddy warmth blazing through her chest.

He winked and then resumed playing.

Restive, Meredith fiddled with the fabric of her skirts. The duchess had noted Meredith and Barry's time together. Of course, Barry's mother had, in her own mind, explained away the reason for their connection.

What connection? a voice taunted. *You're the one who's become hopelessly captivated by the man who is your assignment.* Whereas Barry? Aside from that earliest embrace, he'd given her no reason to believe he was anything but committed to the terms of their arrangement that would see him married and in control of the land he sought here at Berkshire.

Feeling eyes upon her, Meredith forced her gaze away from Barry and over to the cluster of five frowning ladies who'd directed all that displeasure in her direction.

Her heart plummeted all the way to her toes, stirring up panic and unease.

The other guests had noticed her attention.

She forced a smile and then made a show of watching Emilia's in-laws as they played.

Meredith stole another peek at the cluster of five, and some of the tension left her. The gaggle was back to firmly ogling the future duke at his game.

They didn't necessarily know how hopelessly enrapt Meredith had become by Barry Aberdeen. The rogue who wasn't so roguish. The gentleman who wasn't just the athletic one to pursue the requisite gentlemanly pastimes, but was also an intellect.

And a man, who despite his station, had looked closely enough at Meredith to see how she'd built up walls to keep herself from feeling. And hurting. And in doing so, he'd reminded her of how to simply be alive and enjoy the moments in the here and now without mourning the lost, happiest ones of the past.

Now she was faced with a new question about Barry Aberdeen…

How am I going to let him go?

As if to taunt her with that very question, the latest round ended and new matches were made.

Lady Ivy Clarence, mallet in hand, went rushing off to greet Barry for their set.

Plastering a smile on her face that strained the muscles in her cheeks, Meredith made herself stand there and watch.

The pair of them were glorious golden perfection together. Barry, tall and broadly muscular, and Lady Ivy, slender and delicate in all the ways Meredith had never been, presented as a striking couple.

Barry sent his ball sailing, and the young lady clapped lightly, then laughed at whatever witty jest he'd no doubt delivered.

Because that was who Barry was. That was what he did. He could make a widow at her just-departed husband's services laugh.

Meredith had gone and made those kindnesses out to be something special that he did for her, when in truth, that was the manner of man Barry Aberdeen was. He showed that depth of warmth to all. Just as he had when he'd been almost sixteen and she just twenty. It was just one of the reasons she loved him.

Gravel crunched behind her.

She prayed the person would continue on.

Alas, was she to expect anything else of this day?

Lady Ivy's companion, her spinster sister, smiled at her. "Hullo."

"Hello, my lady," Meredith said, dropping a belated curtsy.

"Please, there's no need for those formalities." The woman's large brown eyes held a kindly warmth. "After all, we're not so very different, Miss Duranseau."

They were entirely different. Meredith offered a smile. "Though that is kind of you, we're not quite the same, my lady," she said gently, glancing out to the pall-mall courts and promptly wishing she hadn't.

Lady Ivy, making her namesake a reality, clung to Barry's arm, crushing her generous breasts against him.

"Because I'm noble born?" the other woman drawled, bringing Meredith's gaze quickly back.

"Yes."

"Miss Duranseau, I'm thirty-two years old. I'm serving in the role of companion for my younger sister. And for those reasons, I'm largely invisible to the other guests present. I'd say, for all those reasons, we're very much the same," the lady said with a forthrightness Meredith could appreciate.

"As you put it that way…"

"I did."

They shared a smile.

"Then I shall call you Lady Agatha."

They fell into a companionable silence, both watching the same pair of players. However, their focuses, Meredith wagered, were entirely different.

Barry and Lady Ivy had found themselves halfway down the court. As before, Emilia and her husband, Lord Heath, had the advantage. Playing as the four of them offered a glimpse of a future with the family joined.

"You are the matchmaker, are you not?"

She stiffened. Mayhap she'd given greater credit to another woman seeking her out. "I am."

"I trust my sister is at the top of the duchess's list?" Lady Agatha ventured.

Meredith started. "My lady?"

"Agatha," the lady corrected. She discreetly motioned to the collection of guests assembled—the row of ladies hovering on the sidelines and the disproportionate number of unattached gentlemen. "It doesn't take much to look at Her Grace's guest list and determine her intentions in bringing together the ladies she did."

"I… couldn't say either way," she demurred.

The taller woman waved her off. "I'd not ask you to violate the duchess's confidence," she said, having perfectly followed Meredith's thoughts. The lady's eyes twinkled. "Especially as I already know the answer," she said, startling another laugh from Meredith.

Lady Agatha joined in, and hers wasn't the trilling, practiced giggle, but raw and honest. "My sister asked that I speak with you on a potential match between her and Lord Tenwhestle. She's... noted that he seems to greatly value your opinion and time together."

This time, she did not imagine the knowing in the other woman's eyes.

"Our families were very close," she explained. "Our history is long." Meredith sought to redirect them toward a safer, and yet, still no less miserable, source of discussion. "What do you think of a match between them?" she asked carefully.

"Truthfully?"

Meredith nodded. A bee circled before her eyes, and she lightly swatted at it, shooing it away.

"I know nothing about him aside from the reputation he has amongst the *ton* as a rogue."

He was so much more than that. He was an intellect, with many passions. He was clever.

"I'd have my sister marry not with a future title in mind."

The woman grew tenfold in her estimation.

Another trilling laugh echoed around the gardens, clear and bell-like and blending with the deeper, more robust masculine chuckle belonging to Barry.

Meredith and Lady Agatha stared out.

"They do appear lovely together," Lady Agatha murmured.

"Yes," she said softly, torturing herself with the sight of that lovely pair playing on to the next point. Who knew jealousy had a taste? Like vinegar, it was overwhelming in its bitterness. Sharp. And left the mouth soured. Even after Patrin's betrayal, she'd not felt... this. There'd been fury and outrage and hurt... but she'd not envied the woman who'd won him as she envied the lady upon the pall-mall field now.

The bee returned, serving as almost a bull's-eye target on the couple in the distance, and Meredith gave it another angry swat.

"You needn't worry, you know."

Her stomach muscles twisted. "I'm not worried." *I'm jealous and hurting.*

"You keep swatting at it."

What was the other woman on about? She cocked her head.

"The honeybee," Lady Agatha clarified.

Heat went rushing to her cheeks.

Giving no outward reaction to Meredith's sudden blush, she rattled on. "If you look close between him and"—turning, she surveyed the row of flowers behind them—"that one there, you'll see he's larger. He has no stinger."

That managed to penetrate her earlier misery. Meredith's intrigue stirred. "Indeed?" she asked, squinting first at one creature and then the other, attempting to bring them into better focus.

"None of the males do. They do no work, and all they do is… mate." Her lips twitched. "One might say they're not much different than a nobleman in that regard."

A laugh exploded from Meredith's lips, and the other woman joined in. When her amusement faded, Meredith wiped the mirth from her eyes. How much more fascinating these past years would have been had she the company of one such as Agatha Clarence. "How do you know this?"

Lady Agatha smiled. "My father was an amateur naturalist. Since I was a girl, he had a sizable collection of bees, and I, to my late mother's shame and horror, held a like fascination. She despised it…"

"Your pastime or the bees?" Meredith inquired.

"Both." A twinkle lit Lady Agatha's eyes. "We helped her see the mutual relationship between her prized roses and the bees, and she came to an uneasy truce with them."

"Agatha, I've need of you."

They glanced off to the young lady now stalking toward them. At some point, Barry's pall-mall partner had quit the courts.

Agatha sighed. "She is not one for the sun. If you'll excuse me?" Giving Meredith a regretful look, the other woman hurried to join her sister.

Meredith watched an exchange that was all too familiar.

No matter what the Duchess of Gayle expected of either the ladies she'd hand-picked for Barry or Meredith's task, Meredith would never see Barry wed such a woman.

From the field, more laughter met her ears.

Barry had been joined by another partner.

Nay, even if Barry didn't make a match with Lady Ivy, there was a whole number of options here, as specially invited guests of the duchess, no less.

This time, unlike before, Meredith couldn't make herself suffer through any more of the flirting between the duchess's young, glowing guests and the future Duke of Gayle.

Turning on her heel, she left.

CHAPTER 13

$\mathcal{S}$HE WAS LATE.

It was the first instance in a week that Meredith had failed to arrive at the agreed-upon morning meeting.

Barry consulted his timepiece for the tenth time. Twenty-six minutes after six o'clock. He tucked the watch back inside his jacket and resumed his search of the terrace above for some hint of her.

Nay, not only was she late this morn, she'd also failed to appear for their evening appointment.

Meredith Durant remained elusive. Just as she had since their game of pall-mall. That agonizingly seductive match in which she'd been so endearingly competitive, thrilling in the game, smiling in a way that met her eyes and erased the wary, somber creature who'd first arrived.

Once again, he reached inside his jacket for his timepiece…

He felt her before he heard her.

Barry looked up.

His heart knocked around in his chest at the sight of her. The chignon had returned to its painful-looking, tightened state. Her features were set in an equally severe expression.

And he could not have hungered for her any more than he did in that moment.

The women he'd kept company with were content to live lives of leisure. They didn't rise early. They didn't sweat or laugh exuberantly over games of pall-mall. The world was there for their pleasures, but they were measured in how they claimed them. And they'd certainly never take on work, even if their own survival depended upon it… as Meredith's had.

"Hullo," he called up.

Meredith bowed her head. "My lord," she returned. Clasping the rail, she started her descent.

Ah, she saw this as a working meeting, then. It was a detail he'd come to note about her in their time together. She'd been able to carefully delineate the moments when they found pleasure from the moments when she so diligently saw to the task his mother had foisted upon her.

As soon as Meredith reached his side, Barry proffered his elbow.

"I cannot take your arm."

He wagged it. "Of course you can."

She ignored that offering. That had always been Meredith. As stubborn as the English sun.

With a sigh, he let his arm fall. "Very well. On we go." Barry started forward.

Meredith easily matched his strides. "What activity do you have planned for the morn?"

He'd have to be as deaf as Lady Jersey to fail to hear that slight timbre of anticipation in her voice. This was how he preferred her. This was how she should be. Lively. Eager for life. Barry glanced at her from the corner of his eye. "Excited, love?"

"I might be… curious."

He snorted. "Indeed."

She wrinkled her nose, and he bit back a grin.

"Do you intend to tell me or not?"

"Or not…" He stretched the pause on.

Meredith punched him in the arm, and he winced. "God, you are ruthless," he muttered, rubbing the aggrieved flesh.

She directed her gaze forward.

"Very well," he said. "*Riding*. We're going riding." Because a woman who'd loved to ride, and who'd been as glorious at it as Meredith Durant, deserved to do so again.

Barry had walked five paces, reaching the quiet stable yard where the head stable master waited with the reins of two mounts: his and Meredith's beloved mare, Gabby. He glanced at Meredith to assess her reaction to again seeing her horse.

All the color had leached from her cheeks, leaving her skin ashen.

He frowned. "I'm sorry, I thought to surprise…"

Only, Meredith's slightly unfocused eyes were directed just beyond Gabby to the stable master holding the reins.

"Patrin," Barry said quietly, "that is all."

When the expert stable master made no move to follow his directives, Barry looked over.

The servant's features were stamped in surprise. And something more… pain.

Barry's gaze went from Patrin to Meredith and back to the servant.

Gathering her skirts, Meredith bolted.

And Barry knew. Born of an intuitiveness that came from knowing Meredith as he did.

Patrin was the one.

The knowledge hit him like a kick to the chest.

Barry remained frozen for a moment and then hurried to hand the reins off to Patrin before taking off after Meredith. "Meredith," he called, his heart thundering.

He'd forgotten how damned quick she was.

Like summer lightning, she streaked across the graveled paths and had already put sizable distance between them and continued running.

Barry stretched his legs, lengthening his strides. All the while, his gaze remained fixed on her figure.

Meredith stumbled through the arbor leading to the rose garden.

Skidding to a halt a moment later, Barry did a sweep of the insulated grounds… and found her.

She stood alongside the watering fountain. "I didn't think I'd see him again," she said quietly, confirming everything Barry suspected.

But he didn't know what to make of Meredith's admission.

Had she wanted to see Patrin Scott again? Did she love him even now?

That latter question had the same effect as a dull blade being dragged around his chest.

It is not about you. It is only about her.

She hugged her arms to her chest. "I knew he was going to return." Meredith angled her head back slightly, meeting Barry's gaze. He searched, trying to read anything in those brown depths. "He'd written as much," she explained.

Barry balled his hands into tight fists at his sides. The other man had broken it off with her in a damned note.

"I just didn't imagine he'd be here still," she murmured.

"Do you love him?" The question slipped out. He needed the answer.

Meredith didn't pretend to misunderstand. "I loved the time we had," she said, her gaze distant and contemplative. "I loved the thrill of being in love." She flashed a wry smile. "I didn't love anything that came after it." Her smile fell. "And I learned early on that I loved the idea of being in love. But seeing him? It reminded me of the greatest mistake I've made, Barry. What a fool I was."

Barry eyed her for a moment.

Then, fishing his gardening shears from his pocket, he snipped a nearby bloom. "Do you know all the varieties of roses, Meredith?"

At the abrupt shift away from talk of Patrin, Meredith shook her head. "Do I…?"

"There are the China roses. They have more than one hundred petals. A bit of a look of a cabbage to them." He held the flower up. "Is there not?"

Meredith nodded slowly. "I…"

"Then, there are the mosses." He wandered several paces and carefully snipped another bud. Barry evaluated the petals for a moment. "Now, this is a peculiar one. They, in fact, get their name because, well, they are very mosslike in appearance. The stem, calyx, and sepals…" He ran his fingers over each of part of the flower, highlighting those structures for her. "They all have a sticky, glandular structure. Gives them the look"—he guided the flower under her nose—"and smell, of moss."

Meredith inhaled, and the slight puff of air that she exhaled stirred the purple petals.

"Do you smell it?" he murmured.

She nodded. "A woodsy scent."

"So very different, and yet, as intoxicating as the sweet smell of the prior rose, isn't it?"

This moment with Barry held her fully ensnared. In ways Patrin never had. She knew that now.

Barry, however, proved almost clinical in his methodical lesson. He gathered another bud. "There's also the Portland rose, named after the Duchess of Portland. They're bright red and bloom every six weeks through the summer and autumn." He slid the rose into her fingers so he could collect another. "The bourbon is a newer one. Not very long ago, it was formed by crossing an autumn damask and the Old Blush China rose and has traits of both that make it unique." Barry continued on with his lesson, plucking a white flower from the back of a porcelain vase and turning it over in his hands. "Now, this... this has long been for me the most fascinating of all the flowers."

Meredith studied his bent head. "Why that one?" she asked, wanting to know everything there was about Barry Aberdeen, willing to admit that fascination came not from her work as a matchmaker, but from who Barry was as a man.

"Many botanists believe the rugosa is the oldest of the roses. Unlike the other flowers before you, the rugosa is quite hardy. It doesn't require much attention. And even with that, it blooms frequently. It's also very rare." He held the flower out, and she took it with her free hand. "In fact, there are few of its kind in England. And some have prickles."

Meredith adjusted the stems still damp from the dew, organizing them so they were easier to hold. "Prickles?" She lowered her nose to breathe in that eclectic blend of scents when Barry spoke, freezing her.

"The world tends to think of them as thorns." With greater care, Barry eased another flower from its bush. She reached for it, but he made no attempt to hand this one over.

"The truth is there's more than thirty genera of roses that do not have prickles. And it would be deuced unfair to believe they're all the same and that they all might hurt you."

Her heart hammered in her chest as his meaning became clear. And she fell in love with him all over again.

"Barry," she whispered, and stepping close, she leaned up and kissed him.

His body tensed. "What was that for?" he whispered.

"Because there is no one like you," she said simply. Because he made her smile and her heart melt and her belly flutter and she loved him.

Barry's gaze worked over her face, and then he took her in his arms.

There was nothing tender or gentle about their coming together.

He guided her down, and she went with him, the cloud-studded summer-blue sky overhead a canvas behind him.

Looping her arms about his neck, she clung tight and kissed him.

Barry licked at her lips. Tracing the seam. Teasing and tormenting until she moaned incoherently from the desire that pulsed sharply between her legs. At the feel of him in her arms. At the honey taste of him. So sweet and intoxicating that she whimpered. Barry swept inside, fiercely taking her mouth. Laying claim to it, and she wanted him to take it. To own it.

And he did.

His tongue lashed boldly, possessively against hers, just as he brought the neckline of her dress down and exposed her skin to the soft summer air.

He closed his lips around one swollen peak. Meredith stiffened. And then she hissed through her teeth. He suckled that oversensitized tip until she was bucking against him. Needing more. Needing to be closer to him and the gift he held out.

"Do you like that, Meredith?" he whispered, his breath as ragged as her own.

"Barry," she pleaded.

"Yes, love. Tell me." He teased his thumb around her areola. "Show me."

And she did. Twining her fingers in his long, silken strands, she guided him down to the previously neglected tip.

Her eyes slid closed as he worshipped that bud.

And then he palmed her through her garments. Meredith's eyes went flying open.

Her breath came in hard, fast pants as he teased her center.

She bit her lip, those ministrations maddening for what they offered and worse for what they prevented. "I need to feel you." She struggled to get air into her lungs. "I need to feel us together, Barry."

Passion had turned his blue irises a shade that was nearly black. He got to work divesting her of her garments. First, he rolled her stockings down, kissing each swath of exposed skin that he left bare to his worshipful gaze and the hot summer sun.

Closing her eyes, Meredith draped a forearm over them to shield them from the bright early morn's rays.

"You are beauty personified, Meredith Durant. Your skin the silk of a rose in bloom." His words, whispered in a silken baritone, cascaded over her. There was a poetry to his touch and in his words, and it compelled her to open her eyes.

Leaning over her as he now was, he blocked the light of the sun, and instead, it hung like a halo about him.

With a hand that shook, she brushed at the sweaty lock that had tumbled over his brow. How she loved him.

She suspected she always had.

Not taking her eyes from his, Meredith reached her hands up between them and loosened the buttons of his jacket. Once the soft wool article fell agape, she shoved it from his shoulders.

His throat muscles moved.

"Am I scandalizing you, Barry?" she whispered. Untying his cravat and pulling the white scrap free, she tossed it to the ground beside them, forgotten.

"Entrancing me," he croaked as she tugged his lawn shirttails free of his trousers. "Be-bewitching me." She drew the garment overhead and added it to the pile beside them. "Captivating me. But—" Air hissed between his teeth on what might have been a prayer or a curse as she slid her palms over the hard wall of the muscles of his chest.

Meredith pressed her lips against one of his flat nipples. "You were saying?" she breathed against his chest, and the faint whorl of curls upon it stirred.

"I–I've no idea," he groaned, and then his eyes flew open. "But you're not scandalizing me," he rasped out. "I recall now."

Meredith expected some part of her should be appalled at her own boldness, and yet, it had been the man whose arms she lay in now who'd opened her eyes to the walls she'd erected and the need to be free of those constraints. She'd not forgive herself if she left Berkshire without having known Barry in her arms.

And mayhap it was wanton and wrong, but it felt only right.

With jerky movements, Barry wrestled out of his trousers and kicked them aside until he was naked before her.

She drew back so she might see him as she'd longed to, taking in the solid muscle-hewn frame, from his taut shoulders and defined biceps, to the flat muscles of his belly. He was... perfection. "*You are so beautiful,*" she said softly.

Desire sparked in his eyes, and they moved in harmony, Meredith lifting her arms up for him just as he came down over her.

Barry lowered his head to her right breast and flicked his tongue over the tip.

Moaning, she stroked a palm over his cheek and let herself feel.

Then he threaded his fingers through her growing wetness and teased her with slow, agonizing strokes. She lifted her hips up, urging him with her body. It had never been like this.

There'd been a thrill of excitement, but not this all-consuming hunger.

Meredith's body shook. Biting her lip hard, she lifted her hips up, arching into his touch.

He slipped another finger inside, and she cried out.

Barry swallowed that sound of desire with his mouth, taking her lips in a frantic joining. Lashing his tongue against hers. And then he eased some of the franticness of that kiss. He stroked more slowly, in a deliberate rhythm, and matched that with the skilled fingers that explored her center, destroying the little that had remained of clear thought. He reduced her to a puddle of heightened nerves and feeling.

His eyes slid closed. "Meredith, I want to go slow. I—"

She let her legs splay, and he immediately slid into position, bringing himself to rest against her. "I want you, Barry."

It was all he needed. He plunged himself deep, burying his length inside her damp channel.

She cried out in beautiful bliss, the sound splintering across the early morn sky, sending birds into noisy flight.

Barry began to move, thrusting inside her, and she rocked her hips, matching his pace.

Sweat beaded his brow, and all the muscles of his face remained taut and pained. And that evidence of his desire sent further heat low into her belly.

Their pace grew increasingly frenzied. Only, she wanted this moment to go on forever, and yet, the sharp ache building at her core begged for surcease.

"Barry," she moaned imploringly.

He thrust frantically, and she felt herself climbing. In ways her body never had before. In ways she'd not believed possible, and then her entire body jerked. Crying out once more, she went tumbling over the edge of passion, exploding in a flash of color like the Vauxhall fireworks. That went on forever. That she wanted to go on forever. And then her body went limp.

A guttural groan resonated in Barry's chest, and he withdrew, spilling himself in warm rivulets upon her belly before he collapsed atop her.

They lay there. Their breaths came together in fast, shaky spurts as they clung to each other.

A dreamy smile hovered on her lips as she wrapped her arms about his waist. "I never knew it could be like that."

He drew back, and she went cold at the slight separation. "I never did either, Meredith," he said with a somberness that brought her eyes open.

She didn't want the spell to break. She wanted the illusion. She wanted the illusion of a future with him and this garden they'd transformed into Eden to remain a place where make-believe won out.

In the end, reality intruded, as it invariably did.

"I'm s—"

"Don't you dare apologize to me, Barry Aberdeen," she said tersely. Pushing herself up onto her elbows, she glared at him. "You're the one who spoke to me about living life fully." And there could be no doubting that she'd never, and never would again, feel more alive than she did in Barry's arms.

He lightly palmed her cheek. "You deserved the privacy and comfort of a bedroom."

"Ah, but I wanted this. That is the difference, Barry." She rested her cheek atop his chest.

"My father didn't send your father away."

She picked her head up. "What?"

"Yesterday, when we were playing pall-mall, I... demanded answers for his treatment of you and your father. Your father... he confided in mine about your broken heart. Your father sought to protect you. He wanted you away, and now that timing"—with Patrin's return—"makes sense. And yet, my family failed you both by not trying to find you. He sought to protect you."

Tears glimmered in her eyes, and she brushed them away.

"I don't say that to in any way pardon my parents and me for failing to—"

Meredith touched her lips to his. "I don't want apologies, Barry. I was as capable of seeking out your family... more so." She'd not have him play any manner of guilty party. "I can't stay."

Barry stiffened. "Because of him."

"Because I gave my virtue to a stable lad who is now your stable master," she said.

Reaching for his jacket, Barry fished out a kerchief, and with an infinite tenderness that stole the remainder of her heart, he cleaned her between her legs. He used the soiled scrap to next clean himself.

"You're running away. Again."

Biting the inside of her cheek, Meredith forced herself to sit up. "I'm not."

"Aren't you?"

He didn't know anything about it. Was this truly about the fear of her past being discovered? Or the pain of having to bear witness to Barry making a match with another? He caught her by the shoulders. "All I know, Meredith, is that I—"

Mutterings just outside the rose gardens reached them, interrupting whatever he'd been about to say. "I think this is a disastrous idea," a familiar and decidedly regal voice intoned.

Meredith and Barry froze.

She felt the blood leave her face as those voices grew increasingly closer.

"A summer concert in the gardens?" the duke went on. "I'll have you know you're the reason for Barry's fascination with flowers.'"

"Your parents," Meredith mouthed, searching frantically for a place to run. A place to crawl. Any form of escape.

Barry remained motionless, and she sent an elbow into his side. "Your parents," she said silently once more, springing him into action.

"Oh, bloody hell," Barry whispered, frantically wrestling into his jacket.

"None of my ideas are disastrous." The Duchess of Gayle clipped out those six words. "What could be disastrous about my gard..."

Arm in arm, the duke and duchess entered and drew to an abrupt stop. The duchess sharpened her gaze on Meredith's wrinkled dress, her disheveled hair hanging loose about her shoulders, and an equally rumpled Barry.

Who at last managed to slide his jacket on.

The silence was deafening, and Meredith curled her toes into the soft earth as shame, horror, and mortification whipped through her.

The duchess tightened her mouth. "I stand corrected."

CHAPTER 14

IT HAD TAKEN MEREDITH EIGHT and a half years to build her career.

And but a day to destroy it.

Numb, she sat at her desk with her notebook open before her.

Though, numbness was far preferable to the nausea that had roiled in her belly since the duke and duchess had stumbled upon them.

In flagrante delicto.

In a way and place by which there could be absolutely no doubt as to what they'd been doing.

From out in the hall, the chiming clock rang the top of the hour, and she jumped, her heart racing.

She briefly pressed her eyes shut and then forced them back open to stare once again at the blank page before her.

She didn't know what she'd expected.

For the duchess to storm Meredith's guest chambers and call her out as a harlot? To be thrown out unceremoniously?

Only, the duke and duchess would never resort to such a display. Not when doing so would only raise gossip, and His and Her Grace would never permit that. No, they'd smile through gritted teeth, even knowing their son had been caught in the family gardens with a thirty-year-old servant.

With a groan, she dropped her head atop her desk and lightly banged it.

She'd been discovered with Barry. By his parents, of all people.

And what was worse... she had no regrets. That was, with regards to everything that had come before they were discovered. Not true regrets anyway. She loved him. She loved being with him and laughing with him and making love with him. Her body still tingled and burned with the memory of Barry's hands upon her.

"Enough," she whispered.

In coming here, she'd made a promise to both his mother and him. And even now, as the duchess's opinion and three thousand pounds did not matter... Barry did.

Biting her lower lip, Meredith picked up the list the Duchess of Gayle had given her... ten days ago? A lifetime. This same list, Meredith had committed to memory, and yet, she made herself read it again, as a reminder.

Setting it down, Meredith hastily scratched a handful of sentences. She tore the page carefully along the seam, and after she'd read over it several times, she folded it.

She reached for another sheet, and her fingers tightened so hard about her pencil, the charcoal scrap left indentations upon her callused palm.

And then she began to write. And write. And she continued writing until the numbness went away, and her fingers and neck both ached.

There was a sharp, perfunctory knock, and Meredith whipped her head up.

It had been inevitable.

There'd be no summons, but a visit in her rooms, away from the prying eyes of other guests.

Knock-knock-knock.

Her stomach flipped over, and Meredith forced herself to stand. "Just a m–moment," she called. She hurriedly finished off her words, signed the note, and then folded the three sheets of paper. Searching for time. Anything to delay the impending meeting. Even for just a handful of moments.

She reached the door and took a steadying breath and braced herself to face—

"Emilia?" she blurted.

The way Emilia could not meet her gaze confirmed... her friend knew. "May I come in?"

"Of course." Meredith stepped out of the way and motioned the other woman inside. She closed the door behind them, and when she turned back, she found Emilia studying the two valises beside the armoire.

"You have four valises," her friend whispered.

"Had," she softly corrected, and to escape the emotion in Emilia's eyes, she returned to the armoire to continue with her packing. "I had four. I only require two now."

"I... overheard my parents speaking."

And there it was.

Meredith paused in midfold. "Oh." Because, really, what else was there to say to Barry's sister? She swiped a hand across her eyes. If Barry's family was speaking so freely about her scandal, how much longer before all the world knew?

Emilia removed a dress from the armoire and effortlessly folded the garment. "Do you love him?"

Her lower lip trembled, and Meredith caught it hard between her teeth. Drawing in an unsteady breath, she knelt and packed away the garment. "It does not matter."

"Because your happiness does not matter?"

"Because your brother's future is not mine." He was destined to wed a lady who shared his interests, not one with a scandalous past. Not when his experimental gardens were contingent upon him wedding the right woman.

"That is not what I asked," Emilia said matter-of-factly, laying the article she'd folded atop Meredith's. Then, climbing to her feet, she went and gathered a chemise.

Meredith studied the floor and then nodded. "I do."

"Have you told him?"

"Of course not."

"And why ever not?" her friend shot back.

Meredith jumped up. "Because it is not as simple as you'd have it seem. Titles and rank..." And in her case, lack thereof. "They matter." She began to pace. "Nor, for that matter, do I have reason to believe your brother would even want a future with me."

Emilia frowned. "Barry isn't one to go... go..." Her friend blanched. "I can't say it," she said around a grimace. "And I don't even want to begin thinking about it. Not about my brother. But... but you know what I'm saying. He wouldn't do *that* unless he cared."

Despite the misery at her impending departure, and the loss of Barry, Meredith found herself smiling.

They were interrupted by a light scratch.

"The scratch," Emilia muttered.

"How could I have forgotten?" Emilia's earlier, more direct knock could have never been confused with the catlike clawing on the other side of the panel.

They shared a smile, and Meredith found some strength in that show of support.

The duchess didn't bother to wait for an invitation—but then, a woman of her stature wouldn't. She swept in, her gaze reserved for Meredith. "Out, Emilia."

Emilia positioned herself alongside Meredith. "I'm not leaving. Whatever you are going to say, Mother, you'll say—"

Meredith set a hand on her friend's forearm. "It is fine," she said softly. Grateful as she was for that display of solidarity, she'd not have Emilia fight with her family. Not on Meredith's behalf.

"But—"

"I'd speak with your mother," Meredith insisted in her firmer tones. Her gaze remained locked with the duchess. "Alone."

Her friend hesitated, and then with a tense nod, she quit the rooms.

As soon as the door had closed behind her, the duchess pounced. "I invited you with one assignment laid out before you."

"I know that, Your Grace," she said quietly. Only, it had never been about what the duchess had wanted. Not truly. Yes, the funds had represented security, but ultimately, she'd taken on the role so she might help Barry wed a woman who would bring him happiness. An idea that now threatened to cleave her in two.

Peering down the length of her straight nose, the duchess eyed the mess of garments and valises. "Were my instructions somehow... unclear?"

"They were not," she said softly. "I did not anticipate, however, falling in love with your son."

The duchess made no outward reaction to that admission.

Meredith took a steadying breath. "I love your son," she went on. "And I want him to be happy." Because his happiness meant more than even her own. And for all the pain of this moment and the ones that had come before—and the ones that would undoubtedly come after—anger whipped through her. Not for Meredith, but rather for Barry. Because of this woman and her husband. "I want Barry to be happy, which is far more than I can say for you and His Grace."

The duchess sputtered. "I *beg* your pardon?"

Enlivened, Meredith stalked over to Her Grace. "You and your husband have asked Barry, since he was no more than a child, to conform to societal expectations. You'd have him do only that which Society deems appropriate and make him feel shame for ever daring to pursue intellectual interests that you find lacking."

"How dare you?"

"I dare because it is true." She took another step toward the duchess, this woman she'd bowed to since she'd been a child. "You'd craft a list of women whom you wish your son to marry, without a single consideration for who might be deserving of your son." *None. There is not a single woman.* "You'd hold over him land, forcing him to barter one happiness for another," she said, trying to will Her Grace to see, "all to satisfy you and your husband's concern for the Gayle title." Her chest rose and fell. "Without ever a thought that Barry should come first, before anything."

The duchess went slack-jawed and then slapped a hand against her chest. "Well, I never."

"No." Meredith looked her up and down. "I trust you've never had anyone truly tell you how they feel." She thrust a folded page at the duchess.

Her Grace made no move to take it. "What is this?"

"I've considered that which you've not. I'd ask that you give it to Barry." She forced the sheet into the other woman's hand. "I am done here. You needn't worry about ever again seeing me." At best, she could hope her long-ago connection would afford her the duchess's silence so that Meredith could continue on to London in her role of matchmaker. She'd bring about unions for young ladies, while going back to the same, sad, lonely existence she'd had before Barry.

Surprise rounded the duchess's eyes. "You are leaving."

She was. And it was going to destroy her. Oh, God. Her heart wrenched; the weight of her pain threatened to drag her under.

But she'd be damned if she let Barry's mother see her suffering. She'd not allow her that satisfaction. Meredith clenched and unclenched her jaw. "I'm not leaving because of you. I'm not making this decision for you or His Grace or Emilia. I'm doing this for Barry. Because I love him. and I'd see him have the grounds he desires and the future he d-deserves." Her voice broke, and she hated herself in that instant for revealing weakness before this woman.

Unfolding the small, neatly torn sheet from Meredith's notebook, Barry's mother read the words written there and promptly refolded it. "I see." With that, she turned on her heel and left.

Meredith didn't move for several long moments.

Then, her shoulders slumped.

Yes, she suspected the Duchess of Gayle indeed did see. Meredith would go, Barry would marry, and in that, the duchess had won.

With tears stinging her eyes, Meredith resumed packing.

CHAPTER 15

$\mathcal{S}$EATED IN THE $\mathcal{D}$UKE OF Gayle's office, with the austere duke and duchess on one side of the desk and Barry on the other, Barry knew there could be only one certainty.

His parents were displeased.

Nay, they sat before him as he'd never seen them. Enraged. From the high color in their cheeks, to the matching glowers etched on their faces, fury simmered from the regal pair, on the cusp of boiling over.

Which was saying a good deal, since as a rule, they ascribed to an existence where they showed no emotion.

In the end, his mother broke the tense impasse. "I told you he was a shameful rogue. *This* is why I insisted he marry."

Barry shot up a hand. "If I may—"

His parents snapped in unison, "You may not."

"You insisted he marry?" his father went on, not missing a beat. "I was the one losing sleep over his escapades in the gossip columns."

His mother snorted. "You've never lost sleep a day in your life, Geoffrey."

The duke thumped the desk. "That is unfair."

"Is that the reason you've called this meeting, Geoffrey? To lament your loss of sleep?"

As his parents proceeded to bicker, Barry stared on in something akin to shock. Nay, it *was* shock. Unalloyed shock. In the whole of his existence, his parents had never succumbed to "plebian responses," as his mother called them. Under other circumstances,

Barry might have otherwise enjoyed their descent into normality.

Alas, all this was secondary. His parents' feelings and opinions, in this instant, were secondary.

"If I may?" he called out, interrupting them once more.

His father nudged out his chin. "Go on."

"I am sorry you…" He yanked at his cravat, hopelessly wrinkling the fabric. "That is…"

"For all the rumors of him being a rogue, he's deuced bad at this," his father muttered.

"Indeed," his mother said on a like whisper.

"I hear you," Barry said, feeling like he'd wandered onto a stage production of a farcical drama.

His father gestured with his hand. "You were saying?"

Barry sat up. "I regret that you came upon me—"

"It wasn't *just* you."

"—as I was earlier," he finished, refusing to take his mother's bait.

"That is what you're sorry for?" his mother asked archly. "Being *discovered*?"

Yes, but not for the reasons she thought. It was because he'd not change that moment with Meredith for any damned botanical garden or horticultural society or anything. He was greedy, however. He didn't want a single, stolen night with Meredith. His throat moved. He wanted a lifetime.

His mother narrowed her eyes on his face. "Meredith was… quite eloquent in communicating her feelings for you…" She wrinkled her nose. "As well as her opinion of your father and I."

He could only begin to imagine what words Meredith had hurled. There was no woman more magnificent than Meredith Durant. Barry managed his first smile since his parents had come upon him in the gardens.

"And I'll have you know, hers would hardly constitute as a favorable opinion of your father and I," his mother said, merely confirming that which Barry had suspected.

"I trusted it wasn't," Barry said.

The duke sputtered. "What in blazes did *I* do?"

"Apparently, we've not supported Barry in his endeavors."

Despite the risk posed to her career and her future and her security, Meredith had gone toe-to-toe with Barry's parents—for him.

God, he didn't know whether to kiss her or shake her for not caring after herself first before all. She was what mattered.

"I must commend her, though. She did fulfill her obligation."

"Her…"

His mother held out a folded sheet. Barry was out of his chair and across the room in three strides.

"Barry," his father scolded as he ripped the note from his mother's fingers.

Ignoring him, Barry read the handful of lines.

He'd been wrong. He knew precisely what he wanted to do. The minx deserved a damned good shaking. But only after he kissed her thoroughly.

"What is that?" the duke demanded, looking from his wife, over to Barry, and then back again.

He seethed. "It appears Meredith Durant has selected my bride." Just like that.

His father's face lit up. "That is splendid!"

Barry and his mother spoke over each other.

"Enough, husband."

"No. It isn't."

"Barry has found his match," the duchess explained. "Isn't that right, Barry?"

Yes, he'd found her. Long ago. He'd just not known it then. Now, he knew. Just as he knew he'd never be happy with another.

"And she certainly isn't that stranger on the sheet that Meredith insisted I give you," his mother went on, cutting into his musings.

He creased his brow and tried to make sense of what his mother was saying.

And then he went absolutely motionless. Impossible. Surely not… And then he caught the smug glimmer in his mother's eyes. All the air left him on a slow exhale. "It was *you*."

His mother smirked. "Well, it wasn't *just* me."

"You brought her here."

A wide, unrestrained smile wreathed her face.

"I don't…"

"Understand?" She patted his arm. "Gentlemen never do."

The duke grumbled, "I understood quite well."

Barry was gobsmacked a second time for their exchange. "You, too?"

"Hmph. Needn't sound so shocked about it."

His mother slipped her hand through the duke's and drew it close to her heart. "I'd be remiss if I didn't give credit where credit was due. When you arrived several months ago, indicating that you'd seen Meredith, your father pointed out that he'd never seen you react so about any woman and suggested we bring her to visit."

The duke stared affectionately at the top of his wife's head. "At which point, your mother pointed out that any lady we suggested for you would send you fleeing."

Flummoxed, Barry rocked back on his heels. "Good God, you set me up?"

With matching smiles, husband and wife looked at each other. "Indeed."

His mind spinning, Barry resumed reading the sentences written in Meredith's neat hand. "She's mad," he whispered.

The duke guffawed. "Alas, if your intentions are to win the lady, might I recommend 'keeper of my heart' or 'dear heart'? Really, anything other than 'mad.'"

There'd be time enough for endearments later. Hopefully. If he was successful. Barry was already tearing across the room.

His heart thundering, he bolted through the corridors. Passing servants and the straggling guest.

My God, my parents saw and knew. Reaching the stairs, he didn't break his stride, taking them two at a time. The moment he reached the landing, he took off until he reached her room.

Barry skidded to a stop.

He didn't bother knocking.

Meredith gasped. "Barry, what are you…?"

He shoved the door closed with the heel of his boot. Narrowing his gaze on the two valises at her feet and then the partially white chemise in her fingers, he started forward. "I trust the better question is, what are *you* doing?" It didn't require clarifying. It was quite obvious she intended to leave. And equal parts panic and outrage pounded away in his chest.

She followed his stare and stood. "This? I think it should be fairly obvious, Barry… I'm folding…"

Barry stopped before her.

Meredith wetted her lips. "Oh. You refer to my leaving."

Her leaving. She'd said it. How casually she spoke of her departure that would cleave him open and leave him forever destroyed. And what was worse… she was choosing to go. For all that they'd shared these past days, she'd simply… pack up… and walk out of his life?

"We're not done here, Meredith," he said silkily.

She hugged the chemise close to her chest. "Barry, please don't make this harder than it is."

If she thought he was going to make this easy, she didn't know a thing about anything.

Unfolding the pages, he proceeded to read them aloud.

"'Dearest Barry…'"

"I know what I wrote, Barry."

He continued on, "'I promised I'd help you make a match with a woman who'd have you deliriously happy, and I confess I've failed you. Not because I do not believe there isn't a woman who could make you happy. Nor because I don't believe there exists a woman out there who'd appreciate your wit, and your skills, and your… everything. Because there is such a woman. And you are so very deserving of her.'"

Barry ceased reading and refolded the pages along the seams. "I fear you've not done yourself credit," he said.

She wetted her lips again. "I've not?"

"Yes, you found me the perfect match."

She should be only elated.

She'd done it. Of the guests invited by the duchess, and the young women selected as potential brides, Meredith had found the one woman who'd not been on his mother's list, and yet, who, with her appreciation for botany, shared Barry's passions. And she would be a companion and friend to him.

He'd have those lands his parents had dangled over him.

Tears stung her eyes, and she made a show of refolding the chemise in her hands. "Lady Agatha will make a fine wife."

He dropped a shoulder against her armoire. "I'm certain."

Her face crumpled.

"For some gentleman, she will."

She froze. For some gentleman? Which implied…

"I'm not, however, going to be that gentleman."

Her heart did a funny little leap and then settled into a normal beat. "But you don't know her, Barry," she said quietly. "She is witty and clever and kind and—"

Barry kissed her, and all thought fled. The taste of him, sweet and spellbinding, pulled her deeper into his hold.

He drew back, and Meredith's lashes fluttered.

"You promised you'd help me make a match with a woman who'd have me deliriously happy, and you did, Meredith," he said hoarsely. "You promised there was a woman who'd make me happy and appreciate me. And I found her."

Her lips quivered. "Me?" She wanted it to be her. Since she'd come upon him at the Royal Horticultural Society, reading poetry among the roses, her heart had belonged to him. Nay, longer.

"Yes, you daft woman." A pained-sounding laugh rumbled in his chest as he took her by the shoulders and gave a light squeeze. "It is you."

He went on, "I'm not looking for someone who has the same interests. I'm looking for someone with whom I can share my life and who wants to share mine. I want a partnership in which we learn from each other. I always knew it was you, Meredith." Barry drew out his watch fob and pressed the metal clasp. The case sprang open. Wordlessly, he turned the gold piece so she could see it, and Meredith brought her palms up, stifling a gasp.

A crystal case covered a pressed rose, aged brown by time.

"You know they say yellow roses signify friendship shared."

Tears spilled, unchecked, down Meredith's cheeks, and she struggled to see his beloved face.

With the pad of his thumb, Barry wiped away the remaining drops.

"But your gardens…"

He crushed the pages in his fist and shook it at her. "Do you think I give a jot about the horticultural society?" he snapped.

Her eyes widened. "Why, yes. Yes, I do." When he spoke of flowers, he did so with reverence.

He frowned. "Fine, I do give a jot about it." Barry waved the wrinkled pages at her once more. "But do you truly believe I care about it and any land or anything more than you?"

She tried to make her mouth move, but there were no words.

"Alas, you've been outmatchmade, love. It was my parents' grand plan all along to bring us together."

Meredith drew back. "Impossible." His mother had been clear in her expectations. Hadn't she?

"Oh, I assure you. It was quite masterful, really. Impressive. Even if I'd not bring myself to admit as much to them." All hint of teasing fled his features, and emotion rippled over Barry's face. He let her note drop to his side. "How do you not know that I am so desperately in love with you?"

Her breath caught, and she shot a palm behind her to catch herself on a chair. "Mayhap because you've never said it?" she ventured hesitantly.

"You are the only woman who has seen beyond the image of rogue and scapegrace. You are the only one to see more. And the lies I allowed Society to believe." His gaze touched her like a physical caress. "You are the only woman I've ever known"—he paused—"in any way, Meredith."

Her heart fluttered. "You…"

Barry dropped his brow against hers. "You are the only woman I've ever made love to, because I wanted that moment to be with a woman who loves me in return, just as I am. Not as the current title or the future duke. And if you weren't so stubborn, you would just marry me."

Meredith lifted trembling fingers to the heart locket at her throat. She fiddled with the latch, and it sprang open.

He sucked in a breath. "Meredith."

She stroked a finger lovingly over the casing that covered a tiny piece of a lone rose petal. "In those days when life was hardest, when I was alone, Barry, I touched this locket and remembered you."

He groaned, the sound low and primal.

"I love you." She wept. "Yes, I will marry you." She launched herself into his arms. Barry staggered back, colliding with the armoire and keeping them upright. "Yes, I'll marry you. I love you, Barry. I want a future with you. And gardens. And babies. And pathetically poor matches of pall-mall. All of it."

He looped an arm around her waist and drew her closer. "It is all yours, love. All of it."

THE END

ENJOYED, A MATCHMAKER FOR A Marquess? Be sure and check out Christi Caldwell's next book coming August 2019, *The Minx Who Met Her Match*, Book 4 in The Brethren series!!

And also coming from Christi....
September 2019

THE SPITFIRE,

Book 5 in the Wicked Wallflowers series

Her dream is to open a music hall. Only one thing stands in her way—the man she loves.

The final Wicked Wallflowers novel from *USA Today* **bestselling author Christi Caldwell.**

LEAVING BEHIND HER LIFE AS a courtesan and madam, Clara Winters is moving far from the sinful life to which she was accustomed in the gaming hell the Devil's Den. Her more reputable and fulfilling endeavor is a music hall for the masses. One night, when she sees a man injured on the streets of East London, she rushes to his aid and brings him home. It's then that she discovers he's Henry March, Earl of Waterson, and a member of Parliament. No good can come from playing nursemaid to a nobleman.

When Henry rouses to meet his savior in blonde curls, he is dazzled. This smart and loving spitfire challenges his every notion of the lower classes—and every moment together is a thrill. But after Henry returns to his well-ordered existence, he strikes a political compromise that has unintended consequences. Will his vision for London mean dashing the dreams of his lovely guardian angel?

OTHER BOOKS BY CHRISTI CALDWELL

Martha Donaldson went from being a nobleman's wife, and respected young mother, to the scandal of her village. After learning the dark lie perpetuated against her by her 'husband', she knows better than to ever trust a man. Her children are her life and she'll protect them at all costs. When a stranger arrives seeking the post of stable master, everything says to turn him out. So why does she let him stay?

Lord Sheldon Graham Whitworth has lived with the constant reminders of his many failings. The third son of a duke, he's long been underestimated: that however, proves a valuable asset as he serves the Brethren, an illustrious division in the Home Office. When Graham's first mission sees him assigned the role of guard to a young widow and her son, he wants nothing more than to finish quickly and then move on to another, more meaningful assignment.

Except, as the secrets between them begin to unravel, Martha's trust is shattered, and Graham is left with the most vital mission he'll ever face—winning Martha's heart.

THE LADY WHO LOVED HIM
Book 2 in the "Brethren" Series by Christi Caldwell

In this passionate, emotional Regency romance by Christi Caldwell, society's most wicked rake meets his match in the clever Lady Chloe Edgerton! And nothing will ever be the same!

She doesn't believe in marriage....

The cruelty of men is something Lady Chloe Edgerton understands. Even in her quest to better her life and forget the past, men always seem determined to control her. Overhearing the latest plan to wed her to a proper gentleman, Chloe finally has enough...but one misstep lands her in the arms of the most notorious rake in London.

The Marquess of Tennyson doesn't believe in love....

Leopold Dunlop is a ruthless, coldhearted rake... a reputation he has cultivated. As a member of The Brethren, a secret spy network, he's committed his life to serving the Crown, but his rakish reputation threatens to overshadow that service. When he's caught in a compromising position with Chloe, it could be the last nail in the coffin of his career unless he's willing to enter into a marriage of convenience.

A necessary arrangement...

A loveless match from the start, it soon becomes something more. As Chloe and Leo endeavor to continue with the plans for their lives prior to their marriage, Leo finds himself not so immune to his wife – or to the prospect of losing her.

THE SPY WHO SEDUCED HER
Book 1 in the "Brethren" Series by Christi Caldwell

A widow with a past... The last thing Victoria Barrett, the

Viscountess Waters, has any interest in is romance. When the only man she's ever loved was killed she endured an arranged marriage to a cruel man in order to survive. Now widowed, her only focus is on clearing her son's name from the charge of murder. That is until the love of her life returns from the grave.

A leader of a once great agency... Nathaniel Archer, the Earl of Exeter head of the Crown's elite organization, The Brethren, is back on British soil. Captured and tortured 20 years ago, he clung to memories of his first love until he could escape. Discovering she has married whilst he was captive, Nathaniel sets aside the distractions of love...until an unexpected case is thrust upon him—to solve the murder of the Viscount Waters. There is just one complication: the prime suspect's mother is none other than Victoria, the woman he once loved with his very soul.

Secrets will be uncovered and passions rekindled. Victoria and Nathaniel must trust one another if they hope to start anew—in love and life. But will duty destroy their last chance?

ROGUES RUSH IN
A Regency Duet by Tessa Dare & Christi Caldwell

New York Times and *USA Today* Bestselling authors Tessa Dare and Christi Caldwell come together in this smart, sexy, not-to-be-missed Regency Duet!

Two scandalous brides...
Two rogues who won't be denied...
His Bride for the Taking by NYT Bestselling author Tessa Dare
It's the first rule of friendship among gentlemen: Don't even think about touching your best friend's sister. But Sebastian, Lord Byrne, has never been one for rules. He's thought about touching Mary Clayton—a lot—and struggled to resist temptation. But when Mary's bridegroom leaves her waiting at the altar, only Sebastian can save her from ruin. By marrying her himself.

In eleven years, he's never laid a finger on his best friend's sister. Now he's going to take her with both hands. To have, to hold... and to love.

His Duchess for a Day by USA Today Bestseller Christi Caldwell
It was never meant to be...

That's what Elizabeth Terry has told herself while trying to forget the man she married—her once best friend. Passing herself off as a widow, Elizabeth has since built a life for herself as an instructor at a finishing school, far away from that greatest of mistakes. But the past has a way of finding you, and now that her husband has found her, Elizabeth must face the man she's tried to forget.

It was time to right a wrong...

Crispin Ferguson, the Duke of Huntington, has spent the past years living with regret. The young woman he married left without a by-your-leave, and his hasty elopement had devastating repercussions. Despite everything, Crispin never stopped thinking about Elizabeth. Now that he's found her, he has one request—be his duchess, publicly, just for a day.

Can spending time together as husband and wife rekindle the bond they once shared? Or will a shocking discovery tear them apart...this time, forever?

THE VIXEN

Book 2 in the "Wicked Wallflowers" Series by Christi Caldwell

Set apart by her ethereal beauty and fearless demeanor, Ophelia Killoran has always been a mystery to those around her—and a woman they underestimated. No one would guess that she spends her nights protecting the street urchins of St. Giles. Ophelia knows what horrors these children face. As a young girl, she faced those horrors herself, and she would have died...if not for the orphan boy who saved her life.

A notorious investigator, Connor Steele never expected to encounter Ophelia Killoran on his latest case. It has been years since he sacrificed himself for her. Now, she hires orphans from the street to work in her brother's gaming hell. But where does she find the children...and what are her intentions?

Ophelia and Connor are at odds. After all, Connor now serves the nobility, and that is a class of people Ophelia knows firsthand not to trust. But if they can set aside their misgivings and work

together, they may discover that their purposes—and their hearts—
are perfectly aligned.

THE HELLION
Book 1 in the "Wicked Wallflowers" Series by Christi Caldwell

Adair Thorne has just watched his gaming-hell dream disappear
into a blaze of fire and ash, and he's certain that his competitors,
the Killorans, are behind it. His fury and passion burn even hotter
when he meets Cleopatra Killoran, a tart-mouthed vixen who
mocks him at every turn. If she were anyone else but the enemy,
she'd ignite a desire in him that would be impossible to control.

No one can make Cleopatra do anything. That said, she'll do
whatever it takes to protect her siblings—even if that means being
sponsored by their rivals for a season in order to land a noble
husband. But she will not allow her head to be turned by the
infuriating and darkly handsome Adair Thorne.

There's only one thing that threatens the rules of the game:
Cleopatra's secret. It could unravel the families' tenuous truce and
shatter the unpredictably sinful romance mounting between the
hellion…and a scoundrel who could pass for the devil himself.

TO TEMPT A SCOUNDREL
Book 15 in the "Heart of a Duke" Series by Christi Caldwell

Never trust a gentleman…

Once before, Lady Alice Winterbourne trusted her heart to
an honorable, respectable man… only to be jilted in the scandal
of the Season. Longing for an escape from all the whispers and
humiliation, Alice eagerly accepts an invitation to her friend's
house party. In the country, she hopes to find some peace from
the embarrassment left in London… Unfortunately, she finds her
former betrothed and his new bride in attendance.

Never love a lady…

Lord Rhys Brookfield has no interest in marriage. Ever. He's worked quite hard at building both his fortune and his reputation as a rogue—and intends to enjoy all that they can offer him. That is if his match-making mother will stop pairing him with prospective brides. When Rhys and Alice meet, sparks flare. But with every new encounter, their first impressions of one another are challenged and an unlikely friendship is forged.

Desperate, Rhys proposes a pretend courtship, one meant to spite Alice's former betrothed and prevent any matchmaking attempts toward Rhys. What neither expects is that a pretense can become so much more. Or that a burning passion can heal… and hurt.

BEGUILED BY A BARON
Book 14 in the "Heart of a Duke" Series by Christi Caldwell

A Lady with a Secret… Partially deaf, with a birthmark marring her face, Bridget Hamilton is content with her life, even if she's been cast out of her family. But her peaceful existence—expanding her mind with her study of rare books—is threatened with an ultimatum from her evil brother—steal a valuable book or give up her son. Bridget has no choice; her son is her world.

A Lord with a Purpose… Vail Basingstoke, Baron Chilton is known throughout London as the Bastard Baron. After battling at Waterloo, he establishes himself as the foremost dealer in rare books and builds a fortune, determined to never be like the self-serving duke who sired him. He devotes his life to growing his fortune to care for his illegitimate siblings, also fathered by the duke. The chance to sell a highly coveted book for a financial windfall is his only thought.

Two Paths Collide… When Bridget masquerades as the baron's newest housekeeper, he's hopelessly intrigued by her quick wit and her skill with antique tomes. Wary from having his heart broken in the past, it should be easy enough to keep Bridget at arm's length, yet desire for her dogs his steps. As they spend time in each other's company, understanding for life grows as does love, but when Bridget's integrity is called into question, Vail's world is shattered—as is his heart again. Now Bridget and Vail will have to overcome the horrendous secrets and lies between them to grasp a love—and life—together.

To Enchant a Wicked Duke
Book 13 in the "Heart of a Duke" Series by Christi Caldwell

A Devil in Disguise

Years ago, when Nick Tallings, the recent Duke of Huntly, watched his family destroyed at the hands of a merciless nobleman, he vowed revenge. But his efforts had been futile, as his enemy, Lord Rutland is without weakness.

Until now…

With his rival finally happily married, Nick is able to set his ruthless scheme into motion. His plot hinges upon Lord Rutland's innocent, empty-headed sister-in-law, Justina Barrett. Nick will ruin her, marry her, and then leave her brokenhearted.

A Lady Dreaming of Love

From the moment Justina Barrett makes her Come Out, she is labeled a Diamond. Even with her ruthless father determined to sell her off to the highest bidder, Justina never gives up on her hope for a good, honorable gentleman who values her wit more than her looks.

A Not-So-Chance Meeting

Nick's ploy to ensnare Justina falls neatly into place in the streets of London. With each carefully orchestrated encounter, he slips further and further inside the lady's heart, never anticipating that Justina, with her quick wit and strength, will break down his own defenses. As Nick's plans begins to unravel, he's left to determine which is more important—Justina's love or his vow for vengeance. But can Justina ever forgive the duke who deceived her?

One Winter with a Baron
Book 12 in the "Heart of a Duke" Series by Christi Caldwell

A clever spinster:

Content with her spinster lifestyle, Miss Sybil Cunning wants to prove that a future as an unmarried woman is the only life for her. As a bluestocking who values hard, empirical data, Sybil needs help with her research. Nolan Pratt, Baron Webb, one of society's most scandalous rakes, is the perfect gentleman to help her. After all, he inspires fear in proper mothers and desire within their daughters.

A notorious rake:

Society may be aware of Nolan Pratt, Baron's Webb's wicked ways, but what he has carefully hidden is his miserable handling of his family's finances. When Sybil presents him the opportunity to earn much-needed funds, he can't refuse.

A winter to remember:

However, what begins as a business arrangement becomes something more and with every meeting, Sybil slips inside his heart. Can this clever woman look beneath the veneer of a coldhearted rake to see the man Nolan truly is?

To Redeem a Rake
Book 11 in the "Heart of a Duke" Series by Christi Caldwell

He's spent years scandalizing society.
Now, this rake must change his ways.

Society's most infamous scoundrel, Daniel Winterbourne, the Earl of Montfort, has been promised a small fortune if he can relinquish his wayward, carousing lifestyle. And behaving means he must also help find a respectable companion for his youngest sister—someone who will guide her and whom she can emulate. However, Daniel knows no such woman. But when he encounters a childhood friend, Daniel believes she may just be the answer to all of his problems.

Having been secretly humiliated by an unscrupulous blackguard years earlier, Miss Daphne Smith dreams of finding work at Ladies of Hope, an institution that provides an education for disabled women. With her sordid past and a disfigured leg, few opportunities arise for a woman such as she. Knowing Daniel's history, she wishes to avoid him, but working for his sister is exactly the stepping stone she needs.

Their attraction intensifies as Daniel and Daphne grow closer, preparing his sister for the London Season. But Daniel must resist his desire for a woman tarnished by scandal while Daphne is reminded of the boy she once knew. Can society's most notorious rake redeem his reputation and become the man Daphne deserves?

TO WOO A WIDOW
Book 10 in the "Heart of a Duke" Series by Christi Caldwell

They see a brokenhearted widow.
She's far from shattered.

Lady Philippa Winston is never marrying again. After her late husband's cruelty that she kept so well hidden, she has no desire to search for love.

Years ago, Miles Brookfield, the Marquess of Guilford, made a frivolous vow he never thought would come to fruition—he promised to marry his mother's goddaughter if he was unwed by the age of thirty. Now, to his dismay, he's faced with honoring that pledge. But when he encounters the beautiful and intriguing Lady Philippa, Miles knows his true path in life. It's up to him to break down every belief Philippa carries about gentlemen, proving that not only is love real, but that he is the man deserving of her sheltered heart.

Will Philippa let down her guard and allow Miles to woo a widow in desperate need of his love?

THE LURE OF A RAKE
Book 9 in the "Heart of a Duke" Series by Christi Caldwell

A Lady Dreaming of Love
Lady Genevieve Farendale has a scandalous past. Jilted at the

altar years earlier and exiled by her family, she's now returned to London to prove she can be a proper lady. Even though she's not given up on the hope of marrying for love, she's wary of trusting again. Then she meets Cedric Falcot, the Marquess of St. Albans whose seductive ways set her heart aflutter. But with her sordid history, Genevieve knows a rake can also easily destroy her.

An Unlikely Pairing

What begins as a chance encounter between Cedric and Genevieve becomes something more. As they continue to meet, passions stir. But with Genevieve's hope for true love, she fears Cedric will be unable to give up his wayward lifestyle. After all, Cedric has spent years protecting his heart, and keeping everyone out. Slowly, she chips away at all the walls he's built, but when he falters, Genevieve can't offer him redemption. Now, it's up to Cedric to prove to Genevieve that the love of a man is far more powerful than the lure of a rake.

TO TRUST A ROGUE
Book 8 in the "Heart of a Duke" Series by Christi Caldwell

A rogue

Marcus, the Viscount Wessex has carefully crafted the image of rogue and charmer for Polite Society. Under that façade, however, dwells a man whose dreams were shattered almost eight years earlier by a young lady who captured his heart, pledged her love, and then left him, with nothing more than a curt note.

A widow

Eight years earlier, faced with no other choice, Mrs. Eleanor Collins, fled London and the only man she ever loved, Marcus, Viscount Wessex. She has now returned to serve as a companion for her elderly aunt with a daughter in tow. Even though they're next door neighbors, there is little reason for her to move in the same circles as Marcus, just in case, she vows to avoid him, for he reminds her of all she lost when she left.

Reunited

As their paths continue to cross, Marcus finds his desire for

Eleanor just as strong, but he learned long ago she's not to be trusted. He will offer her a place in his bed, but not anything more. Only, Eleanor has no interest in this new, roguish man. The more time they spend together, the protective wall they've constructed to keep the other out, begin to break. With all the betrayals and secrets between them, Marcus has to open his heart again. And Eleanor must decide if it's ever safe to trust a rogue.

To Wed His Christmas Lady
Book 7 in the "Heart of a Duke" Series by Christi Caldwell

She's longing to be loved:
Lady Cara Falcot has only served one purpose to her loathsome father—to increase his power through a marriage to the future Duke of Billingsley. As such, she's built protective walls about her heart, and presents an icy facade to the world around her. Journeying home from her finishing school for the Christmas holidays, Cara's carriage is stranded during a winter storm. She's forced to tarry at a ramshackle inn, where she immediately antagonizes another patron—William.

He's avoiding his duty in favor of one last adventure:
William Hargrove, the Marquess of Grafton has wanted only one thing in life—to avoid the future match his parents would have him make to a cold, duke's daughter. He's returning home from a blissful eight years of traveling the world to see to his responsibilities. But when a winter storm interrupts his trip and lands him at a falling-down inn, he's forced to share company with a commanding Lady Cara who initially reminds him exactly of the woman he so desperately wants to avoid.

A Christmas snowstorm ushers in the spirit of the season:
At the holiday time, these two people who despise each other due to first perceptions are offered renewed beginnings and fresh starts. As this gruff stranger breaks down the walls she's built about herself, Cara has to determine whether she can truly open her heart to trusting that any man is capable of good and that she herself is capable of love. And William has to set aside all previous

thoughts he's carried of the polished ladies like Cara, to be the man to show her that love.

THE HEART OF A SCOUNDREL
Book 6 in the "Heart of a Duke" Series by Christi Caldwell

Ruthless, wicked, and dark, the Marquess of Rutland rouses terror in the breast of ladies and nobleman alike. All Edmund wants in life is power. After he was publically humiliated by his one love Lady Margaret, he vowed vengeance, using Margaret's niece, as his pawn. Except, he's thwarted by another, more enticing target—Miss Phoebe Barrett.

Miss Phoebe Barrett knows precisely the shame she's been born to. Because her father is a shocking letch she's learned to form her own opinions on a person's worth. After a chance meeting with the Marquess of Rutland, she is captivated by the mysterious man. He, too, is a victim of society's scorn, but the more encounters she has with Edmund, the more she knows there is powerful depth and emotion to the jaded marquess.

The lady wreaks havoc on Edmund's plans for revenge and he finds he wants Phoebe, at all costs. As she's drawn into the darkness of his world, Phoebe risks being destroyed by Edmund's ruthlessness. And Phoebe who desires love at all costs, has to determine if she can ever truly trust the heart of a scoundrel.

TO LOVE A LORD
Book 5 in the "Heart of a Duke" Series by Christi Caldwell

All she wants is security:
The last place finishing school instructor Mrs. Jane Munroe belongs, is in polite Society. Vowing to never wed, she's been scuttled around from post to post. Now she finds herself in the Marquess of Waverly's household. She's never met a nobleman

she liked, and when she meets the pompous, arrogant marquess, she remembers why. But soon, she discovers Gabriel is unlike any gentleman she's ever known.

All he wants is a companion for his sister:

What Gabriel finds himself with instead, is a fiery spirited, bespectacled woman who entices him at every corner and challenges his age-old vow to never trust his heart to a woman. But…there is something suspicious about his sister's companion. And he is determined to find out just what it is.

All they need is each other:

As Gabriel and Jane confront the truth of their feelings, the lies and secrets between them begin to unravel. And Jane is left to decide whether or not it is ever truly safe to love a lord.

LOVED BY A DUKE
Book 4 in the "Heart of a Duke" Series by Christi Caldwell

For ten years, Lady Daisy Meadows has been in love with Auric, the Duke of Crawford. Ever since his gallant rescue years earlier, Daisy knew she was destined to be his Duchess. Unfortunately, Auric sees her as his best friend's sister and nothing more. But perhaps, if she can manage to find the fabled heart of a duke pendant, she will win over the heart of her duke.

Auric, the Duke of Crawford enjoys Daisy's company. The last thing he is interested in however, is pursuing a romance with a woman he's known since she was in leading strings. This season, Daisy is turning up in the oddest places and he cannot help but notice that she is no longer a girl. But Auric wouldn't do something as foolhardy as to fall in love with Daisy. He couldn't. Not with the guilt he carries over his past sins… Not when he has no right to her heart…But perhaps, just perhaps, she can forgive the past and trust that he'd forever cherish her heart—but will she let him?

THE LOVE OF A ROGUE
Book 3 in the "Heart of a Duke" Series by Christi Caldwell

Lady Imogen Moore hasn't had an easy time of it since she made her Come Out. With her betrothed, a powerful duke breaking it off to wed her sister, she's become the *tons* favorite piece of gossip. Never again wanting to experience the pain of a broken heart, she's resolved to make a match with a polite, respectable gentleman. The last thing she wants is another reckless rogue.

Lord Alex Edgerton has a problem. His brother, tired of Alex's carousing has charged him with chaperoning their remaining, unwed sister about *ton* events. Shopping? No, thank you. Attending the theatre? He'd rather be at Forbidden Pleasures with a scantily clad beauty upon his lap. The task of *chaperone* becomes even more of a bother when his sister drags along her dearest friend, Lady Imogen to social functions. The last thing he wants in his life is a young, innocent English miss.

Except, as Alex and Imogen are thrown together, passions flare and Alex comes to find he not only wants Imogen in his bed, but also in his heart. Yet now he must convince Imogen to risk all, on the heart of a rogue.

MORE THAN A DUKE
Book 2 in the "Heart of a Duke" Series by Christi Caldwell

Polite Society doesn't take Lady Anne Adamson seriously. However, Anne isn't just another pretty young miss. When she discovers her father betrayed her mother's love and her family descended into poverty, Anne comes up with a plan to marry a respectable, powerful, and honorable gentleman—a man nothing like her philandering father.

Armed with the heart of a duke pendant, fabled to land the wearer a duke's heart, she decides to enlist the aid of the notorious Harry, 6th Earl of Stanhope. A scoundrel with a scandalous past, he is the last gentleman she'd ever wed…however, his reputation marks him the perfect man to school her in the art of seduction so she might ensnare the illustrious Duke of Crawford.

Harry, the Earl of Stanhope is a jaded, cynical rogue who lives for his own pleasures. Having been thrown over by the only woman he ever loved so she could wed a duke, he's not at all surprised when Lady Anne approaches him with her scheme to capture another duke's affection. He's come to appreciate that all women are in fact greedy, title-grasping, self-indulgent creatures. And with Anne's history of grating on his every last nerve, she is the last woman he'd ever agree to school in the art of seduction. Only his friendship with the lady's sister compels him to help.

What begins as a pretend courtship, born of lessons on seduction, becomes something more leaving Anne to decide if she can give her heart to a reckless rogue, and Harry must decide if he's willing to again trust in a lady's love.

ᖴOR ᒪOVE OF THE ᗪUKE
First Full-Length Book in the "Heart of a Duke" Series
by Christi Caldwell

After the tragic death of his wife, Jasper, the 8th Duke of Bainbridge buried himself away in the dark cold walls of his home, Castle Blackwood. When he's coaxed out of his self-imposed exile to attend the amusements of the Frost Fair, his life is irrevocably changed by his fateful meeting with Lady Katherine Adamson.

With her tight brown ringlets and silly white-ruffled gowns, Lady Katherine Adamson has found her dance card empty for two Seasons. After her father's passing, Katherine learned the unreliability of men, and is determined to depend on no one, except herself. Until she meets Jasper…

In a desperate bid to avoid a match arranged by her family, Katherine makes the Duke of Bainbridge a shocking proposition— one that he accepts.

Only, as Katherine begins to love Jasper, she finds the arrangement agreed upon is not enough. And Jasper is left to decide if protecting his heart is more important than fighting for Katherine's love.

IN NEED OF A DUKE
A Prequel Novella to "The Heart of a Duke" Series
by Christi Caldwell

In Need of a Duke: (Author's Note: This is a prequel novella to "The Heart of a Duke" series by Christi Caldwell. It was originally available in "The Heart of a Duke" Collection and is now being published as an individual novella.

~★~

It features a new prologue and epilogue.

Years earlier, a gypsy woman passed to Lady Aldora Adamson and her friends a heart pendant that promised them each the heart of a duke.

Now, a young lady, with her family facing ruin and scandal, Lady Aldora doesn't have time for mythical stories about cheap baubles. She needs to save her sisters and brother by marrying a titled gentleman with wealth and power to his name. She sets her bespectacled sights upon the Marquess of St. James.

Turned out by his father after a tragic scandal, Lord Michael Knightly has grown into a powerful, but self-made man. With the whispers and stares that still follow him, he would rather be anywhere but London...

Until he meets Lady Aldora, a young woman who mistakes him for his brother, the Marquess of St. James. The connection between Aldora and Michael is immediate and as they come to know one another, Aldora's feelings for Michael war with her sisterly responsibilities. With her family's dire situation, a man of Michael's scandalous past will never do.

Ultimately, Aldora must choose between her responsibilities as a sister and her love for Michael.

ONCE A WALLFLOWER, AT LAST HIS LOVE

Book 6 in the Scandalous Seasons Series

Responsible, practical Miss Hermione Rogers, has been crafting stories as the notorious Mr. Michael Michaelmas and selling them for a meager wage to support her siblings. The only real way to ensure her family's ruinous debts are paid, however, is to marry. Tall, thin, and plain, she has no expectation of success. In London for her first Season she seizes the chance to write the tale of a brooding duke. In her research, she finds Sebastian Fitzhugh, the 5th Duke of Mallen, who unfortunately is perfectly affable, charming, and so nicely… configured… he takes her breath away. He lacks all the character traits she needs for her story, but alas, any duke will have to do.

Sebastian Fitzhugh, the 5th Duke of Mallen has been deceived so many times during the high-stakes game of courtship, he's lost faith in Society women. Yet, after a chance encounter with Hermione, he finds himself intrigued. Not a woman he'd normally consider beautiful, the young lady's practical bent, her forthright nature and her tendency to turn up in the oddest places has his interests… roused. He'd like to trust her, he'd like to do a whole lot more with her too, but should he?

A Marquess For Christmas

Book 5 in the Scandalous Seasons Series

Lady Patrina Tidemore gave up on the ridiculous notion of true love after having her heart shattered and her trust destroyed by a black-hearted cad. Used as a pawn in a game of revenge against her brother, Patrina returns to London from a failed elopement with a tattered reputation and little hope for a respectable match. The only peace she finds is in her solitude on the cold winter days at Hyde Park. And even that is yanked from her by two little hellions who just happen to have a devastatingly handsome, but coldly aloof father, the Marquess of Beaufort. Something about the lord stirs the dreams she'd once carried for an honorable gentleman's love.

Weston Aldridge, the 4th Marquess of Beaufort was deceived and betrayed by his late wife. In her faithlessness, he's come to view women as self-serving, indulgent creatures. Except, after a series of chance encounters with Patrina, he comes to appreciate how uniquely different she is than all women he's ever known.

At the Christmastide season, a time of hope and new beginnings, Patrina and Weston, unexpectedly learn true love in one another. However, as Patrina's scandalous past threatens their future and the happiness of his children, they are both left to determine if love is enough.

Always a Rogue, Forever Her Love
Book 4 in the Scandalous Seasons Series

Miss Juliet Marshville is spitting mad. With one guardian missing, and the other singularly uninterested in her fate, she is at the mercy of her wastrel brother who loses her beloved childhood home to a man known as Sin. Determined to reclaim control of Rosecliff Cottage and her own fate, Juliet arranges a meeting with the notorious rogue and demands the return of her property.

Jonathan Tidemore, 5th Earl of Sinclair, known to the *ton* as Sin, is exceptionally lucky in life and at the gaming tables. He has just one problem. Well…four, really. His incorrigible sisters have driven off yet another governess. This time, however, his mother demands he find an appropriate replacement.

When Miss Juliet Marshville boldly demands the return of her precious cottage, he takes advantage of his sudden good fortune and puts an offer to her; turn his sisters into proper English ladies, and he'll return Rosecliff Cottage to Juliet's possession.

Jonathan comes to appreciate Juliet's spirit, courage, and clever wit, and decides to claim the fiery beauty as his mistress. Juliet, however, will be mistress for no man. Nor could she ever love a man who callously stole her home in a game of cards. As Jonathan begins to see Juliet as more than a spirited beauty to warm his bed, he realizes she could be a lady he could love the rest of his life, if only he can convince the proud Juliet that he's worthy of her hand and heart.

ALWAYS PROPER, SUDDENLY SCANDALOUS
Book 3 in the Scandalous Seasons Series

Geoffrey Winters, Viscount Redbrooke was not always the hard, unrelenting lord driven by propriety. After a tragic mistake, he resolved to honor his responsibility to the Redbrooke line and live a life, free of scandal. Knowing his duty is to wed a proper, respectable English miss, he selects Lady Beatrice Dennington, daughter of the Duke of Somerset, the perfect woman for him. Until he meets Miss Abigail Stone…

To distance herself from a personal scandal, Abigail Stone flees America to visit her uncle, the Duke of Somerset. Determined to never trust a man again, she is helplessly intrigued by the hard, too-proper Geoffrey. With his strict appreciation for decorum and order, he is nothing like the man' she's always dreamed of.

Abigail is everything Geoffrey does not need. She upends his carefully ordered world at every encounter. As they begin to care for one another, Abigail carefully guards the secret that resulted in her journey to England.

Only, if Geoffrey learns the truth about Abigail, he must decide which he holds most dear: his place in Society or Abigail's place in his heart.

NEVER COURTED, SUDDENLY WED
Book 2 in the Scandalous Seasons Series

Christopher Ansley, Earl of Waxham, has constructed a perfect image for the *ton*—the ladies love him and his company is desired by all. Only two people know the truth about Waxham's secret. Unfortunately, one of them is Miss Sophie Winters.

Sophie Winters has known Christopher since she was in leading strings. As children, they delighted in tormenting each other. Now at two and twenty, she still has a tendency to find herself in scrapes, and her marital prospects are slim.

When his father threatens to expose his shame to the *ton*, unless he weds Sophie for her dowry, Christopher concocts a plan to remain a bachelor. What he didn't plan on was falling in love with the lively, impetuous Sophie. As secrets are exposed, will Christopher's love be enough when she discovers his role in his father's scheme?

FOREVER BETROTHED, NEVER THE BRIDE
Book 1 in the Scandalous Seasons Series

Hopeless romantic Lady Emmaline Fitzhugh is tired of sitting with the wallflowers, waiting for her betrothed to come to his senses and marry her. When Emmaline reads one too many reports of his scandalous liaisons in the gossip rags, she takes matters into her own hands.

War-torn veteran Lord Drake devotes himself to forgetting his days on the Peninsula through an endless round of meaningless associations. He no longer wants to feel anything, but Lady Emmaline is making it hard to maintain a state of numbness. With her zest for life, she awakens his passion and desire for love.

The one woman Drake has spent the better part of his life avoiding is now the only woman he needs, but he is no longer a man worthy of his Emmaline. It is up to her to show him the healing power of love.

A SEASON OF HOPE
A Danby Novella

Five years ago when her love, Marcus Wheatley, failed to return from fighting Napoleon's forces, Lady Olivia Foster buried her heart. Unable to betray Marcus's memory, Olivia has gone out of her way to run off prospective suitors. At three and twenty she considers herself firmly on the shelf. Her father, however, disagrees and accepts an offer for Olivia's hand in marriage. Yet it's Christmas, when anything can happen…

Olivia receives a well-timed summons from her grandfather, the Duke of Danby, and eagerly embraces the reprieve from her betrothal.

Only, when Olivia arrives at Danby Castle she realizes the Christmas season represents hope, second chances, and even miracles.

"WINNING A LADY'S HEART"
A Danby Novella

Author's Note: This is a novella that was originally available in A Summons From The Castle (The Regency Christmas Summons Collection). It is being published as an individual novella.

For Lady Alexandra, being the source of a cold, calculated wager is bad enough…but when it is waged by Nathaniel Michael Winters, 5th Earl of Pembroke, the man she's in love with, it results in a broken heart, the scandal of the season, and a summons from her grandfather – the Duke of Danby.

To escape Society's gossip, she hurries to her meeting with the duke, determined to put memories of the earl far behind. Except the duke has other plans for Alexandra…plans which include the 5th Earl of Pembroke!

TEMPTED BY A LADY'S SMILE
Book 4 in the "Lords of Honor" Series

Richard Jonas has loved but one woman—a woman who belongs to his brother. Refusing to suffer any longer, he evades his family in order to barricade his heart from unrequited love. While attending a friend's summer party, Richard's approach to love is changed after sharing a passionate and life-altering kiss with a vibrant and mysterious woman. Believing he was incapable of loving again, Richard finds himself tempted by a young lady determined to marry his best friend.

Gemma Reed has not been treated kindly by the *ton*. Often disregarded for her appearance and interests unlike those of a proper lady, Gemma heads to house party to win the heart of Lord Westfield, the man she's loved for years. But her plan is set off course by the tempting and intriguing, Richard Jonas.

A chance meeting creates a new path for Richard and Gemma to forage—but can two people, scorned and shunned by those they've loved from afar, let down their guards to find true happiness?

"RESCUED BY A LADY'S LOVE"
Book 3 in the "Lords of Honor" Series

Destitute and determined to finally be free of any man's shackles, Lily Benedict sets out to salvage her honor. With no choice but to commit a crime that will save her from her past, she enters the home of the recluse, Derek Winters, the new Duke of Blackthorne. But entering the "Beast of Blackthorne's" lair proves more threatening than she ever imagined.

With half a face and a mangled leg, Derek—once rugged and charming—only exists within the confines of his home. Shunned by society, Derek is leery of the hauntingly beautiful Lily Benedict. As time passes, she slips past his defenses, reminding him how to live again. But when Lily's sordid past comes back, threatening her life, it's up to Derek to find the strength to become the hero he once was. Can they overcome the darkness of their sins to find a life of love and redemption?

CAPTIVATED BY A LADY'S CHARM
Book 2 in the "Lords of Honor" Series

In need of a wife…

Christian Villiers, the Marquess of St. Cyr, despises the role he's been cast into as fortune hunter but requires the funds to keep his marquisate solvent. Yet, the sins of his past cloud his future, preventing him from seeing beyond his fateful actions at the Battle of Toulouse. For he knows inevitably it will catch up with him, and everyone will remember his actions on the battlefield that cost so many so much—particularly his best friend.

In want of a husband…

Lady Prudence Tidemore's life is plagued by familial scandals, which makes her own marital prospects rather grim. Surely there is one gentleman of the ton who can look past her family and see just her and all she has to offer?

When Prudence runs into Christian on a London street, the charming, roguish gentleman immediately captures her attention. But then a chance meeting becomes a waltz, and now…

A Perfect Match…

All she must do is convince Christian to forget the cold requirements he has for his future marchioness. But the demons in his past prevent him from turning himself over to love. One thing is certain—Prudence wants the marquess and is determined to have him in her life, now and forever. It's just a matter of convincing Christian he wants the same.

SEDUCED BY A LADY'S HEART
Book 1 in the "Lords of Honor" Series

You met Lieutenant Lucien Jones in "Forever Betrothed, Never the Bride" when he was a broken soldier returned from fighting Boney's forces. This is his story of triumph and happily-ever-after!

~★~

Lieutenant Lucien Jones, son of a viscount, returned from war, to find his wife and child dead. Blaming his father for the commission that sent him off to fight Boney's forces, he was content to languish at London Hospital… until offered employment on the Marquess of Drake's staff. Through his position, Lucien found purpose in life and is content to keep his past buried.

Lady Eloise Yardley has loved Lucien since they were children. Having long ago given up on the dream of him, she married another. Years later, she is a young, lonely widow who does not fit in with the ton. When Lucien's family enlists her aid to reunite father and son, she leaps at the opportunity to not only aid her former friend, but to also escape London.

Lucien doesn't know what scheme Eloise has concocted, but knowing her as he does, when she pays a visit to his employer, he knows she's up to something. The last thing he wants is the temptation that this new, older, mature Eloise presents; a tantalizing reminder of happier times and peace.

Yet Eloise is determined to win Lucien's love once and for all… if only Lucien can set aside the pain of his past and risk all on a lady's heart.

ONLY FOR THEIR LOVE
Book 3 in the "The Theodosia Sword" Series

Miss Carol Cresswall bore witness to her parents' loveless union and is determined to avoid that same miserable fate. Her mother has altogether different plans—plans that include a match between Carol and Lord Gregory Renshaw. Despite his wealth and power, Carol has no interest in marrying a pompous man who goes out of his way to ignore her. Now, with their families coming together for the Christmastide season it's her mother's last-ditch effort to get them together. And Carol plans to avoid Gregory at all costs.

Lord Gregory Renshaw has no intentions of falling prey to his mother's schemes to marry him off to a proper debutante she's picked out. Over the years, he has carefully sidestepped all endeavors to be matched with any of the grasping ladies.

But a sudden Christmastide Scandal has the potential show Carol and Gregory that they've spent years running from the one thing they've always needed.

ONLY FOR HER HONOR
Book 2 in the "The Theodosia Sword" Series

A wounded soldier:

When Captain Lucas Rayne returned from fighting Boney's forces, he was a shell of a man. A recluse who doesn't leave his family's estate, he's content to shut himself away. Until he meets Eve...

A woman alone in the world:

Eve Ormond spent most of her life following the drum alongside her late father. When his shameful actions bring death and pain to English soldiers, Eve is forced back to England, an outcast. With no family or marital prospects she needs employment and finds it in Captain Lucas Rayne's home. A man whose life was ruined by her father, Eve has no place inside his household. With few options available, however, Eve takes the post. What she never anticipates is how with their every meeting, this honorable, hurting soldier slips inside her heart.

The Secrets Between Them:

The more time Lucas spends with Eve, he remembers what it is to be alive and he lets the walls protecting his heart down. When the secrets between them come to light will their love be enough? Or are they two destined for heartbreak?

ONLY FOR HIS LADY
Book 1 in the "The Theodosia Sword" Series

A curse. A sword. And the thief who stole her heart.

The Rayne family is trapped in a rut of bad luck. And now, it's up to Lady Theodosia Rayne to steal back the Theodosia sword, a gladius that was pilfered by the rival, loathed Renshaw family. Hopefully, recovering the stolen sword will break the cycle and reverse her family's fate.

Damian Renshaw, the Duke of Devlin, is feared by all—all, that is, except Lady Theodosia, the brazen spitfire who enters his home and wrestles an ancient relic from his wall. Intrigued by the vivacious woman, Devlin has no intentions of relinquishing the sword to her.

As Theodosia and Damian battle for ownership, passion ignites. Now, they are torn between their age-old feud and the fire that burns between them. Can two forbidden lovers find a way to make amends before their families' war tears them apart?

My Lady of Deception
Book 1 in the "Brethren of the Lords" Series

This dark, sweeping Regency novel was previously only offered as part of the limited edition box sets: "From the Ballroom and Beyond", "Romancing the Rogue", and "Dark Deceptions". Now, available for the first time on its own, exclusively through Amazon is "My Lady of Deception".

~★~

Everybody has a secret. Some are more dangerous than others.

For Georgina Wilcox, only child of the notorious traitor known as "The Fox", there are too many secrets to count. However, after her interference results in great tragedy, she resolves to never help another… until she meets Adam Markham.

Lord Adam Markham is captured by The Fox. Imprisoned, Adam loses everything he holds dear. As his days in captivity grow, he finds himself fascinated by the young maid, Georgina, who cares for him.

When the carefully crafted lies she's built between them begin to crumble, Georgina realizes she will do anything to prove her love and loyalty to Adam—even it means at the expense of her own life.

NON-FICTION WORKS BY
CHRISTI CALDWELL

Uninterrupted Joy: Memoir: My Journey through Infertility, Pregnancy, and Special Needs

The following journey was never intended for publication. It was written from a mother, to her unborn child. The words detailed her struggle through infertility and the joy of finally being pregnant. A stunning revelation at her son's birth opened a world of both fear and discovery. This is the story of one mother's love and hope and…her quest for uninterrupted joy.

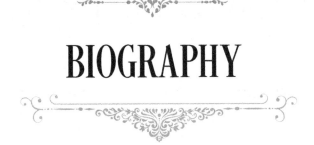

BIOGRAPHY

Christi Caldwell is the bestselling author of historical romance novels set in the Regency era. Christi blames Judith McNaught's "Whitney, My Love," for luring her into the world of historical romance. While sitting in her graduate school apartment at the University of Connecticut, Christi decided to set aside her notes and try her hand at writing romance. She believes the most perfect heroes and heroines have imperfections and rather enjoys tormenting them before crafing a well-deserved happily ever after!

When Christi isn't writing the stories of flawed heroes and heroines, she can be found in her Southern Connecticut home chasing around her eight-year-old son, and caring for twin princesses-in-training!

Visit *www.christicaldwellauthor.com* to learn more about what Christi is working on, or join her on Facebook at Christi Caldwell Author, and Twitter @ChristiCaldwell